The Hawk Circles

A Danielle Baker and Nigel Hawksworth Series, Volume 1

Debbra Anderson

Published by Debbra Anderson, 2022.

This is a work of fiction. Similarities to real people, places, or events are entirely coincidental.

THE HAWK CIRCLES

First edition. September 5, 2022.

ISBN: 979-8215636091

Written by Debbra Anderson.

Table of Contents

To my children

who have walked with me

through it all,

Thank you!

Chapter 1

But I Like My Prom Dress!

I was paying bills at the desk in my bedroom when I heard the front door slam and wondered if I should find out who was in my house. I recognized my daughter's footsteps as she trudged up the stairs. In just a moment, my daughter, Shelly, dragged herself through the door.

"I'm an idiot. A fool. I can't go to Prom, can't return to that school. You're going to have to homeschool me again, Mom." She threw herself down onto the bed. "I'm going to have to take my beautiful dress back –"

"Buy a habit and get thee to a convent, oh, beautiful young woman?" I couldn't resist.

Shelly sat up and glared. "Don't joke, Mom. I'm serious here."

"I'm sorry, sweetie," I smiled at her, "but you were being kind of melodramatic. Tell me what's wrong and how I can help."

"You're so snarky sometimes." A smile tried to break through, but I could see she was seriously upset.

"I know, and I'm sorry. But I'm listening. Please tell me what happened."

She sighed deeply. "Well, you know Jamie Sneider." I nodded. "She went around school telling everyone she found this beautiful dress that she's going to buy for Prom, and it's the same one I bought." Tears welled up and spilled over. I jumped up and gathered her into a hug.

"Aw, babe, don't cry. It'll be okay. I promise."

"How can it be okay?" She wailed against my shoulder. "I can't wear the same dress to Prom that Jamie's wearing. She's, like, super tall and skinny, and she'll look better than me. I'll look short and... and *dumpy.*"

Our big galumph of a dog, Ramon, trotted into the room and placed his wet nose in Shelly's hands. She quickly wiped them on my back. As I waited for the tears to subside, I prayed for wisdom, stroking her hair, so different from mine. It led me to think again of the wonder of genetics.

Shelly and I look alike in the face, but she's a couple of inches shorter than I am. She has ash blond hair, straight as a pin (so pretty!) where mine is medium brown with big corkscrew curls. *How can we be so different yet so similar?* I wondered. As I thought this, Shelly hiccupped and pulled away, ready to talk.

"Are you sure she's getting the same dress?" I asked.

Shelly rolled her eyes. "I saw a picture of it on her phone – long, light blue with beadwork on the bodice and crossed straps in the back. It's the exact same dress. It even has the little elastic pull over the butt."

It certainly sounded like the same dress. Rats. I really liked what we'd chosen for her. "All right, Shelly, I want to tell you three things. Are you ready to listen?" She sniffed one last time and sat up straighter. "Good. First, honey, I understand your dilemma. And we'll work this out together, okay?"

Shelly nodded, hopeful but not convinced. "Second," I continued, "you are not dumpy. You aren't as skinny as Jamie, but you are tall, and beautiful, and not everyone likes skinny. I know you don't believe me on this, but trust me, it's true. I *never* lacked for dates when I was in college." Shelly flashed her lopsided smile and snuffled into the tissue I handed her.

"Third, Jamie hasn't purchased the dress, yet. And when she does, she will probably tell everyone in school, right? Like she's been telling everyone what she's *going* to buy."

"Yeah?"

"Yeah," I repeated. "So, if she buys the same dress, we'll take this one back and get you a different one. Okay?"

Shelly's eyes grew large. "We could do that?"

"You mean, would I? Of course, sweetie. It's what Moms do."

She looked down at her hands clasped tightly together. "But I *like* my dress. I don't want to buy a different one."

"I know honey. Let's just pray she finds a different one she likes better."

Two big tears spilled over as Shelly wrapped her arms around me. "Thank you, Mom. You're awesome." She jumped up to leave only to turn at the door. "I don't mind when you're snarky. It's kind of cute. Thanks again." And with a smile she was gone.

I chuckled as I returned to the bills. I would find out later why she thought she was an idiot and a fool, unless that was all just part of the melodrama. As I finished the last bill, the phone rang. It was my best friend, Natalie.

"Hey, Danielle," she said breezily. "Are you up to taking a walk?"

"How long have we been walking, twenty years?" I asked with a smile.

"And you still have to ask?"

"More like five," she retorted. "The previous fifteen years were spent running – first, after cute guys and then after babies."

We laughed comfortably, and I said I'd meet her in ten minutes. As I laced up my shoes, I thought of our friendship. Natalie and I met just as we both graduated from college. Our lives have taken very different courses professionally, but our friendship has held firm – through marriage, divorce, childbirth, job promotions, and job losses. Nothing has been able to come between us. We often joke that we're more like sisters.

Natalie is Vice President of an electronic entertainment company. I'm not sure just what that means, but she certainly has a nice car and beautiful clothes. She works about six hours, four days a week at the corporate office in Eugene, not far from our little town. However, she spends innumerable hours in her home office where she does the rest of her work in order to be accessible to her husband and children.

I've been divorced four years, and paying the bills is an unwelcome aspect of being single again. I wasn't sure how I was going to support the kids after the divorce, but just three months before it was final, I published my first young adult historical novel. That was a crazy time! But the money I earned from it and the other books that have been published since have made it possible for me to live a life I love. Now, I work at home sitting in front of a computer writing for several hours every day, in between homeschooling, doing laundry, cleaning house, taking care of animals...all the things a mom does on a daily basis. The upside is that I can work in my pajamas. The downside is that people don't consider writing "real work" and assume I have hours and hours of free time to help with charities, car pools, kids' activities, and so on. I've had to learn to be strong with my 'no'.

I almost never turned down a walk, though. Not only is the exercise good for me, but the fellowship is, too.

Shoes on, I went in search of my kids to let them know where I was headed. Shelly was on the phone telling her best friend, Amy, about the Prom dress. Hannah was doing an extra science assignment. At fourteen, she was a better student than Shelly would ever be. And my youngest, Mikey, was shooting hoops in our driveway with Natalie's younger son, Danny. The boys were just a few months apart, and they were good friends. I told them where I'd be and turned my feet toward Natalie's house just two blocks away.

The trees were blooming, and through the houses and trees I caught glimpses of the Coburg hills shining in their new spring green. The air smelled fresh, and I breathed deeply. I love spring.

As I approached Natalie's house, I could see her doing some weird gyrations. Her back was to me, and her long, black hair was swishing from side to side as she moved. Turning into her driveway, I saw that she was scooping up dog vomit. I quickly turned my back. I don't handle that kind of thing well.

"I can come back another time," I told her.

"Oh, hi, Danielle," she said. "I'll be done in a sec." She joined me in about five, and we started walking the two-mile loop. "You'd think I'd have someone to clean up the messes, wouldn't you?"

"What, you need a housekeeper *and* someone to clean up the messes the neighbor's dog leaves?" I grinned at her. "How about a personal shopper, too? Or do you have one already? You're all of five-four and a size two. It should be easy to shop for you." I always think that, at five-eight and a size twelve, I should feel like an Amazon woman next to Natalie, yet she somehow manages to make me forget the size difference . . . and the income difference, too.

In a haughty tone, she informed me, "We executives need someone to take care of the menial labor."

We both laughed. Quickly, I sobered. "Did you have to let anyone go today?"

Chapter 2
Which One?

"No," she answered with a sigh of relief. "It looks like the company will be doing okay for a while. We won a contract with a small entertainment company based in Seattle that's seen an increase in their sales and profits. I guess people turn to escapism when times are bad. Anyway, we'll be able to give them the technical support for their systems, and it means we need all the people we have right now. Everyone is jumping up and down with joy."

"I'm so glad. You really get touchy when you have to fire someone."

"You would, too." She defended herself. I nodded as she continued, "What happened in your world?"

I told her about the prom dress mishap and Jamie Sneider.

"Didn't you tell her that what's inside is far more important than what's outside, and she has every right to wear what she wants to wear to the prom? Did you tell her - "

"I told her what she needed to hear at the moment, Aunty-Mommy." It was my children's favorite nickname for her. "And she's already heard our sermons on image, the media, and all the lies we have to face on a daily basis about how 'young and thin' is the definition of beauty. What she needed to hear me tell her is that while what is on the outside isn't as important as what is on the inside, the outside is important, too, sometimes."

"You're right," she waved to someone in a blue minivan as it drove past. Obediently, I waved, too. In a small town, it's a good idea to wave, even if you can't see who it is. You're probably on a committee or go to church with the person.

Natalie continued, "She hasn't asked someone, yet?"

I shook my head. "She's still trying to decide."

She smiled. "I remember my prom..."

"Which one?" I teased. Natalie had managed to go to six proms. *Six!* Can you imagine?

Natalie laughed. "I think it was my second or third prom, probably my sophomore year. I went with this guy from school who I thought of as a friend. I guess he thought we had something special." She shook her head. "That was really weird.

"You know Matt Smythe, right? He works for city hall."

I nodded. "I've seen him around town for years, working on water systems and setting up for our huge 4th of July celebration. In fact, isn't that him?" I pointed discreetly to a city pick-up as it drove by.

She nodded and we waved again. "I went with him. He was devastated that I wasn't interested in him and left me at the dance. He went home with someone else."

"He left you behind?" I exclaimed. "What did you do?"

She grinned in remembrance. "Well, the DJ was really cute, so I flirted with him for a while, and he took me home.

"To my house," she answered my sideways look with a mock frown. "Anyway, I was wearing the same dress as a girl who was a year ahead of me. She was a plain girl, a little heavy, and I was a lot prettier and thinner than she was. It ruined her whole evening. Poor girl. Her name was Patricia Flower. Some of the mean kids called her Fat Pat. She moved away a week after graduation and hasn't been back. Not that I blame her."

"You didn't preach to her your sermon on body image?"

Natalie hesitated. "I didn't have my sermon then. In fact, I'd bought into the whole body image thing that the media projected - and so had she." We walked quietly for a while.

"What about your prom? I know you only went to one. What was it like?" Natalie asked as we waved yet again, this time to her favorite hairdresser,

I shrugged. "It was fun getting ready, I guess," I answered. "I had to wear a dress I didn't like, because my mom said it was a good deal. And my date didn't drive, so we went with some of his friends. They weren't friends of mine. The dance was boring...well, it was okay, but it wasn't any more special than any other dance. I don't know, I guess it wasn't all that great. I hope Shelly isn't as disappointed as I was."

"If she chooses her date wisely, she'll have a great time," Natalie replied with confidence.

Later that evening, Shelly came into the kitchen for a snack. "What are you making?"

I looked up from the cookbook. "Nothing, I guess. It all looks like the same food I always cook with just a couple of different ingredients. Does that make it more interesting?"

Shelly peered over my shoulder and grimaced.

"I take it I should just make my usual and find a new hobby," I laughed.

"I was going to ask you," I continued, "what it was that made you feel like an idiot and a fool today. Do you mind talking about it?"

She leaned against the counter and squinted at me. "Oh, you mean when I came home?"

I nodded.

"Well . . . when I heard Jamie Sneider talking about the dress she wants to buy, it was no big deal. But when I saw that it's exactly like the one I have, I, well, I'm sorry, but I might have cussed. Under my breath."

I raised my eyebrows. "And?"

Shelly's face grew red and she shifted uncomfortably. "And I have a reputation for not cussing."

"And? Honey, I'd like to understand why you're so uncomfortable right now."

Shelly sighed. "I have a reputation for not cussing because of you."

I may have stared as I pondered that. Then I got it. "Oh, you mean because of my lecture series on Naughty Words."

She sighed with relief and nodded.

I pondered a moment longer. "Nope, I still don't get it. Why are you so uncomfortable using a naughty word in a moment of high stress?"

"Well, when you put it like that, I guess I feel better. But I don't like to cuss."

I leaned over and kissed her forehead. "I understand, sweetie, and I'm glad you don't like to cuss. But did you curse her?"

She shook her head.

"Then I think an apology to the Lord might be sufficient. And I'm not going to chew you out for expressing your emotion in an un-Christian-like manner." I smiled at her obvious relief.

It was time to change the subject. "Have you decided who you're going to ask to prom?" Shelly sat at the table with crackers, cheese, and grape juice.

"Nah," she answered. "I thought about asking Jacob. You remember him? He's pretty cool, and I think he's cute, but he really likes this sophomore. I think he'll ask her."

I nodded but stayed silent. Shelly brushed our inquisitive cat, Tom, off the table and continued. "So I kind of wondered if I should just go with a group of my friends, you know, like, girl power." She popped a cracker in her mouth and pumped the air as she chewed. "Then again, I thought maybe I could invite Abe."

"Natalie's Abe?"

"The very one." She grinned at me. "He's really cool, a *great* dresser, and I wouldn't feel uncomfortable with him at all. I mean, he's like a brother, and he talks a lot, so there wouldn't be those weird pauses in conversation, you know what I mean?" I carefully kept my face neutral and nodded.

"Besides," she continued through another mouthful of cracker, "my friends think he's okay, and I wouldn't have to worry about him thinking I should kiss him at the end of the date...I mean, he's like a brother. But he isn't a brother, so dancing with him wouldn't be like...well, it wouldn't be, like, weird or anything." She watched me eagerly.

I folded my hands on the table top. "Abe is very cool, and he'd be a lot of fun to take with you – safe fun, too. I think he's a good choice for taking to a dance."

"Yeah," she began again as I paused for breath, "and he's got this great voice, kind of deep and resonant. And his hair is awesome. And he knows how to dance 'cause he's in that new musical, and they're taking dance lessons for it."

"That's all very true, Love." I hesitated, marshaling my thoughts. "But let's look at the downside of asking him. First, he's a freshman and you're a junior. Would your friends think it's weird? Or would you run into teasing or even people thinking you're seriously interested in each other?"

Shelly made a face. "Ew. Gross." She considered it a moment longer. "Yeah, maybe not." She shook her head, gathered up her snack and headed out of the kitchen.

"Where are you going with that food?" I asked. "And I haven't covered the other points with you."

"Homework," she called back. "And your first point was enough."

I sat at the table a few more minutes. Going from homeschool to public high school had been an adjustment, but it was working well with my first child. Shelly had made some very good friends over the years in band and sports, and they had been thrilled when she finally joined them in their classes. I was planning to do the same with Hannah and Mikey. Hannah will be in ninth grade next year, but Mikey will be in sixth grade, so I still get to keep him with me for a little longer. I sighed and returned the cookbook to the cupboard.

As I closed up the house, gave the animals a little snack, and turned out the lights, I considered Shelly's friends, wondering who she should take to prom. Actually, Abe would be an excellent choice for all of the reasons Shelly had stated. I wished I had kept my mouth shut about why he might not be the perfect prom date.

The next morning, I supervised the feeding of Tom and Jerry, the cats. It's Mikey's job, and they often charm him into giving them extra. I may be a push-over at times, giving them snacks they don't need, but Mikey is much worse than I am. The feeding of Ramon the Wonder Dog is Hannah's job. She needs no supervision. I sent Shelly off to school and got Hannah and Mikey settled in the dining room with their school work.

With a sigh, I sat back down to finish the bills. As I paid the last one, I wondered when our Cockatiel, Asia, had last been fed and watered. The front door slammed, interrupting my thought.

"Mom!" Shelly shouted. She was in a full-out panic. I rushed from my bedroom and flew down the stairs.

"What is it, Shelly?" She was a mess – hair tangled; red, puffy eyes; and mascara ran down her face mixed with tears. "Honey, what's happened?" I asked as she threw herself into my arms, sobbing.

Hannah and Mikey had run from the dining room. I held Shelly, rubbed her tangled hair, and tried to throw reassuring looks at my other children whose eyes were riveted on their older sister.

Finally, Shelly tried to talk. She was still incoherent, so I led her to the living room and pulled her down onto the couch with me, my arms wrapped around her. "What is it, honey?" I still had to wait a few minutes for her to calm down enough to speak.

"Mom," Shelly hiccupped and tried again. "Mom...Jamie Sneider's *dead!*" Shelly wailed and continued sobbing.

Chapter 3
Jamie Sneider's Dead!

J*amie?* I thought. *Jamie Sneider's dead? What in the world?* Finally, as Shelly's sobs lessened somewhat, I asked, "How do you know?"

Shelly's voice was muffled against my shoulder. "Some *idiot* told us over the intercom in school this morning, during the announcements." She shuddered. "Mom, she was mixed in with the band concert and the football game. It was so dumb. How could they do it that way?"

I continued to rub her back. "Do you know how she died? Did they say?"

Shelly shook her head. A disturbing thought (another disturbing thought) came to me. "Shelly, it's only, what, 10:15? Does the school know you're here?"

Still crying, she shook her head, and Hannah ran for the phone. As she brought it to me, she also had the box of tissues in her hand. I took the phone and Hannah silently placed the tissues on the floor next to Shelly. Her eyes were large as she backed up to the wall next to Mikey.

"Hi," I said to the secretary. "This is Danielle Baker, Shelly's mom. I just wanted to let you know Shelly's with me. She heard of the death of Jamie Sneider this morning during announcements, and it's upset her tremendously."

"Oh, thank you for calling, Danielle," the secretary said. "We were wondering if she had gone home. Is she okay? I know a lot of the kids were upset by how the announcement was handled. I'll go ahead and mark her down as at an appointment so she won't be unexcused. Just have her check in at the office when she comes back, okay?"

I shook my head in awe as I hung up the phone. "A student dies overnight. Another student is so upset by the news she runs home to Mom," (*Why*, I wondered, *was she so upset?*), "and all the secretary is concerned about is protocol. This is a strange world we live in." Hannah and Mikey nodded their heads.

I continued to hold Shelly for a while longer. I noticed with a corner of my mind that Ramon and Tom and Jerry were all sitting in a line just inside the door to the living room. Mikey's hand rested on Ramon's head. The cats were sitting on Hannah's feet. I was thankful for them.

That evening, Natalie came over for a latte and a cookie. (Can you imagine; she only ever eats one.) We talked about Jamie's death and Shelly's reaction.

"Why was she so upset?" Natalie asked, carefully fishing coffee grounds out of her mug.

I looked for grounds in my own coffee as I answered. "I guess she had a dream in which she had throttled Jamie with the prom dress. She was extra cranky this morning, but I thought she was just starting her period and let it go. The dream was so vivid, though, that when they announced Jamie's death, for one horrifying moment, she wondered if it was a memory and not a dream. Besides, Shelly had been frustrated and angry with Jamie, and the guilt – on top of the dream – completely unnerved her. She ran home where sanity and Mom are always available."

Natalie looked around. "Mom, yes, I'll give you that. You are usually here. But sanity? You have Ramon the Wonder Dog, Tom and Jerry the insane cats, and a very loud bird." She grinned. "I'm not sure that 'sanity' is the right word."

I smiled and sighed. "I know, you're amazing. Your house is always clean, and you always looks like you're ready to enter a board meeting, not a hair out of place, not a spot or wrinkle." I looked pointedly at her pristine jeans and blouse and shrugged. "Sanity is relative, I guess. When I called the school to let them know she was home with me, all they cared about was making sure she checked in at the office when she came back."

Natalie was shocked. "No way! I'd expect that from a large city, but not from a small town like ours. What's their problem?"

"Well, I guess a few of the kids had run home, like Shelly, and the office was overwhelmed with parents calling and kids missing. I finally talked with the principal. She was furious with whoever did the announcements for how it was handled – she wouldn't say who it was. And because it was botched, they have to bring in extra counselors to help clean up the mess. It's going to cost the school time and money."

Natalie shook her head. "They were going to have to bring in counselors anyway. But wow. Do we know how Jamie died?" She reached for a cookie.

"Oh, my goodness, this is the first time you've ever eaten a second cookie. Are they that good, or are you just that upset? Are you sick, maybe?" I feigned concern, reaching out a hand to feel her forehead.

Natalie slapped my hand away and gave me The Look. It's stopped CEOs of major corporations in its time, but I was almost immune to it. After twenty years, I should be. "Yes, it's good. Your cookies are always good. And, yes, I am upset about Jamie's death. Her mom is probably overwhelmed right now. I wonder what we can do to help."

I had been so wrapped up in calming Shelly and giving hugs to Hannah and Mikey that I hadn't thought about Jamie's mom. Guilt. Guilt. Guilt. *Go away*, I told it, *I'll think of her now.*

And I did think of her, as I absently chewed. Jamie and Linda Sneider live . . . lived together in the trailer park on the edge of town. After a brief marriage, rumored to have lasted about a year, it had been just the two of them, and a single mom doesn't earn a very good living in a small town. But Linda had decided that the meager pay was worth it for Jamie to have the small town life that engendered good, lasting friendships.

"Do you think we should call?" I asked, taking my third cookie.

Natalie shrugged. "Maybe we should take her a casserole or flowers. Or do you think that would be tacky? We really don't know her."

"Doesn't the executive's handbook tell you anything about small town bereavement?" I jibed.

Once again, Natalie gave me The Look. "Executives don't die," she replied loftily. "Except of extreme old age, surrounded by their loving families."

"Right." I snorted (in a genteel and lady-like way).

She chewed a moment. "What about your Pastor Ted? Can't he advise you?"

"What about your Father Bingham? Can't he advise *you?*"

Shelly stormed into the kitchen. "How can you joke about it?" She stood with hands on hips.

Natalie said gently, "If we don't joke, Shelly, we'll cry. And I don't want to cry. It won't help Jamie's mom, and it certainly won't help you. And I do want to help. How are you doing?"

"Oh, Aunty Mommy, I don't know." She flopped into a chair, the tears spilling over again. "I want to be as detached as you and Mom are, but all I do is cry." Large tears rolled down Shelly's cheeks as her face crumpled. Tom (or was it Jerry? They look identical) leaped into her lap. He reached out a soft, gray paw and touched her wet cheek. Shelly buried her face in his soft fur for a moment, wiping her tears on him.

Natalie walked over and hugged Shelly. "You will, sweetie. You will, and sooner than you think, too."

Shelly clung to Natalie for a few moments. She sat at the table with us as we talked about benign subjects like Prom, graduation, the daffodils that were blooming all the way up Highway 99 between Harrisburg and Halsey, a couple of farm towns like ours. As we visited, Shelly stroked Jerry (or was it Tom?).

"Thanks," Shelly finally said as she took four cookies. "I needed that." She dumped the cat onto the floor and headed back to her room.

"I'd better head home," Natalie watched Shelly's retreating form. "How does she eat four cookies and still fit into her jeans?"

"We both did at her age," I replied. "Why did we want to get older? Please remind me. I can't remember."

Natalie smiled at me as she stood. "Because we're wiser when we're older. We make more money. People treat us with more respect. We will eventually not care how much we weigh or what we look like. When we both have mustaches, sagging breasts, varicose veins, and false teeth, we'll eat all the cookies we want."

"Speak for yourself," I retorted. "I plan to die with all my teeth."

As we walked to the door, I grabbed another cookie and declared, "And I think I'd rather eat all the cookies I want to eat now, rather than wait until I can't taste them because I'm so old my taste buds have died."

Natalie laughed and headed out the door. I sat back down to eat my cookie and finish my latte. I would take Linda Sneider a casserole tomorrow.

AT BASEBALL PRACTICE the next afternoon, I was waiting for Mikey; Natalie's son, Danny; and the other boys I had promised to take home. For a while, I pondered Jamie's life and death, and I wondered how her mom was getting through the ordeal. When I had dropped the casserole by, I had been happy to learn that a couple of women were staying with her.

I was distracted by Danny when he caught a pop fly. He had been named after me, the most humiliating fact of his ten-year-old life. Natalie and I were under threat of death, decapitation, and dismemberment if we ever, *ever* mentioned this to anyone.

I smiled, remembering the day we had told Danny where he got his name. He had gone white, red, and white again. His eyes had teared up, and he had bolted from the room, slamming his bedroom door. It was three weeks before he had spoken to me again, and then only to swear me to secrecy.

Gradually, we'd been able to tease each other about our names, and recently, he'd seemed okay with it all. He still didn't want anyone to know, though, that he'd been named after...a *girl*.

"You look like you have a scrumptious secret," Peggy Sue grunted as she seated herself on the bleachers next to me.

Large, blonde, and too old (she said) to care about men, Peggy Sue nonetheless tried to match single men up with the single women in town every chance she got. Never crude but always romantic, she continued, "Is he good looking?"

"Yes," I sighed. "He's got a cute nose...beautiful eyes...a stunning smile."

"No kidding?" Peggy Sue was all ears. "What's he do for a living? How old is he? What's his name?"

"He's in school right now. He's ten years old, and his name is Danny," I answered. "He's out there in left field, wearing his mitt on his head."

Peggy Sue's rollicking laugh rang out. "You got me." I've always loved Peggy Sue's infectious laugh. "I was hoping this time, really hoping, you'd actually started dating, with that smile on your face. What is it that Danny has that no one else has...besides your name?"

I met her twinkling eyes. "I never said a word," I told her. "And you won't, either."

"Of course not," she answered. "But the whole town knows."

"Shh. I've been sworn to secrecy." Again, Peggy Sue's laugh rang out. "Besides, next to Mikey, he's the cutest kid out there. What are you doing here, anyway? This certainly isn't the best seat in town."

"It is for me. I'm picking up the best-looking man in my life," she answered and pointed to a puny little kid standing at third base. Proudly she announced, "He's my grandson, LeRoy."

"No way," I hugged her. "I didn't know you had a grandson. Why have you been keeping this from me?"

"I couldn't hide what I didn't know," she retorted. "I just found out a couple of months ago, and he and my daughter moved in with me last week."

"Daughter?"

Peggy Sue smiled. "Yeah, a small indiscretion when I was in high school." She grimaced. "I was still in Jackson, Mississippi, so no one here in town knows – knew – I was a teenage mother. I gave her up for adoption. And she finally found me." She grinned triumphantly.

Sobering, she continued thoughtfully, "I'm glad she did. I was never given the chance for another child."

"I'm sorry, sweetie," I gave her a one-armed hug.

"People like you don't know the longing for a lost child," she answered without animosity. "You've been blessed with a normal marriage, a normal divorce, a normal motherhood." She sighed and shook her head.

"Then again," she continued in a lighter tone, "I missed out on the pain of raising a brat and get to move right into grandmothering someone else's." And she laughed again, always eager to face forward.

"Sue Ellen's adoptive parents died in a car accident a couple of years ago, so she went looking for me," Peggy Sue sobered. "She said their death ripped her world apart. I'm sorry she lost them, but I can't even *begin* to explain how happy I am to have them here with me. Sue Ellen's working for the motor coach company in Junction City, and I get to run LeRoy around."

"I'm so happy for you." I felt tears prick my eyes and blinked.

She grinned. "I have, like, thirty years of missed memories to make up for. And am I having fun? Girlfriend, we're making memories galore!"

We spent the rest of practice talking about the memories they were making, but it finally ended. As six stinky fifth- and sixth- grade boys jockeyed for seats in my minivan, Peggy Sue said, "It sure is a sad thing about Jamie Sneider, isn't it?"

"Yeah, it is." I looked at her. "You're only just now mentioning Jamie?"

"Hey, I'm all wrapped up in my new family," she protested.

I grinned. "I totally understand."

Peggy Sue continued, "I feel sorry for her parents, though. They don't live together, and Jamie hardly ever saw that loser of a dad of hers, but if that had happened to my kid, even one I didn't know very well, I'd be spittin' mad. Shoot, I might even go lookin' for someone to blame."

I didn't quite understand, but the kids had finally settled in with their seat belts on, and I wanted to get them home. My stomach was growling, and my van already smelled ripe. "I know what you mean," I answered as I looked at Mikey.

Peggy Sue chuckled. "You probably have a *very* slow boil, but I'll bet when you finally explode, everyone scatters out of your way. I'll see you soon, *Danny*." She winked at me and called to her grandson to get into the car as I opened every window before getting in.

As we pulled into our driveway, Mikey asked what was for dinner.

"Well, I thought we'd do tater tots and chicken nuggets," I answered blithely, hoping I still had some in the freezer.

Mikey whooped and ran into the house. "Shower first," I hollered.

I turned as I heard a car stop behind me. It was a brown deputy sheriff's car with two officers inside. I groaned quietly and stood where I was, waiting until they had approached me. I don't have a great love for policemen, and this one had no great love for me.

"Ma'am," the older one asked. "Are you *Mrs*. Baker?" I didn't miss the emphasis on 'Mrs.'

"Yes, I am," I answered, just managing not to roll my eyes. Bruce Carey is a male chauvinist pig, a jerk, and a great friend of my ex-husband, but he had another officer with him who I hadn't met, so I waited patiently to see how this would play out.

"We'd like to speak to you. I'm Officer Carey. This is Officer Nichols."

Chapter 4

The Spruce Bruce and the Hawk

I raised an eyebrow at him and led them to the porch of my beautiful Victorian home. "Would you take a seat? I won't ask you inside, so the children won't be upset." I wondered how often my ex-husband had conducted interviews on someone's porch.

"What can I do for you, Bruce – Officer Carey?" I asked as we sat.

"*Mrs.* Baker, we're looking into the death of Jamie Sneider." I raised my eyebrows.

"Wasn't her death natural?" I asked.

"No, it wasn't. She was..." he looked at me closely. "She was strangled."

"Oh, no! That must have been what Peggy Sue meant when she said Jamie's parents must be especially upset. Her poor parents. I had no idea."

Officer Nichols grimaced. "I take it you aren't on the main grapevine." His voice was higher pitched than the older man's.

At a glare from his partner, he murmured, "Sorry."

I smiled at him. "No, I'm not on the *main* grapevine, Officer Nichols. I can see you understand small town life."

"Yes, ma'am," he answered, relief flooding his face.

Officer Carey took over again. "May we ask you a few questions, *Mrs.* Baker?" I nodded, my temper rising.

"First, are you aware that Jamie and your daughter, Shelly, were involved in an altercation on the last day of Jamie's life?"

I rolled my eyes as my temper finally flared. "For crying out loud, Bruce Carey, that was yesterday. Perhaps you could stop talking like a detective novel and speak to me like a normal human being."

"*Mrs.* Baker, this is a murder investigation." His face reddened more with each word. "You control your attitude and just answer a few questions. If you don't we will take you to *the police station*," he bellowed. Officer Nichols looked scandalized.

Bruce Carey doesn't know the meaning of words larger than two syllables, so my best defense against his posturing is to use as many large words as possible. I took a deep breath and spoke softly. "Bruce Carey, if you are unable to sublimate your emotional ties to my ex-husband for the duration of this investigation, you know you need to request a substitute. I'm not going to accept your blundering antidote to this second-hand offense in salving your wounded feelings. I don't deserve it and neither does Jamie."

I walked into the house and closed the door softly, just to emphasize my self-control over that *creep*. The *nerve* of that man. The phone rang while I was still raving against the lunacy of Officer Bruce Carey.

"Hello?" I nearly shouted into the phone.

It was Natalie. "I heard you had a visit from the police, and you made them sit outside."

"You heard nothing of the sort." I grinned. "You were standing behind the hedge across the street. I saw you."

"Okay, I admit it. But you didn't let them into the house."

"Of course I didn't. It was that . . . that *jerk* Bruce Carey and his new partner. You know how I feel about the Spruce Bruce."

"Good for you. I'll be right over. I want all the details."

"Wait!" I shouted. "Are they gone?"

Natalie laughed. "Officer Nichols practically dragged the Spruce Bruce to their car. I'm not sure he would have left, even then, but they got a call."

She hung up the phone as I sighed in relief, and I started a pot of coffee.

Shelly glided into the room. "Did I hear you talking to that creepy friend of Dad's?"

"Yes, you did, love. He was here to talk to me about Jamie's death."

"Why?" she asked warily.

Thinking quickly, I opted for discretion. "In the event of a sudden death, the police have to investigate. You know that from what your dad used to say." Shelly nodded, grabbed a box of crackers, and glided back out of the room, practicing her Hollywood walk as Natalie burst through the door.

"I want to hear every word," she demanded.

I laughed. "Did you run all the way over here? Sit down, and give yourself a chance to breathe more slowly." I deposited a plate of cookies and our coffee mugs on the table.

We talked through the evening, discussing every aspect of Jamie's life, death, parents, friends, everything. Natalie said, "Jamie had very few rules at home, and she broke those she had."

"Like what?" I asked curiously.

"What do you mean, 'like what?'" Natalie shot back.

I shifted in my seat. "I mean, what kind of rules did she have, and how did she break them?"

"Does it matter?"

"No," I smiled. "I'm really just curious."

Natalie fished a coffee ground out of her cup. "Well, she didn't have a curfew, although she was supposed to sleep at home on school nights."

"So she would sometimes not come home?" I asked. Natalie nodded. "Where would she sleep, then?"

Natalie shrugged. "No clue," she said, "but knowing Jamie, probably at a boy's house."

I nodded. "What else?"

"Well, I know she didn't have her driver's license, and I've seen her driving every now and then."

I groaned. "That doesn't feel safe at all!"

Natalie grinned. "Want to hear more?"

I shook my head. "I've heard enough. I knew Jamie was a rule-breaker, but I never asked what rules she was breaking. I just assumed if she was told to eat her veggies, she'd have potato chips instead."

Natalie laughed. "Close enough. She was certainly a rebellious teen."

We sighed together.

Natalie continued, "Her mom is an alcoholic."

I nodded. That wasn't news, so Natalie continued, "And no one knows how she died. Except the police, of course, and they're being unnaturally closed-mouthed about it. We usually hear *some*thing, but nothing has hit the grapevine so far."

I blinked. "That's weird." Natalie nodded agreement. "I wonder why."

Natalie shrugged. "No idea. I usually hear the gossip -"

"I hate gossip," I interrupted.

"I know," Natalie grinned. "You hate gossip, you homeschool so you don't go to PTO meetings and other school functions, and even if you did, you would stay away from those who exchange the news."

I scoffed, "Whereas *you* -"

"*Whereas?*" Natalie laughed.

"*You*," I repeated, "hear a lot more gossip because you visit with as many people as possible every day, *and* you attend every school meeting offered."

"I get lonely," Natalie shrugged. "Being an executive in a private office can be isolating. So I talk when I can."

"Of course," I answered. "That's why you gossip." We smiled at each other, that comfortable smile of acceptance between lifelong friends.

We continued to talk for another hour or so. Finally, Natalie sighed. "We still know almost nothing, and I'm exhausted. I'm going home and to bed."

Monday morning, I got Shelly out the door for school and Hannah and Mikey going for the day. I changed the litter box and let Ramon out for his run through the back yard. Then it was time for me to work on my newest book.

Being a writer allows me to work from home, exercising the creative brain that God gave me, while offering me the chance to travel every now and then. I love to travel, and it's all in the name of research. And I do like research. Mostly, I write young adult historical fiction; but recently I've branched out into teen historical adventures. Hannah and Mikey can interrupt me if they have questions dealing with their school assignments, but the curriculum I'd chosen for them was working very well, and this far into the school year, they rarely needed help.

Two hours later, there was a knock on the door. Until this morning, I had been enjoying writing this particular story of a teen-age Irish girl who had immigrated to the U.S. in the early 1900s. I sighed as I looked away from the computer screen. My teen-age heroine was sounding and acting a lot like Jamie, real life intruding into my work. I would probably have to rewrite everything I'd done. I clicked "save" anyway, just in case it wasn't as bad as I feared.

On my way to the door, I glanced into the dining room – home school central – and laughed at the dog's hopeful attitude. He wasn't going to see even a small crumb of food today. I opened the door to an attractive man in a suit. He had dark hair and blue eyes, and he said nothing for a moment.

"Can I help you?" I smiled at him.

"Oh, yes, so sorry," he snapped out of his reverie. "Ah you Danielle Bak-uh?" I nodded. "I'm D.C.I. Hokeswuth. This is my nappie-changuh, D.C. Smith."

My American brain took a moment to translate the plummy English accent.

"My name is Smythe, sir," smiled the female officer I hadn't noticed. I thought about my Prom conversation with Natalie the other day and wondered if Officer Smythe was a niece or younger sister of the boy Natalie had gone to prom with. She would be too old to be a daughter.

D.C.I. Hokeswuth (Hokes*worth*?) glanced over. "Ah you shu-ah?"

Officer Smythe's smile widened. "Yes, sir."

"Ah. Thank you. " D.C.I. Hokesworth (Hokes*wuth*?) answered.

Turning back to me, he asked, "May we speak with you a moment?" I was loving the English accent. And then he smiled. Dimples! Deep dimples, dark brown hair, blue eyes. I nearly swooned.

"Please?" he asked.

I pulled myself together and answered. "Oh, yes, please do come in, Detective..."

"Hokeswuth, spelled H-A-W-K-S-W-O-AH-T-H."

"Detective Hawksworth, yes, please do come in." I led the officers into the living room. The kids came out, curious (and cautious) about our visitors, only one of whom was in uniform. "These are two of my children, Hannah and Mikey."

"Michael," Mikey muttered.

"Michael, Hannah," Detective Hawksworth said. "It's very nice to meet you." It almost sounded like "verra nice". I decided I'd have to exercise extra self-control to concentrate on his words rather than his accent.

"Won't you please sit down, Detective Hawksworth? Officer Smythe?"

Detective Hawksworth chose the sofa, Officer Smythe a straight-backed chair, and I chose a wing back chair facing the dimples. . . the detective.

Mikey asked, "What does D.C.I. stand for?"

Detective Hawksworth looked surprised. "Did I use that title? Dear me, I must have thought I was back home for a moment. I'm from England, you know, and there I have the title Detective Chief Inspector. You don't use that title here in the States. I suppose you should just call me Detective Hawksworth."

"What's a 'nappie-chang-uh'?" Mikey asked.

Officer Smythe grinned as the detective laughed and answered, "A 'nappie-chang-uh' is someone who changes nappies. What you might call diapers. It was an unprofessional phrase to use, so don't give me away, okay, mate? Officer Smythe is my American escort, here to show me how to conduct myself in the U.S. We don't want to get me into any trouble culturally, do we?"

"Why are you here?" Mikey asked.

"Mikey, don't be rude," I admonished.

Detective Hawksworth smiled again. "I don't mind the questions. They're very good ones. Actually," (it sounded like 'akshully'), "I'm here on attachment...You Americans call it a job exchange, for two years of service while someone from your country is doing my job in the U.K. This gives us intimate experience of each other's police procedural methods and is good for public relations."

"Oh, cool," Mikey said. He perched on the arm of the chair Hannah was sitting in. They were ready to listen.

"Ah you two ill? Is that why you ahn't in school?" asked Detective Hawksworth.

"No, we're homeschooled," Hannah answered. "That means Mom's our teacher here at home."

He nodded. "Do you like it?"

Mikey shrugged and answered, "Usually. We have shorter school days, and we get to go on a lot of field trips."

Hannah smiled shyly. "And we still do band and sports at the public school, so we have a lot of friends. Besides, we learn at our own pace, whether that's a little ahead of our peers or slightly behind."

"Which we aren't." Mikey boasted. "We're both a little ahead." He looked to see if the detective was impressed.

"Fascinating. I would love to learn more about it, but if you don't mind, I need to talk to your muthuh for a moment." Detective Hawksworth smiled at the children again, and Hannah breathed a sigh, undoubtedly smitten by those dimples. Mikey stood quickly, and he and Hannah walked from the room.

"It was nice to meet you, Detective Hawksworth," Hannah said softly as she walked out.

I noticed they left the door open.

As I watched the kids leave, I glanced with affection around my old Victorian house. Sometimes, it just hits me – out of the blue – that I'm living in my dream house. It's one of the oldest in our small town. The United States, and especially Oregon, doesn't have the history of England or other European countries, but I'm very proud of my house. The small rooms, the upper middle class opulence of 1876, when the house was built, and my decorating skills (if I do say so myself) all combine to create a homey atmosphere. I was sure Detective Hawksworth, with four-hundred-year-old buildings common in his birth place, hadn't noticed the care and love we used to bring the old house back from the brink of the grave, but the kids and I love it, especially the "character" – crooked walls, sloping floors, funky nooks and crannies. And doors, many doors. Every room has a door; they served to keep the rooms warm before central heating.

Before Detective Hawksworth spoke, I moved over to close the door, checking to see that there were no eavesdroppers standing on the other side. Coming back, I sat again facing him, and waited for him to start the conversation.

"Thank you, Mrs. . . Ms Baker?"

"Missus is fine," I said. "I am divorced, but everyone still calls me Missus, and I don't mind."

"Well, then, thank you, Mrs. Baker, for speaking with me." It sounded like 'Bakuh', so cool. And then he smiled, and I nearly fell off my chair. Mentally, I shook myself. "This conversation isn't compulsory, you understand, and you may choose not to answer questions." I nodded a little nervously as Officer Smythe took out her notebook.

"Have you lived here long?" he continued.

"Most of my adult life," I answered. "Detective Hawksworth, may I ask you a question?"

He nodded.

"Are you here to ask questions about Jamie Sneider's death?"

He hesitated a moment. "Yes. I understand Officer Carey and you were unable to complete an interview yesterday."

"Yes, we were," I answered. "He was offensive. Our small town doesn't have a detective branch, so I assume you're from Albany, serving Linn County. Am I correct?"

"Yes." He waited for me to continue. When I didn't, he asked, "Did Officer Carey ask you about the disagreement that took place between your daughter, Shelly, and her friend Jamie?"

"He tried to, but I'm afraid I'd used up all my patience on his posturing, and I didn't answer him." I smiled. "I have great stores of patience, Detective Hawksworth. I have to; I'm a mom. However, I don't suffer fools gladly."

Chapter 5
I Can Ask Someone Else

Officer Smythe snorted and quickly covered her mouth as Detective Hawksworth grinned then sobered almost immediately. The dimples nearly sent me into orbit again. I'm sure people beg to tell him things, just so they can see him smile.

"Mrs. Baker, I shall have to ask you about that disagreement. I've not spoken with Shelly, yet..."

"And you want to corroborate our stories. No, don't bother to deny it; I know a little something about police detection. Not much, I admit, but a little something." I sighed.

"I wasn't going to deny it, actually. I was merely going to tell you that Shelly isn't, at this point, a suspect. Right now, we're trying to piece together Jamie Sneider's last days." It sounded like, "Right now, we'uh trying to piece togethuh Jamie Sniduh's lahst days."

Pay attention, I told myself.

"Detective, Shelly didn't tell me about any fight the two girls may have had. She came home from school upset because Jamie was planning to buy the same dress for Prom that Shelly had purchased. She felt that she would be short and chubby next to the taller, slimmer Jamie."

I realized I was being a bit aggressive, so I smiled and softened my voice. "After I promised to go with her to exchange the dress for another one if Jamie did in fact buy that dress, she was much happier.

Within an hour, the whole thing was forgotten in thoughts of who she would invite to the dance."

"So she was very upset when she came home from school," Detective Hawksworth clarified. "But after a conversation with you, she felt better. Did she, do you think, forget the whole thing in favor of choosing an escort . . . a date? Why was she choosing her date? Don't the young men ask the young ladies to dances here in the States?"

"Well, normally, yes. But Shelly has made it clear from the very beginning of high school that she doesn't and won't date until she's ready to choose a husband. And then she plans to be courted.

"It was her idea, one she got from a book," I answered his skeptical look with a smile, "but if some young man catches her eye, she may change her mind instantly."

"And her attitude that evening?"

"She was fine. In fact, we discussed several of her friends as possible dates."

"Well, thank you very much, Mrs. Baker." He stood to go, Officer Smythe following. "I shall let you get back to homeschooling your children. May I return this evening to interview Shelly? You are welcome to be present at the interview, of course."

I considered the ramifications. "It isn't that I don't want you to interview her," I answered slowly. Detective Hawksworth sat back down. Choosing my words carefully, I said, "It's just that policemen in the house bring back painful memories of my ex-husband. I don't want to complicate this matter with another." I thought a moment.

"Would you mind meeting us at my friend Natalie's house? Natalie Shalligan is a close friend of the family. I'm sure Shelly would be fine, emotionally, speaking to you there. I'm pretty sure, anyway."

Detective Hawksworth was watching me closely. Any policeman who heard the words I'd spoken would be concerned. But he smiled again and said, "That should be fine."

I told him where Natalie lived and he left the house, calling good-bye to Hannah and Mikey who were standing outside the dining room door. They looked a bit anxious.

I reassured them that both Detective Hawksworth and Officer Smythe were respectful and that all they wanted was to ask about Jamie, nothing else.

That evening, Mikey and Hannah argued that they should go to Natalie's, too. It was obvious they wanted to try to protect Shelly and me from what the police might say and do. And to see those dimples again, if I knew my Hannah. Both children had been impressed with Detective Hawksworth, I could tell, but they didn't fully trust him. I finally had to threaten them with a ten-page research assignment on the troglobites of southern New Zealand if they didn't stay home. I'd discovered the cave-dwelling animals while doing research for a book on sheep ranching in New Zealand during World War II and thought they'd sounded interesting. After weighing the costs, they reluctantly agreed to stay behind.

I left quickly, before they changed their minds.

"Now, tell me everything," Natalie said. "And I mean *everything*."

Moving my mug of coffee in a circle on the dining room table, I told her everything that was said. She listened attentively, interrupting just a few times to ask how Detective Hawksworth had looked or sounded as he asked a question.

Finally, she asked, "What does he look like?"

I'd hoped she wouldn't ask me that. I wanted the fun of watching her face when she saw his dimples, dark hair, and blue eyes.

"Oh, man, well," I exaggerated shamelessly. "He's about six feet tall, dark hair, you know, just a man. And a policeman at that," I added with disgust. "He'll be here in about ten minutes, so you'll see then."

Natalie was disappointed. "Oh, well," she sounded resigned. "He'll have an English accent, and that covers a multitude of sins."

I smiled to myself. I seriously didn't like policemen after my marriage and divorce, but she was kind of right. That plummy English accent, the good looks, those dimples . . . yes, it all combined to cover the multitude of sins of the job title alone.

As Detective Hawksworth's car pulled into Natalie's driveway, I called to Shelly to come downstairs. She and Abe, Natalie's oldest, were playing a computer game in the games room (only the rich have a games room, right?), and I wanted her to be there when the detective walked in. I was sure her *sang froid* would be much greater than Natalie's.

And it was. Shelly was nonplussed for a moment, but Natalie's mouth actually hung open. I nudged her aside and invited Detective Hawksworth into the house. He was alone this time and had the grace to pretend not to notice Natalie staring. I took a moment to wonder how often he faced this kind of reaction and if he was totally conceited about himself because of it. I hoped not. Natalie's mouth snapped shut as she smacked my arm, and she asked if the Detective would like a cup of coffee or if he preferred tea.

"American tea, or English?" he asked with a twinkle in his eye.

"American, I'm afraid," answered Natalie, her own eyes twinkling. Obviously she had recovered. "And to add insult to injury, the coffee is decaf."

Natalie gasped at the dimples as Detective Hawksworth smiled and said, "Coffee would be wonderful, thank you."

He turned to Shelly and me. "As you can see, I came alone, so this will be an informal interview. No note-taking, just a quiet conversation, all right?"

Shelly nodded, obviously nervous. As we all sat down in the living room of Natalie's craftsman-style home, Detective Hawksworth looked around with obvious pleasure. "Another beautiful home," he said as Natalie handed him his coffee. She beamed and sat down in a chair, slightly removed from the three of us.

The detective frowned but didn't tell Natalie to leave.

"Shelly," he began, "please tell me a bit about your school."

"Is this supposed to make me feel more comfortable with you?" Shelly asked defensively. "Because it won't work, so just ask the questions."

Detective Hawksworth didn't even blink. He answered quietly, pleasantly, and with respect, even. "Actually, I'm still new here and hoped you could help me – genuinely help, not just waste time – with the relationships between different age groups. I can ask someone else, however, if you prefer not to answer."

Shelly looked at me, slightly confused. This wasn't what she was expecting. Finally, she shrugged and looked at the detective. "All right, well, what do you want to know?"

"Let's just say I have no idea how it all works here, shall we? Tell me how the different forms interact, er, the different grades."

Shelly thought a moment. "Well, most of the classes we take are with our own grade, but some classes, like band, art, and some of the honors classes have more than one grade in them." She paused a moment. "Is that what you're looking for?"

"Yes, that's exactly what I'm hoping for," answered the detective with a smile. "So, would Jamie have classes with students outside of her grade level?"

Shelly thought a moment. "I don't know all of the classes she's taking . . . took. I know she wasn't in band or the honors classes I'm in. She might have been in art, and I'm pretty sure she wasn't in leadership class . . . I just don't know."

Shelly waited for the next question, obviously more relaxed than she had been a few minutes before. Detective Hawksworth took her through the last day of Jamie's life, asking her what had upset her about the prom dress, what she had done about it, what the argument was really about, the prom dress or something else.

Shelly leaned forward, her shoulders hunched. "I didn't argue with Jamie."

"Several people saw you arguing with her," the detective countered.

Shelly shook her head. "They saw wrong. I didn't talk to Jamie that day at all."

"According to witnesses, the altercation between you and Jamie was quite loud. Some even described it as 'a screaming match.'"

Again, she shook her head, crossing her arms. "Didn't happen."

Quietly but with increased intensity, the detective continued, "Witnesses place you at the argument with Jamie. You can't deny what so many others saw."

"I *can* deny what isn't true." Shelly bounced in irritation. "I will tell you the truth every time, and I didn't argue with Jamie. I didn't even talk to her. I can't argue with someone I never spoke to."

"And *I* can't deny the witnesses, Shelly," Detective Hawksworth said a bit more sharply.

Shelly stood, arms crossed. "Who are these witnesses, huh? Who are they?"

Detective Hawksworth looked up at Shelly. "I can't tell you who the witnesses are . . ."

Shelly made a "Pfft" noise and waved her arm. "Great. I can be accused, but I can't know my accuser? That is totally unjust." She flopped back down into the chair, eyes bright with unshed tears.

"All I want to know," began the detective.

"No," I interrupted. Shelly and Detective Hawksworth looked at me. My hands were shaking, defying this policeman, but I would protect my daughter. "We are done with this interview. Shelly has given you the information you sought. Whether you believe her or not, she is nearly in tears, and I will not have her browbeaten."

Detective Hawksworth smiled gently. "I would never browbeat Shelly, Mrs. Baker."

"Whatever you want to call it, we're done for tonight."

He nodded, and Natalie breathed a sigh of relief. I had seen her look at the door a couple of times, wishing her husband, Shea, were here with us.

"Can we continue this interview tomorrow morning at the school?" the detective asked. Shelly looked at me. I nodded, so she agreed on ten o'clock, during her least favorite class, American Government.

Before he left, Detective Hawksworth shook Shelly's hand and said, "You have been very helpful, Shelly. You know, though, that if you didn't argue with Jamie, someone who looks like you did. I should really like to speak with that young woman. If you know who she is, or if you discover her name, please tell your mum or me. I want to find out what truly happened to Jamie. No one should end her life so young and so violently."

Eyes bright with tears, Shelly looked the detective in the eye and simply said, "Thank you." And she turned and hugged me for a long moment.

Natalie let the detective out and put frozen pizzas in the oven. An hour later, smiling again and full of pizza and donuts, Shelly went home to bed, and Natalie and I shared another pot of coffee at the dining room table.

"You are so mean," Natalie exclaimed as soon as the door closed behind Shelly. "'Just a man,' you said. 'He's okay,' you said. You...you don't lie. Except, you *lied*. I'm devastated." She lay back in the dining chair, the back of her hand on her forehead.

"I didn't lie, I prevaricated," I grinned at her sound of disgust. "I wanted you to be surprised. Isn't he gorgeous? You drooled."

"Yes, he's gorgeous," she sat up instantly. "And I didn't drool. But those dimples."

"Those eyes."

"Those dimples."

"That accent."

"Those *dimples.*"

We laughed. Natalie's husband walked into the room. "I don't have dimples, so you aren't talking about me." Shea (pronounced Shay) Shalligan is an amiable teddy bear, muscular, tanned, a carpenter of highest quality. Italian by ancestry, Shea and Natalie often tell their story to confused strangers when they meet.

Shea's great-grandfather was Irish. He married an Italian. Their son married an Italian, their son married an Italian, and *their* son married an Italian. They often joke that their sons, Abe and Danny, will have to marry Italian women. "They're the only ones who know how to cook," Natalie jokes. (Says the woman with frozen pizzas.)

Natalie tugged him into the chair next to her. "We're talking about the new detective. He came here to interview Shelly about Jamie Sneider's death."

Shea instantly looked concerned. "How did that go?"

"Not too badly," I answered. "He was patient and respectful," I smiled at Shea's look of pleased surprise, "but I should go home. I just wanted a few minutes to ask Natalie what she thought of our new limey."

As I closed the door, I heard Shea ask, "What's a limey?"

I laughed softly. Shea doesn't have the intelligence of Natalie, but he's a wonderful husband and father. *No competition there,* I thought. And I thanked God for giving my children this example of a good marriage.

The next morning, I was preparing for the meeting with Detective Hawksworth. We were to meet at the school in forty-five minutes, and I felt like I was running out of time. Hannah entered my bedroom.

"Mom, can I do another extra science experiment . . .why are all these clothes on your bed?"

"I'm having trouble deciding what to wear," I answered.

"I don't understand," she stared at me. "You always just throw on jeans and a t-shirt."

"Well, I don't want to wear jeans and a t-shirt for a meeting at the school." I turned around to find Tom (or was it Jerry?) sitting on a blouse. "Get off, cat!"

"Why? You've never cared before. Mom," Hannah gasped. "You like Detective Hawksworth, don't you? I mean, like, *like.* Ew. That's gross. You're too old for him."

She stomped from the room. I stood and stared after her, my pretty, curly-haired daughter, and hoped my 14-year-old wasn't smitten with a 40-something-year-old detective from another country. An image of those dimples floated in front of my eyes, and I decided to forgive her if she were.

But, I asked myself, *could she possibly be right*? I shook my head. There was *no way* I was going to get involved with another policeman. And I was perfectly content with my life as it was. "On the other hand, little missy, I am not too old for him," I muttered to the absent Hannah. "He's at least my age, if not a little older. And he's an attractive man...fun to look at." Time passed as I sat and smiled to myself, and I had to rush to reach the school on time. The tailored outfit I wore was chosen - not because it looked good on me (it did), but for professional reasons only.

Mary's Peak, the tallest hill in our part of Oregon's coastal mountain range, rose majestically over the top of the high school as I parked. *The Willamette Valley is a beautiful place to live,* I thought with a contented sigh. The daffodils and tulips were blooming around the school sign, and the flowering plum trees shaded the quad, shedding pretty pink petals on the green grass.

As I walked toward the school office to check in, I saw several girls I didn't know sitting at a picnic table in the sunshine. They were giggling about something, but I wasn't interested in what it might be. It's a sad truth that the very atmosphere of a high school can and does take me back to my own insecure youth. If I never walk on a high school campus again for the rest of my life, I will be perfectly happy.

The secretary showed me where to sign my name, gave me a visitor's pass, and pointed me to the conference room. Shelly wasn't there, yet, but Detective Hawksworth and Officer Smythe were. The detective looked even more stunning in the morning light.

"Good morning, Mrs. Baker. Thank you for coming," he smiled at me. I realized I was early after all as I returned the greeting, and we visited for a couple of minutes as we waited for Shelly. A movement at the door caught my attention.

"Good morning, Danielle. Good morning, Detective Hawksworth," Natalie breezed in wearing her power meeting suit with an emerald green silk blouse. "I hope you don't mind, but Shelly is nearly as much my child as Danielle's. I will be a quiet support for both her and Danielle, but I'm going to stay."

Chapter 6

Who Was Arguing With Jamie After School?

Natalie's defiant gaze quickly melted into a smile as she met Detective Hawksworth's amusement. "Thank you," she sighed and her shoulders relaxed.

"I understand your concern for Shelly, Mrs. Shalligan, and I respect it. If Mrs. Baker approves, you are welcome to stay."

Natalie plopped down into a chair as Shelly walked into the room.

"What's this, the Spanish Inquisition?" she asked doubtfully.

"Your mother is here because you are a minor," answered Detective Hawksworth. "Mrs. Shalligan is here as support. Since we are doing a fact-gathering interview, she is welcome to stay if you agree."

Shelly looked at Natalie and gave her that lopsided smile of hers as she sat in the fourth chair. "Aunty-Mommy can stay."

Detective Hawksworth blinked. "Aunty-Mommy? I'm not familiar with that term. Is it an American colloquialism?"

"No, it's a family thing," Shelly looked him in the eye. She seemed more at ease this morning. "She's like Mom's sister, making her our honorary aunt. But she's like our unofficial mom when our mom is busy or sick or something. So she's our Aunty-Mommy."

Detective Hawksworth nodded and the interview went from there, Officer Smythe writing in a notebook spread on her knee. We learned nothing new, and Shelly denied having a fight with Jamie. She explained that they hadn't even talked after Jamie had described the dress she was going to buy.

"With whom do you believe she may have been ahguing?" Detective Hawksworth asked. (*So cute!* I sneaked a glance at Natalie. Her eyes were on Shelly.)

Shelly shrugged. "We-e-l-l," she said. "Are you sure there was a fight? It could have just been a rumor. This school is overrun with them."

I jumped up. "I'll be right back," I called as I ran through the door.

The girls were still sitting at the picnic table. As I approached them, I prayed for wisdom. They looked at me as if I were an alien from some unappetizing planet. *Well,* I thought, *they probably won't want to bite me if I look that bad.*

"Good morning," I smiled at them. "Just a little while ago, you girls were talking about something, and I thought I heard the word, 'fight'. You weren't talking about the fight Jamie Sneider had with someone the other day, were you?"

They just stared at me. I began to despair of getting any answer at all when one of them finally spoke. She had about fourteen piercings on her face. It was hard to concentrate.

"Jamie and this band geek, Shelly Baker, were going at it after school out by the football stands," she said with a sneer. I suspected she knew I was Shelly's mom.

"Did you see them 'going at it'?" I asked.

Another girl snorted. "No, we weren't there. We have better things to do than hang around this dump."

"Then how do you know they were going at it?" I asked.

"Well, everyone knows," a third girl answered. She had green hair that she kept twisting around a paint-stained finger.

"I'm sorry; I'm out of the loop. Who would be 'everyone'?"

A fourth girl, obviously the leader as she was the most attractive of that motley group, said, "Ask the band geeks. They were practicing on the football field – for *next year's* football games. After school, even. They're such losers." She snapped, and they all rose together and left.

I returned to the office and asked the secretary, "Who might be in the marching band who I could talk to?"

"Besides Shelly, you mean?" she asked brightly. "Well, you might talk to –"

"No, thank you," I blushed. "I'll ask Shelly." I returned to the conference room. It looked as if no one had moved.

"Shelly, who was arguing with Jamie after school a couple of days ago?" I demanded as I entered the room.

Immediately, she looked sullen. *Aha!* I thought. *You were hoping I wouldn't ask that.* I sat and waited. The others followed my lead.

Finally, her face red, Shelly said, "From the gossip going around the lunch room, I guess she was fighting with Kelly, but it wasn't about the dress. They were fighting over Jamie's boyfriend."

We waited for her to continue. She looked at me, silently pleading.

"Shelly," I reminded her quietly, "someone killed her. We need to know why. And we need to hear about the things that led up to it, even if it's gossip."

Shelly dropped her gaze with a sigh and said, "Jamie accused Kelly of coming on to her boyfriend. Kelly said Jamie was a disgusting, selfish pig, and Jamie called Kelly a slut...it ended up being a screaming match. I wasn't marching, 'cause I came home to tell you about the dress, but I walked past them while they were yelling at each other.

"I guess everyone thought it was me she was fighting with, since I missed band." Shelly shifted in her chair. "Oh, I need you to excuse the absence, Mom."

"I already did, remember?"

Shelly shook her head. "That was the next day. After school marching for next year's football games is required spring term, and I was home with you."

"Oh, right. I was confusing the days," I answered. "I'll get it excused before I leave today, okay?" She nodded.

Detective Hawksworth asked, "Shelly, who is this Kelly? Does she have a surname?"

"Oh, sure, she's Kelly Green. She's this little freshman and really cute, but she's a...umm..." Shelly's face turned a bright red. "I don't know how to phrase this. Let's just say she'll cuckold any guy she's dating, or any other girl's boyfriend."

I turned to the surprised detective. "That means she sleeps around."

"Mo-om, I *hate* that phrase."

"I know, honey . . ."

Shelly continued, "Because they're doing anything *but*."

"And I understand that, but not everyone . . ."

"I know my Shakespeare, Mrs. Baker," the detective interrupted our spat with a smile. "You are a bright young lady, Shelly. I'm impressed with your understanding of Shakespearian language."

Shelly smiled. "Thank my mom. She taught me."

I hugged Shelly. "Thank you for being honest, honey. I know you wanted to protect Kelly –"

"No, Mom, it isn't that." Shelly protested. "I just hate gossip, and I didn't want to pass it on if I didn't have to. It hurts. You know that." And she leapt from her chair. "May I go, now?"

Detective Hawksworth nodded.

"I'll see you at home," she blew me a kiss. Just before she left the room, she turned and said, "Thank you for coming, Auntie Mommy. And thank *you*, Detective Hawksworth, for leaving the rack back at the station." And with an impish grin, she was gone.

"Why do people think the police still put people on the rack?" Detective Hawksworth asked plaintively. "The Spanish Inquisition wasn't even a police inquiry."

Natalie and I laughed in relief, and the detective asked the secretary to page Kelly Green. As he returned to the room, he said, "Thank you, ladies, for your help. If I need anything else, I will call on you."

"Don't you need a female to be with you during this interview?" I was willing to stay; I cared about these kids, and I didn't want them hurt any more than they already were.

"Yes, I do, but the secretary (he said, 'secretree') has called Kelly's mum, and Officer Smythe will be here with me until she arrives."

Natalie and I left the office – after signing out, of course. The cheerful *sec-re-tree* made sure of it. On our way to the parking lot, we ran into little Kelly Green.

"Hi, Kelly," I said cheerfully. "Are you okay? You look nervous."

"Oh, hi, Mrs. Baker. I'm on my way to the office, but I don't know what I've done wrong."

"Oh, I expect someone wants to ask you about the argument you had with Jamie Sneider the other day."

Kelly looked almost scared now. "Oh, Mrs. B, what should I do? I don't want to talk about it."

I put an arm around her shoulder. "Just tell the truth, Kelly," I told her. "That's all Detective Hawksworth wants. That way he doesn't make any mistakes."

"All right. If you're sure."

I hugged her. "If you want to talk later, you know where I live. I'm here for you."

Kelly smiled her thanks. As she walked into the office, Natalie murmured, "Smooth, Danielle, real smooth."

"I was, wasn't I?" I smiled at her. "I wish she'd said more, though."

Kelly's wobbly smile haunted me for the rest of the day. I tried to write, but only managed to "paint" Kelly into the story.

"Way to go, Danielle," I told myself. "Not only did you put Jamie into the story yesterday, but now you're doing it with Kelly. Behave yourself." I wrote some more, but it was no good. My subconscious mind was working on the real life problem, so I turned off the computer as the phone rang.

"Hi, are you busy?" It was Natalie.

I sighed. "Not right now. I don't seem to be able to write. Why? Aren't you busy?"

"Of course. I'm at work three hours later than usual," she answered. "But you and I need to get together and talk." I could hear her shuffling papers.

"About what? Have I offended you?"

She chuckled. "Of course not. But I don't like seeing Shelly upset, and little Kelly Green looked a little queasy when she left us, and this town needs to see the end of this business. You and I are intelligent women with our ears to the gossip mill. Surely we can come up with some leads on this case."

I laughed. "First, it's been two whole days. Give the police some time to work."

She inhaled to answer me, but I pushed on.

"Second, we aren't the investigators, Natalie. And what do you mean, *we* are part of the gossip mill? You're the one who hears the gossip, not me." I heard papers shuffle and the creak of her chair as she sat back and sighed. "But I know what you mean. Something needs to be done before the entire town falls apart." We settled on eight o'clock that evening, after dinner and homework.

Chapter 7
You Started It!

"Okay," Natalie began our discussion that evening. I was still making coffee, shoving the cats away with my foot. They weren't hungry, and I couldn't imagine them liking the stuff, so they must just be curious. Natalie was rummaging in the cupboards. "Don't you have *anything* to eat?" I opened the freezer and pulled out a zippered baggie of last week's chocolate chocolate chip cookies. Natalie grabbed a plate to put them on.

"Okay," she said again, sitting at the table. I brought the coffee. "We need to look at what we know and go over everything we've heard so far." She looked at our cups, the cookies, napkins, and various school papers on the kitchen table. "Don't you have paper and pen ready?"

I went to the junk drawer and pulled out an old grocery list and a pen. "There's no writing on the back," I said as I sat back down. Natalie wrinkled her nose but said nothing.

"I forgive you."

She looked surprised. "Huh?"

"For being so clean, you don't have old grocery lists or wrinkled bits of paper around your house." I smiled. "Do you even have a junk drawer?"

Natalie rolled her eyes. "Before I forget, I talked with Mrs. Waters today."

"The exchange student coordinator?"

"Yep. I overheard someone at the grocery store say that Jamie was working with her on coordinating field trips for the exchange students."

I raised an eyebrow. "Are you sure?"

Natalie nodded. "I wondered the same thing. I guess she was hoping to be a mentor to Jamie, to help her get her life back on track."

"How long had she worked with Jamie?"

"Only a couple of weeks."

"Oh, too bad. I've always liked her. I hope it did some good."

"I hope so, too. Anyway, let's look at what we know."

I put a hand out. "Wait. Did Jamie know any of the exchange students? Should we talk to them?"

Natalie shook her head. "Mrs. Waters didn't know, but I'll ask my kids and talk to any who knew her. Now, back to our task. First, we know that Jamie and Shelly were at odds about the dress."

"No," I corrected her, "we don't know that. Shelly was upset about the dress, but she didn't say anything to Jamie about it. She came home and talked to me. It wasn't until the next day that people talked about Shelly and the dress being an issue between the girls."

"That's right," Natalie nodded. "I'd forgotten. These are good cookies. Where'd you get the recipe?"

"From Peggy Sue," I answered absently, wondering if we actually knew anything at all.

Natalie took another bite. "They don't taste like Peggy Sue's cookies. They're better."

"I changed the recipe. Can we get back to the murder, now?"

Natalie nodded.

"Good," I said firmly. "I think the big thing we have right now is the problem between Kelly Green and Jamie about Jamie's boyfriend. That's about our only fact, isn't it?"

Natalie chewed for a moment longer. "No, we also know that Jamie was strangled...with her prom dress."

I stared at her, aghast. "No. You mean the same one Shelly has now?" I lay my head on the table. "We're going to have to get another prom dress. Oh, man, oh, man . . . this is so bad. Poor Shelly. Poor Jamie."

"You didn't know?" Natalie stared at me. "How could you not know? Everyone in town knows."

"Except me. And obviously Shelly," I answered. "Come on, tell me the details." I looked at my coffee, but my stomach felt queasy.

"Well, she was found with this dress around her neck. It's long, dark blue, kind of slinky with sequins and a slit all the way up the thigh."

"Oh, my goodness. What a relief," I sighed gustily, spewing cookie crumbs. I placed my forehead in my hands, elbows on the table. "That's not Shelly's dress."

Natalie laughed. "I thought you'd be glad of that. How could you not know?"

"Come on, Natalie, you know why. I homeschool." I sat up. "I talk to parents at baseball practice, band concerts, and things like that. And it wasn't my turn to car pool the baseball kids today. I don't see parents when I drop my kids off at school – 'cause I don't...drop my kids off at school, I mean. I don't see parents when I pick my kids up from school –"

"'Cause you don't pick your kids up from school. I get it. But, Danny, you shop at the local supermarket. You take walks, work in your yard, all those things."

"And usually fail to hear gossip, because I don't pass it on. You *know* this. The gossip chain is very big on give and take, and I don't usually have anything to give. And I like it that way. Besides, you know how I hate gossip...except right now when it's all I have."

Natalie shrugged.

We have never seen eye to eye on the topic of gossip. I don't really want to hear it. If I know someone and care about them, I want to know what's going on, but usually from that person. Natalie has the small town mindset that gossip isn't really gossip, it's *caring through sharing*. She hears a lot more than I do.

"Well, write it down, anyway," she said, passing me the pen and paper. I wrote down:

Argument with Kelly Green re: boyfriend
Strangled with prom dress – dark blue, slinky.

"Is there anything else we know?" I asked, eating a cookie. "You're right, by the way. These are good, even better than when they were fresh. I think I'll freeze the next batch, too."

"Well, we know that Jamie and her dad don't – didn't get along. You could write that down. And we know that Jamie's mom drinks on a daily basis."

"Natalie, those aren't pertinent. They're old news."

"No, they matter. You'll see," Natalie countered through a mouthful of cookie. "Everything that has to do with Jamie's life matters."

I sighed. "Okay, I'll write it down, but we need something *good*, something *definite* or this is a waste of time."

"What about Shelly?" Natalie asked. "Would she know anything?"

"Natalie, you know that Shelly and I share the same antipathy toward gossip. I doubt she'd know much, and she wouldn't want to tell us what she knew. No," I sighed again. "We're going to have to do this on our own."

Natalie rolled her eyes and re-crossed her designer jean-clad legs. "Okay, then, let's look at local news. One, Jamie had few rules at home, and she flaunted breaking the few she had."

"Two," I took up the enumeration. "She had a boyfriend who was paying attention to another girl."

Natalie shook her head. "That would be a good reason for Kelly or the boyfriend to die, but not Jamie. Well, not die, really, but you know what I mean. It wouldn't be Jamie who got hurt; I'd think she'd do the hurting."

"Oh, right. Shoot. Okay, how about this? Two, Jamie was a bit of a spitfire. Maybe one of her friends got tired of hearing her spout off about their faults and did her in."

"Wouldn't they rather just stop being her friend? That would make more sense," Natalie pointed out.

"In a small town? Where you see everyone you know practically every day?"

"Yeah, even in a small town. Especially in a small town. How many suspects can there be in a small town?"

"Fine, then. You try one." I sat back and waited.

"Okay, how about this? Kelly and Jamie's boyfriend were planning to run off together but Jamie found out and...No that's backward, too."

"And now you're suggesting motive instead of facts, Natalie."

"I've run out of facts." Natalie leaned forward, defending herself. "Besides, you started it."

We looked at each other and laughed.

We chewed our cookies a moment before I ventured, "How about this: Jamie and her boyfriend were planning to run off together and Jamie's dad found out. In a fit of temper, he grabbed the prom dress and strangled her."

"Does her dad even know where she lived? He's so seldom around, how do we know he spent any time with her at all? He didn't spend much time with her when Jamie was little. And why go after Jamie? Why not go talk to the boyfriend, warn him off?" Natalie scoffed.

"In this small town? Come on, Natalie, of course he knows where she lived." I shot back. "Maybe he didn't warn the boyfriend off, because he thought he had more authority over Jamie than over him."

The lion's head knocker crashed against the front door and we both jumped. It had grown dark, and suddenly we were nervous. Whoever was at the door knocked again, and I went slowly to answer it.

Chapter 8
Talk to Him Again, and You Die

"Good evening, Mrs. Baker." It was Detective Hawksworth.

"Oh, good evening," I answered with relief. "Won't you please come in?" I closed the front door. "I hope you don't mind the kitchen this time. Natalie and I have been drinking coffee."

"Not at all," Detective Hawksworth answered cheerfully, looking around him. "It's a lovely house."

"Thank you." So he had noticed after all.

As we entered the kitchen, Natalie was placing a mug of coffee and another plate of cookies on the table. She had already refilled our mugs. I wondered how long Tom and Jerry had been sitting on the other end of the table. I shooed them off, and they left the room, tails high.

"Good evening, Detective," Natalie said cheerfully. "Please sit down and have some cookies. You didn't bring Officer Smythe with you?"

"Thank you, ladies," he said as he sat. "I apologize for disturbing your evening. I gave Officer Smythe the evening off. She wanted to watch her nephew's baseball game."

"We're thrilled you've stopped by," Natalie assured him. "We were discussing the situation resulting from Jamie's death, and you're just the person to reassure us that you're close to an arrest and we can all sleep peacefully in our beds tonight."

Leave it up to Natalie to fish for information in a suave yet forceful manner. But Detective Hawksworth wasn't a fish to be caught easily.

"Actually (again, he pronounced it 'ackshully'), I was hoping to glean information from you," he turned to me, effectively cutting Natalie off. *She won't like that*, I thought with a wicked inner smile. "Do you happen to know the name of Jamie's latest boyfriend? Or would Shelly know? It seems everyone in the sixth form is shielding him."

Natalie and I looked at each other in confusion. "What's the sixth form?" I asked.

Detective Hawksworth chuckled. "I got it wrong again, didn't I? What do you call the last two years of high school, for students ages seventeen and eighteen?"

"They're in their junior and senior years," I answered. "Are you saying you interviewed every junior and senior? Why not the freshmen and sophomores?"

"Would they be more helpful than the older students?" he asked, rather naively I thought. "Jamie didn't have any of the mixed-grade classes, so I assumed the younger students would be somewhat segregated and less informed about the older students. They are in England." He ran his hand through his dark curls leaving them deliciously rumpled. "I have so much to learn," he groaned.

Compassionately, I pushed the plate of cookies closer to him. "Here, eat one, and I'll ask Shelly what she knows." I ran upstairs.

As I returned to the kitchen, Natalie and Detective Hawksworth were chatting about life in our small town as compared to the small city in the Peak District of England where he's from. I wondered where I had put the map of England we had gotten during our study of the Middle Ages. It would have the Peak District on it. (Did he say the town was called Duffield?) I wondered if it was a pretty place to live and decided it probably is. *So he'll be going back as soon as he can,*

I told myself. *Stop that. Of course he's going back, and you don't care. Besides, Google Earth would be better than a map.*

"Shelly says the boy's name is Forrest Pearson," I sat down again. "He's a senior, and he hasn't been at school for a couple of days. Um, Detective," I hesitated. "I have no right to ask this, but...would you mind giving me some information on how the investigation is going?

"I know you don't usually do that," I hastened to explain as he opened his mouth to answer. "But, I'm really worried about Shelly...well, about all the kids at the high school. This is beginning to cause a lot of fear. I walk around town a lot, and the kids come here to hang out –"

"Danielle gives great teen parties," Natalie put in. "Nothing any parent wouldn't want to have at the party, but the kids love to come anyway."

I glanced at Natalie and back again. "Well, thanks, but really, I am concerned about the kids. They've all become 'my' kids, and I love them. I'm not enjoying seeing them look scared or talk about 'someone out there' who might want to hurt them." I looked at him with pleading eyes and continued softly. "Several of them have told me, 'This used to be a safe town'. I don't like hearing that, Detective."

Detective Hawksworth chewed on his cookie for another moment, obviously playing for time. Natalie rose from her chair, placed her mug in the sink, and said, "Well, I must head home. Danielle, I'll see you tomorrow." *Call me*, she motioned with her hand to her head. Then she winked and closed the door behind her.

"Detective Hawksworth?" I hesitated. "Please forgive me. I've put you in an awkward position. I retract my request and won't ask again." I sighed and flopped back in the chair. "It's so *hard!*"

"Murder is hard on everyone," he said quietly. He was picking up crumbs and placing them on the plate. "These are excellent biscuits, I must tell you."

Americans call them cookies, I mentally corrected him with a small smile.

He continued quietly, "Everyone involved in a murder investigation is injured in one way or another, because we have to ask so many personal questions. It's difficult for people to have their lives turned inside out to be reviewed by a group of strangers, even if they are police." *Especially if they are police,* I thought, *for our family, anyway.* He paused a moment. With a sigh, he said, "Even young children. Which brings me to the point of my visit. I must ask a favor. It's been suggested that Hannah and Michael may have information for me."

"*What?*" I stared at him.

"I'm so sorry, Mrs. Baker, but more than one person has told me that they knew Jamie Sneider well enough to know what was going on in her life."

I considered this. Then, sighing once more, I went upstairs for my children. They were ready for bed, and I gave them ten minutes to get dressed and join us in the kitchen. When they learned Natalie had gone home and had been replaced by Detective Hawksworth, they were speedy enough to almost beat me back downstairs.

The detective smiled at them as Hannah leaned against my chair and Mikey perched on my leg. I was glad they were happy to see the detective and also that they wanted the comfort of their mom.

"Good evening," he said. "I have some questions for you about Jamie Sneider. I understand you knew her quite well."

Hannah and Mikey both looked at me. They were on guard. I reached a hand out to Hannah and wrapped an arm around Mikey's waist.

"Hey, guys," I smiled gently, "please answer the questions. It'll be all right."

They nodded and turned again to Detective Hawksworth.

"Do you know what was going on in her life?" he began.

Their answers to his questions were enlightening and disturbing. Jamie had told them her dad had hit her, which was one reason she saw him as seldom as possible, and her mom was drunk nearly every night. She hated it but felt stuck. Jamie had also said she was afraid she might be pregnant, and then she told them it was okay, she wasn't. Mikey wasn't sure how she knew, but Hannah understood. *Awesome,* I thought. *Mikey and I are going to have to talk about the facts of life.*

It took about thirty minutes, and Detective Hawksworth did an excellent job of questioning them carefully and gently, but the questions were *very* detailed, and they were exhausted by the end. He agreed to stay while I put them to bed.

Going up the stairs, Mikey asked, "Are we in trouble, Mom?"

"Of course not, sweetie," I put my arm across his shoulders in a bumpy climbing-the-stairs hug. "I'm disturbed that you and Hannah didn't tell me about your friendship with Jamie, especially after her death, but you aren't in trouble." I stopped at the top of the stairs. "Why didn't you?"

Hannah said, "We weren't hiding anything from you, Mom, I promise. But it was really cool how Jamie spent time with us and talked to us. She's in high school. And pretty. And she seemed to need us. We felt important.

"We would have told you about it if we thought it was wrong. Or if she had said something that we thought we couldn't handle."

"I'm sure you would have," I assured them both with a long hug as we stood outside their bedrooms. "And I'm sure you still will." I kissed them, prayed with them, and sent them to bed.

Shelly's bedroom door was closed. I tapped, opened it a few inches, and called out to the darkness, "You awake?" She only grunted, so I said, "Good night, sweetie. I love you," and closed the door again. I went downstairs with a lighter step.

"Well, what did you think of the kids' information?" I asked.

"I'm sorry to have had to put them through that," Detective Hawksworth answered. He sounded sincere. "I don't like having to interview children. The experts tell us they're resilient, but it seems we were created to protect them, and a bobby is only human after all."

I smiled. "A Bobby, a Luke, and a Tom, Dick, and Harry, too."

Detective Hawksworth was surprised into a short laugh. "A bobby is a policeman."

"I know, but you needed a laugh, and I couldn't resist the play on words." I shifted ground. "I did want to ask you, though, about how Jamie was killed. According to Natalie, the grapevine says that she was strangled with a prom dress. Is that right? Can a person even *be* strangled with a dress?"

"The grapevine, as you call it, is somewhat accurate, though how that information was leaked will have to be investigated." He looked irritated. *Oops! Someone is in trouble,* I thought. "And a person can be strangled with a dress, I suppose, but it would depend on the strength of the fabric and the technique used; however, Jamie was not actually strangled with her dress. The dress, we think, was wrapped round her throat to inhibit fingerprints."

"Ick." I looked at my cold coffee and sighed. "Why do I ask questions? That poor child."

"I am trusting that you will refrain from feeding the rumor mill in your town with that information," he said with a deepening of his dimples. "I place myself at your mercy."

I shrugged. "Of course." I rose to put my dishes in the kitchen. Detective Hawksworth did the same with a mug and a plate in his hands and placed them in the sink, just as if he were accustomed to doing the same thing at home. *At home.*

"Detective," I stopped and thought a moment. "Detective, at what time was Jamie killed? At night or in the morning?"

"Late at night," he answered. "Probably between one and three a.m. Why do you ask?"

"Well, I seem to have something in the back of my mind that tells me the timing is important...no, it isn't coming." I shook my head.

"Stop thinking about it, and it will come," he answered confidently.

I smiled at him. "Thank you. And thank you for your gentle approach with my children – all of them. You are helping in their healing process, I'm sure of it."

"That's good," he smiled sadly. "I must be going now," he said more briskly. "The cookies – cookies, right? - were very good. The best I've had since being in the States."

I nodded, "Yes, cookies. But, you called them biscuits earlier."

"Did I? Yes, I think I must have. Biscuits are like your cookies. But we have variations on sweetness." He shook his head with a soft laugh. "We speak the same language, except when we don't."

"It should get easier, the longer you're here. How long have you been here, anyway?" I asked as we walked toward the front door.

"I've been in Albany for nearly a month now," he answered. "I spent a week in Washington, D.C. for a couple of welcome dinners, then I spent a fortnight with the Oregon State Police in Salem for the induction –"

"A fortnight?"

"Yes, two weeks or fourteen nights. A fortnight." He raised his eyebrows, and I nodded. "And now I'm in Albany for the duration. It's a quaint little town. I like it. I like your village, too."

"Village? I thought that term went out toward the end of the Middle Ages."

Detective Hawksworth grinned, and I thought of Natalie's ecstatic, '*But those dimples!*' "The English have been using the terms, 'city', 'town', village', and 'hamlet' for hundreds of years."

"So, what's the difference between them?" As we stood close together in the hallway, I could smell his man-scent. *Yummy. But he's a policeman, remember?*

"A city is the largest place in terms of population and requires the grant of a charter from the reigning monarch." He leaned against the door, relaxed. "Also, a city usually has a cathedral or a university. A town does not have a charter and usually has a smaller population than a city, anywhere from a few thousands of people to upwards of 100,000 people."

He paused. "And a market. Towns have a market, whereas a village does not and has just a few hundreds to perhaps a few thousands of people. Sometimes, a village will have a church, but a hamlet has no market, no church, no pub. . . or perhaps a pub, and usually only a few people. I feel as if I'm teaching a class." We smiled at each other, and I began to consider a book set in England. Maybe in the Peak District. With a research trip. I wondered what my publisher would say about it.

I opened the door and took a deep breath. "Mmm. It smells good outside tonight. Thank you, again, for being so kind."

Detective Hawksworth hesitated at the door. "Thank you, Mrs. Baker, for making me feel welcome. Murder investigations don't generally contribute toward the development of friendships, but you make me feel as if we might be friends."

I grinned at him. "Thank you for the compliment. I do want to be your friend."

We smiled at each other for a moment, then I ducked my head and watched my foot doing a side-to-side tattoo on the porch boards. "Would you like to come to dinner on Sunday? Just as a friend, of course. Or do you need to work? Or am I being too forward?" I blushed and glanced anxiously at his face.

"I should like that very much (again it sounded like 'verra much'). Thank you for the invite. At what time should I call?"

"Call?"

"Yes, what time shall I call?"

"On the phone?"

"No, at your house."

"Oh, come! You want to know when to come." We were laughing now.

"Yes, come. At what time shall I come?"

"How about lunch at one o'clock? We'll be home from church about 12:30, so come early if you'd like. It might be a good idea, actually. You've been so good with my kids, they're starting to trust you, and I *know* they like you. Mikey will be excited when you get here. I think Hannah and Shelly will, too, and a few minutes of noise *before* lunch will make the meal a quieter, more peaceful one." *Stop babbling,* I commanded sternly.

Detective Hawksworth smiled down at me. "I would enjoy that very much, thank you. Good night." And he disappeared into the night.

As soon as his taillights rounded the corner, the landline rang. It could only be one person.

"Hello, Natalie," I answered cheerfully. There was silence on the line. Then I heard heavy breathing.

"Who is this?" I demanded.

Someone whispered, "Talk to him again, and you die, like Jamie died." A high-pitched laugh sounded far away. I hit the off button, shaken.

Chapter 9
I'm Calling It

The phone rang again. I was afraid to answer. I was wishing I had invested in caller ID.

"Hello?" I asked breathlessly just before my old-school answering machine picked up. My heart was racing.

"Danielle, what's wrong?" It was Natalie.

"Oh, Natalie," I breathed in relief. "Oh, my goodness, I'm so glad it's you."

"Who were you expecting, Danielle, the boogey man?" I didn't say anything. The correct answer would be, "yes", of course. "Danielle? Are you okay? Hang on, I'm coming over."

"No." I said sharply and took a deep breath. "No, you don't need to come. I'm okay, only shaky. Someone just called and breathed at me."

"Well, you've been breathed at many times, and it didn't bug you...Oh."

"Right. Things have changed, haven't they?" I took another deep breath, willing myself to calm down. "Then whoever it was whispered, 'Talk to him again, and you die, like Jamie died.' And then someone else laughed." I swallowed a sob.

"That's just wrong." Natalie was angry. "It's stupid, and it's wrong, and . . . and I'm calling it, girlfriend. I call 'bullshit.'"

I gasped. "Natalie!"

"What? You have a problem with that?"

"You can't."

"And why not? Is it a curse? Is it blasphemy? No, it's just a naughty word that perfectly describes what you've just had dumped on you."

"You still can't call it," I said.

"Oh, yeah?"

"It's . . . it's an Eastern Oregon saying, and you were born and raised right here in the Willamette Valley. You're Western Oregon all the way."

"Look," she reasoned, "if I can borrow a cup of sugar from my neighbor, I can borrow a saying from my Eastern Oregon neighbors."

I was laughing, now. "You don't like to cook, Natalie."

"But I do drink coffee," she laughed in return, then sobered. "And no matter how you prefer to word it – poop, feces, dung – what he said to you was nothing more than a pile of smelly waste product. It's worthless, and it stinks."

"I agree, but I'm still a bit scared by that 'pile of smelly waste product.'"

"I know you are, sweetie," Natalie sighed. Then she giggled. "But I shocked you out of your panic, didn't I?"

I laughed. "You did, thanks. But it was a nasty phone call."

"It must have been, by the sound of your voice when you answered. You had me worried for a minute."

I chuckled. "I'm okay, now. But I don't like what this murder is doing to our wonderful little...village, as Detective Hawksworth calls it. Do you think this is a crank call? Or was the guy serious?"

"Was it a man? You said whoever it was whispered."

"It sounded like the deep whisper a man does, but it's hard to tell, isn't it? What do you think I should do? Do you think I should call the detective and tell him right now – I mean, he just left, and what could he do, anyway? Or do you think it's just a crank call, and

I don't need to tell him until Sunday? I'm feeling better already, and I'd hate to look like a fool in front of him."

I could feel Natalie perk up through the phone line. "Do tell!"

Shoot! I was going to save that bit of news for last. Oh, well, maybe I can string it out.

"Detective Hawksworth wanted to talk to Hannah and Mikey about Jamie." Natalie made outraged noises. "No, he was right. I guess they had a sort of friendship with her."

There was a moment of doubtful silence. Natalie said, "Are you sure? That just doesn't seem like Jamie. She was always so involved with her friends and boyfriends."

"Well, it seems to be true." I told her what the kids had said. I finished up with, "So now I have to talk to Mikey about the facts of life...like how a woman knows she isn't pregnant and how pregnancy happens in the first place. Dog-gone-it, Natalie, that's what dads are for."

"Would you like Shea to talk to him? Now that Jim is out of the country, praise the Lord and good riddance, you might like to have Honorary Uncle Shea do some of the daddy work for you. I know Mikey's only eleven, but he isn't too young, even if he *is* homeschooled."

I smiled. Natalie's right; home schooled children don't usually hear the 'facts of life' from friends quite as early as classroom-taught children, if at all. That's usually the privilege of parents. "Thank you, my beautiful friend. You are truly wonderful...No, I think I'll talk to Mikey myself. I can do it; it's just that I'd rather not. You know? Not for another year, anyway." I sighed.

"And you're okay, now?"

"Yeah, I'm okay. That phone call just freaked me out for a minute."

Natalie gave me a moment to change my mind. "So? What's this about Sunday?"

"Oh, yeah, well we were talking about the differences between a city, a town, a village, and a hamlet."

"Yeah? Go on."

"Well, he said he likes our 'little village' even more than he likes Albany. So we visited about that for a while." I teased her with what he had said about the differences between cities, towns, villages, and hamlets, going into details even Detective Hawksworth hadn't given me, making it up as I went along.

"Danielle, are you going to tell me what's happening on Sunday or am I going to have to climb down the phone line and slap you until you do?"

I laughed. "I don't have a phone line, remember? It's cordless." She made strangled noises.

"Okay, okay, I'll tell you. Detective Hawksworth is coming for dinner Sunday. I told him we'll eat at one, but he could come early if he wants, so the kids will get over their excitement before we eat. You know how much they love company."

"Woo-hoo, you move fast, girlfriend. I can't tell you how proud I am of you."

"No, we were talking about his being here alone, knowing no one. He said I had made him feel like he was starting to make a friend." I cocked my head as a thought came to me. "He probably thinks I'm friendly because I don't throw a fit every time he wants to talk to my children. A lot of moms do, you know...especially during murder investigations." I pondered a moment. "Does that make me weird?"

"Yeah, that and a lot of other things," Natalie scoffed. "I don't think that's why he said what he did, my friend. You're friendly, attractive, intelligent and fun. I'm sure he likes you as a person...more than just part of this case."

"I hope so." I sighed. "Is intelligence really third on the list?"

"In no particular order." We laughed at an old joke.

"Then again," I continued, "his being here, in the house, a policeman, no tension, has to be good for the kids."

"True, and good for you, too, especially if he's sweet on you." I made protesting noises, and she quickly said, "Anyway, I have to get some sleep, and so do you. If you feel safe enough."

"I'm fine, now, thanks to you. And we both have to get up in the morning. What time do you want to exercise?"

"How about 6:30? That will give me time to eat breakfast before I have to leave." Natalie loves to eat breakfast. I can cheerfully skip it any day.

I groaned. "Are you sure we need to get up so early? Can't you eat toast and peanut butter?"

"Gag. I haven't had that since grade school."

I sighed again. "Okay, I guess I can drag myself out of bed at 6:30. I'll see you then." I grinned secretly, knowing my guilt trip would make Natalie want to move the time to a half hour later.

I was wrong; she tried a diversion technique instead. "What are you going to have for dinner Sunday?"

Chapter 10
Small Town Life Has a Downside

I yelped. "I don't know. We usually have something simple like burritos. I'm going to have to *cook* something."

Natalie laughed. "Well, good luck, see you in the morning," and she hung up on me. Groaning, I dragged myself to the kitchen cabinet that holds the cookbooks and pulled down two of my favorites. A whimper distracted me, and I let Ramon out for the night before I sat down at the table.

An hour and many recipe books later, I decided I might just have to fall back on burritos. Nothing looked good, and everything required at least an hour of prep time, during which I would be in church.

"Enchiladas!" I suddenly exclaimed to Tom and Jerry. They were sitting on the other end of the table again. "I can make enchiladas. And we can have Spanish rice and salad with it. Hallelujah. Now I can go to bed." I returned the twelve cookbooks to the cabinet, turned off the lights, double checked the front and back doors, pranced up the stairs and into bed.

I read my Bible, a sure way to calm body and mind, but I still couldn't sleep. I kept thinking about the friendship between Jamie and my children. What did Hannah and Mikey give to Jamie that she couldn't get from her other friends? Normally, a sixteen-year-old wouldn't even consider befriending kids two and five years younger, so she must have gotten something out of the relationship. Besides,

Jamie wasn't the kind of girl to be friends with someone unless it was good for her first and foremost.

I considered Hannah's and Mikey's personalities. I was pretty sure I knew what Jamie would like to talk about, and it didn't seem as if Hannah's love of reading or Mikey's love of engineering (taking things apart and putting them back together 'better') would interest her.

So perhaps it was simply that Jamie was an older girl, and they – being younger – were willing to listen to and, yes, admire her. Maybe it was that simple. The girls her age knew Jamie slept around, knew she broke the rules, knew all the bad things about her. Maybe Hannah and Mikey gave Jamie an opportunity to be more herself without the baggage of her lifestyle hanging over her.

Small town life does have a down side. People don't forget what you've done, sometimes forever. I thought about a story I'd heard about an older woman – she must have been in her sixties. She was being criticized for acting as if she were respectable; she taught Sunday School, gave Tupperware parties, and sat on the library board. The people gossiping about her said that when she was sixteen, she'd gotten pregnant. Outside of marriage. Those people thought she should continue to walk with shame more than forty years later. I remember not liking my small town at that moment, even though they were only two sour biddies out of several thousand really nice people.

Which made me think that maybe Jamie wanted friends who didn't know (or care) about what she'd done or what reputation she'd earned. I could see that. And Hannah, two years younger and still in middle school, and Mikey, the tag-along little brother, had been flattered.

How sad, I thought, *to need such young friends in order to escape her own reputation and gain...what? Friendship? Respect?*

The phone rang. I looked at the clock, 12:43 a.m. Too late to be a friend calling for a chat. I hoped nothing was wrong. I picked it up on the second ring.

"Hello?"

Heavy breathing. Before the caller could talk, I slammed the phone down. I sat up against the headboard. "Why are they calling me, Lord? What have I done? I haven't talked to anyone about the murder, except Natalie. I haven't gone around town asking questions, I'm letting the police handle it. I can't think of anything I've done to deserve this, and it's the second call tonight. What is going on?"

I was just starting to gain the upper hand against fear when the phone rang again. Shoot, I was jumpy. I wished Ramon the Wonder Dog was in the house. He would be a little comfort, even if he was worthless as a watch dog.

"Hello?"

Heavy breathing again, but before I could hang up, a raspy voice whispered, "Leave Jamie's death alone. Don't talk to the police again or you'll regret it. You wouldn't want your kids to get hurt." And he (or she) hung up.

"That's it," I muttered as I jumped out of bed. I searched for Detective Hawksworth's card in the near dark. "Tell me not to talk to the police, and that is *exactly* what I am going to do. And don't you *dare* threaten my kids. I wasn't a policeman's wife for nothing. I know that the best way to get rid of danger is to go toward help, not away from it, and police are helpful. Some of them are, anyway, and I know which ones won't be. So I won't call *those* police. And this one will be. Helpful, that is. Oh, God, I'm so upset I'm babbling. Help me, please."

The only light came from the night light in the bathroom down the hall, and it took me several minutes. "Found it."

I reached for the phone, but before I could pick it up, it rang. I jumped so hard, I knocked the receiver onto the floor. I scrabbled after it.

"Hello?"

Once again, there was heavy breathing. I slammed down the phone and waited a few seconds for the line to disconnect. Picking it back up, I tried to dial, but there was no tone.

"Hello?" Now, I was really scared. No one answered, but I could tell there was a person on the other end. I jiggled the toggle switch that hangs up the phone. Still no dial tone.

"Fine," I said and to calm myself carefully hung up the phone. *What should I do?* I prayed.

Then I heard what every mom dreads – someone trying to break in. The front doorknob rattled, then a window. Then another window. I began to search frantically for my cell phone. Usually, I leave it in my purse downstairs, but I distinctly remembered sliding it into my jeans pocket, and they were somewhere on the floor. Or maybe the chair in the corner where so many of my clothes seem to land at night.

"Where is it? Where is it?" I frantically prayed. "Ah. Thank you, Jesus." I pulled it out of my pants pocket and dialed 9-1-1.

And nearly dropped it when Tom and Jerry both jumped on the bed. "Stupid cats," I hissed at them. "Why can't you be a dog and bark?" Even Ramon the useless Wonder Dog would be . . . no, he would probably just lick them to death. Which is why he sleeps outside. That and he has gas.

"9-1-1, please state your emergency." The woman on the other end of the line sounded so relaxed.

"Someone is trying to break into my house." I spoke, quietly frantic. "Please send the police right away. I'm scared."

"What is your address, Ma'am?"

"Um, 416 North Emerald Drive. Please hurry."

"Yes, ma'am, just a moment, please." I heard some typing sounds and a pause. A long pause. I began to despair as the noises continued. "Someone has been dispatched to your house and should arrive in less than three minutes. Do you know who is trying to enter your house?"

"No, I don't." I was trying so hard to stay calm. Then the glass broke, and I screamed. "They're inside. They're inside the house."

"Ma'am, please try to stay calm –"

"You stay calm, I'll panic!"

"Okay, ma'am. Are you in a room where you can close and lock the door? If you can do that, please try. And stay calm."

"I will not leave my children sleeping in their beds while I cower in my bedroom."

"Yes, ma'am, I can understand that. As of this moment, the police are only a couple of blocks away and should reach you in a matter of seconds. Please stay on the line with me and keep telling me what is happening."

I listened. "I can't hear anything now," My voice was quavering. "Do you think they left?"

From downstairs, I heard ripping sounds, and something was knocked over with a thump loud enough to carry over the cell phone to the 9-1-1 operator. Almost on top of the noise, Shelly appeared at my door.

"Mom, what's going on? Who's downstairs?" She whispered fearfully.

I pulled her to me and answered, equally quietly, "I don't know, but the police are on their way. When they arrive, please help Hannah and Mikey stay calm. The police will be here any moment." I was praying nothing of value would be hurt – like us.

And then the sirens *finally* approached our house. Red and blue lights flashed, and we heard the intruders leave through the window. It sounded like two people. A couple of minutes of shouting and running sounds, and there was a knock at the front door. Unmindful of my pajamas and unruly hair, I dropped the cell phone, rushed downstairs, and opened the door to Officer Carey and his partner, Officer Nichols. *Oh, great.* However, I was more resigned to letting them in as I remembered their efforts to protect my children and me. Obviously the intruders had gotten away.

I opened the door wide. The Spruce Bruce swaggered into the house, thumbs hooked into his belt. Officer Nichols followed. It was he who asked how the children and I were.

"Is anyone injured, Mrs. Baker?" he asked me kindly.

"No, thank you, Officer, no one was hurt. They didn't come upstairs." I was touched by his concern, and tears welled up.

The Spruce Bruce shouldered his way into the living room. "It seems they did a pretty good job of scaring you, though, didn't they, *Mrs.* Baker." I looked at his hard, tanned face. His uniform was beautifully ironed and spotless, even at 1:00 in the morning. "Maybe you should have a husband staying here with you, don't you think?"

Anger from the break-in, at being frightened and victimized, at this...this *boar* welled up in me. "Yes, Bruce, a kind, thoughtful, loving husband would be a good kind of man to have. I wish I knew someone like that."

He glared at me, turned on his heel, and headed to the front door. "Obviously, you don't need us. No harm was done to you and your children. No real damage was done to anything but your pride. Have a nice evening, *Mrs.* Baker."

I turned to look into the living room. It was a mess. Chair cushions were ripped, the book case had been knocked over – the loud thump, I presumed – the window was broken. *No harm was done?* I was appalled.

Officer Nichols had followed me to the door of the living room. One look at his thunderstruck face, and I knew he agreed. I wondered how he'd handle this. I knew what I was going to do.

I marched to the kitchen where I had tacked one of Detective Hawksworth's cards and dialed his phone number, happy to hear the dial tone again. I ignored the altercation between the junior partner and the Spruce Bruce.

He answered on the first ring. "Detective Hawksworth, someone broke into my house just now. The Spruce Bruce and his partner are here. Bruce Carey. Officer Carey. He is planning to leave me with a broken window, a disaster of a living room, and no investigation whatsoever. I can't decide if I'm more angry or scared. What do you recommend I do?"

"I'll be right there," he said.

I didn't want to draw the Spruce Bruce's attention, so I stood in the kitchen and waited for the argument to end. Several minutes later, I couldn't stand it any longer and went into the hall where emotions were heated. The Spruce Bruce was threatening Officer Nichol's job. "What you're doing is insubordination," he thundered. "And I'll see to it that you're suspended pending an investigation." *So he does know a few long words,* I thought irreverently.

"Sir, with all due respect," Officer Nichols managed to keep the sarcasm out of his voice, mostly. "Unless we investigate, we can be charged with dereliction of duty. I want to keep my job, so I won't participate in that. If you choose to leave, I can't and won't even try to stop you. I will, however, have to call in a ride back to the station. I'm sure that will cause a few raised eyebrows. Sir."

I interrupted the impending eruption. "Bruce, calm yourself. You're going to have a coronary, and I don't want you doing it in my house. You don't need to investigate anything at this point, so you're off the hook. When you decided to leave, I called Detective Hawksworth. He'll be here soon. When he gets here, you can go back to eating donuts." I looked pointedly at his vast stomach.

Turning to Officer Nichols, I said, "If you would like to stay, I'm sure the detective would be happy to give you a ride back to the station." I turned back to Officer Carey.

"You're free to leave." I walked to the front door, opened it, and pointedly waited for him to go.

Chapter 11
You Will Tell Us What He Says

The Spruce Bruce shifted his weight. "Well, now, Mrs. Baker," no emphasis on 'Mrs.' this time, I noticed. "We don't want to be hasty here, do we? I'm sure if Officer Nichols would like to get the fingerprint powder, we can dust for prints while we wait for Detective Hawksworth."

"I'm sure you could, Officer Carey," I returned sweetly. "But since I know your attitude, and have heard your comments, I don't trust you to do a competent job, and I would hate to see you destroy evidence that might bring about an arrest in this case." His face was dangerously red again. "And since I have already called Detective Hawksworth who continues to treat me with respect and obviously desires to see a *just* conclusion to any investigation he undertakes, you are not needed nor are you welcome.

"So I will state once again, you are free to leave. Should you desire to wait for your partner, you may, of course, do so – in your car."

Summoning up as much dignity as possible for such a fat, obnoxious man, Officer Carey walked out of my front door into a crowd of neighbors. He swaggered importantly to his car, opened the trunk, and started looking at what he might need – as if I would let him back into the house.

Shelly, Hannah, and Mikey came running down the stairs. "Mom, that was awesome." Shelly said, hugging me. "You're so cool."

"Yeah, Mom, you really showed *him* who's boss in this house now." Mikey jumped up and down in his excitement.

Hannah looked at Officer Nichols. "I'm really glad you came," she said quietly. "Will your job be miserable now, since Mom showed Officer Carey to the door but not you?"

Officer Nichols smiled. "Not any more than it already has been," he answered. I could imagine what misery he was suffering at the hands of the Spruce Bruce.

"Officer Nichols, would you like a cup of coffee?" I asked. "Detective Hawksworth probably won't be here for a while. Albany is about thirty minutes away, depending on where he's living."

Officer Nichols looked surprised. "Didn't you know? He moved into an apartment here in town until the investigation is over."

I blinked at him. "No, I didn't know," I answered as the detective himself walked through the door.

And, oh my, did he look angry. His first words were, "Why hasn't anyone put up the scene of crime tape? And when do you plan to dust for prints?"

Officer Nichols saluted and said, "Right away, sir." He scurried away, a slight smile on his lips. Here was someone who knew what to do and expected it done.

Turning to me the detective asked, "Are you and the children well?"

It was a strange way to ask, but I decided it was British, and answered the meaning of the question. "Yes, we're not hurt, just scared." A warmth flowed through me at his concern.

Mikey belied my assertion of fearfulness by jumping up and down. "Can I watch you do your work? I won't be in the way, I promise."

Detective Hawksworth smiled grimly at Mikey and said, "I know it's exciting for you. It was for me, too, at your age, but...you can follow me around another time, okay, chap? Tonight, it's dark and some *cretin* in a brown uniform is standing at the head of your drive regaling the people with stories of his many exploits." I was momentarily amused by his pronunciation of "crettin". Quickly, my mind returned to Mikey and the detective. "I must whip him into shape, and it shan't be a pleasant sight." He thought a moment. "How about you and your sisters sit here on the stairs? You can watch the coming and going, and if you lean up against the wall," he demonstrated, "you should probably be able to see a bit of what we're doing in the lounge – hold up, you call it a living room, correct?"

Mikey raced Hannah to the stair step he had recommended as he continued, "And if, at any time, you feel a bit sleepy, you are welcome to head back to bed, and I won't disturb you until morning for statements. What do you say?"

Mikey grinned and nodded. Hannah said a soft, "Thank you." Shelly followed them more slowly, and all three sat huddled together on the stairs. My heart broke.

Detective Hawksworth turned to me. "Are you all right?" he asked gently. I began to cry. Delayed reaction, no doubt.

"I'm sorry," I said. "I don't know why I'm doing this. My hands are shaking, all of me is shaking. And I don't know why." I wiped at the tears rolling down my face.

Detective Hawksworth pulled me to him and wrapped his muscular arms around me. "Because you've just lived through a frightening experience. And to top it off, that *buffoon* answered your call, and you had to deal with him, too. I stood outside a moment and listened. I can assure you he won't bother you again, or anyone else if I have anything to say about it."

He pulled away and placed his hands on my shoulders. "I know I'm only here for a short time, but I can guarantee you, I will not just sit back and let a bad apple stay in the barrel. No wonder you were hesitant to trust me."

His face was hard, and anger glinted in his blue eyes.

I smiled up at him. "Thank you. You are a healing salve, Detective." He smiled grimly, nodded once, and left to get on with his work. Very soon, I could hear him issuing orders. Several officers were placing crime scene tape, taking pictures, dusting for prints, walking in and out of the front door.

I'd forgotten I was in my pajamas. I'd forgotten my hair was tousled. I'd forgotten I was going to clean up, since there were several men in the house.

I went to the kitchen to make coffee. As I finished pouring water into the machine, I caught movement out of the corner of my eye. I turned quickly, nearly dropping the carafe, my heart in my throat.

"Oh, Natalie," I exclaimed. "I didn't know you were here."

"I had to come; you're my favorite sister-friend," she said as she folded me into a warm, loving hug. "At first I didn't know this circus belonged to you, but as soon as I figured it out, I jumped into some clothes and raced down here." I felt my muscles relax in her embrace. Once again, I cried, a nice, cleansing cry that left me feeling more at peace.

"Nice bed head," she said with a smile. "No, I really mean it. You look...sexy."

"I'm glad you're here." Ignoring her remark, I placed the carafe on the machine and started the coffee brewing. "Come on over to the table. We can at least sit while we wait for the coffee."

"Where are the kids?" she asked.

"They wanted to watch the police work, so Detective Hawksworth gave them a vantage point from the stairs. Didn't you see them when you walked by? You know what Mikey is like. He was jumping up and down like a pogo stick."

Natalie nodded. "Who responded?" One look at my face, and she groaned. "Oh, no. Not the Spruce Bruce. What did you do?"

"Can you believe he actually told me I need a husband for times like these?"

"No."

"Yes. And then he said since no one was hurt and nothing was damaged, except my pride, he and his partner would just go."

"You're kidding. What a... a...." she threw up her hands. "Words fail me" She stood and paced the kitchen. "What did you do?"

"I immediately called Detective Hawksworth." I smiled. "He came really quickly. I guess he stood outside the front door and listened to Officer Nichols argue against leaving and the Spruce Bruce threaten his –Officer Nichols's - job if he didn't leave. I got involved and told the Spruce Bruce off. Actually, I told him he had to leave my house, but Officer Nichols could stay." I grinned at her. "That part was really fun. And the kids heard and approved."

Natalie grinned back. "Way to go. You're getting stronger." I nodded, pleased with myself.

Chapter 12

He's Recording, Guys

"Excuse me, ladies," Detective Hawksworth entered the kitchen. I jumped up and offered him coffee.

"Decaf only, I'm afraid, but warm and fresh." He accepted and sat at the table.

"Don't you dare tell me you're done investigating already." Natalie stood with her hands on her hips. "There should still be a ton of things to do."

Surprised, the detective answered, "No, we're not done, yet. I've sent home the fingerprint experts, and the weapons experts have taken one of your sofa cushions to the lab to run tests on the fabric tears. Do you know how much time it takes to check a crime scene?"

"I haven't been the suspect of a crime, if that's what you mean, or the victim, Detective," Natalie answered pertly. "But Danielle's ex-husband is a police officer, and we've been friends for twenty years, so I'm somewhat familiar with crime scenes – second hand as it were."

Detective Hawksworth nodded and placed a small tape recorder on the table. "Do you think you can go through the evening for me, Mrs. Baker? I need a statement from you." A sleepy-looking Officer Smythe walked in and sat at the table. After saying, "Good morning," she pulled her notebook from her pocket and waited patiently. I noticed she had buttoned her shirt crookedly. With heartfelt thanks, she accepted a cup of coffee from Natalie.

Slowly, I nodded that I was ready, and the detective gently walked me through the evening from the time he left until the time he returned. He wanted to know about the phone calls, the 9-1-1 call, and Officer Carey's words and actions. Officer Smythe wrote everything down, and Detective Hawksworth recorded it all. I didn't like that part, but I know the value of verbatim conversations. I assumed Officer Smythe's notes were in case something happened to the recording – like failed batteries or . . . who-knows-what. Especially where the Spruce Bruce was concerned.

"Why do you think Officer Carey was so antagonistic towards you, Mrs. Baker? Is there something personal between you, or is he this way toward everyone?" Detective Hawksworth asked quietly.

I looked at Natalie. She nodded gently, encouraging me to speak up. I shifted in my chair. As so often happened when I needed to talk about my marriage and divorce, shame swept over me at the thought of describing how I had allowed my husband to treat me. Or maybe it was that I'd allowed it for so long. And as I had done so many times, I fought off the shame, determined not to let it silence me. One day, I would overcome it, would understand the dynamics of abusive relationships, but not yet. It's a long process. And after four years of battling it, the shame was lessened but not gone.

Taking a deep breath, I started. "I think Officer Carey treats most people similarly, but his disrespect is amplified with me. He and my husband were partners at one time." I glanced at Natalie again, then at my hands. The knuckles were white, and I tried to relax. "Jim took the classes and was promoted to the detective branch in Albany, and Officer Carey stayed here. But they maintained their friendship. After the divorce, Officer Carey –"

"That isn't all, Mom," Shelly said as she, Hannah, and Mikey walked into the kitchen. They surrounded my chair. "Tell him all of it. It's time." Shelly placed a comforting hand on my shoulder.

"He's recording, guys," I pleaded with them.

"All of it, Mom," Shelly commanded. "He's either a friend, or he isn't. No more hiding the truth." She smiled at the detective. "I trust him."

Hannah and Mikey nodded their agreement.

"We haven't known him very long," I countered. "And you trust him already? To this extent?"

Shelly said, "Yes," firmly and without reservation. "He isn't like Dad or Bruce Carey."

I wasn't so sure. Flirting and joking and daydreaming are passive and fun. Trust is active and leaves one vulnerable. Was I ready to be vulnerable? To a policeman?

Everyone waited while I battled. Suddenly, a scripture verse from Deuteronomy filled my mind, *Choose you this day life or death, blessings or cursings, fear or faith.* That last bit wasn't scripture, but it sure fit. And I knew what I needed to do.

I sighed and fought back tears. "All right, I'll let out all the dirty laundry for airing, okay?" The kids nodded. Turning back to Detective Hawksworth, I took a shaky breath.

"Officer Jim Baker enjoyed the power of the uniform. He was careful not to abuse that power while he was on the job, but he used it to seduce women. I would find out about his supposedly work-related dates sometimes, through friends. I think he might have bullied people at work who had less seniority, too.

"He and the Spruce Bruce were partners for many years, until Jim was promoted to the detective branch. He and Bruce maintained their friendship, though. Bruce would come over sometimes, and they would mock the victims of sexual assaults and murders. Not Jim's cases, but the cases of other detectives. They would talk as if the victim of a crime deserved what she – usually she – got." I sighed.

"Jim was hard on us, the family," I continued, "but he was very charming in public."

Mikey interrupted. "Mom, let me tell him. I remember a lot of what happened."

"You shouldn't, Mikey. You shouldn't have anything to remember." I looked at him. The pain of this conversation was almost physical.

"I know," he hugged me.

He turned back to Detective Hawksworth. "Dad never actually hit Mom, but he threatened her a lot. I remember he hit the wall next to her head once, but this house was built when they used tongue-and-groove walls, you know?" He put his hands side-by-side horizontally. "They put the boards on either side of the studs, then they put really thin sheetrock over the boards. It made the house sturdier. Anyway, Dad punched the wall once and nearly broke his hand. After that, he would throw things."

Shelly and Mikey snickered at the memory, but Hannah said, "Do you know what would have happened to Mom's head if he'd actually hit her that hard?"

Mikey lay his arm protectively across my shoulders and continued his story, "And he would treat her like dirt when Officer Carey came over. Officer Carey would laugh when Dad said really mean things to mom in front of him. He wasn't like that in public, only here at home and in front of Officer Carey.

"Sometimes," he concentrated on my coffee cup, "Dad would back Mom into a corner and yell at her, tell her how awful she was, for, like, a long time, until she was crying and begging him to stop. He didn't, though, just told her she deserved it, and he wouldn't let her go until he was done telling her just what he thought of her. It was . . ." his arm tightened on my shoulder. "Man, there were times I knew I was just waiting until I was bigger than him."

I looked at him in surprise. "I didn't know that. What were you planning to do?"

Mikey looked at me. "Beat him up."

"Oh, Michael." I pulled him to me and held on tight. And cried. "Honey, you were only seven."

His muffled voice came to me, "Someone needed to protect you, Mom." My tears flowed into his hair for a few moments. Shelly and Hannah sniffed behind me, their hands on my shoulders.

"Then came the time when Officer Carey said mean things to Mom," Hannah said in her soft voice. "Dad just laughed. *He* thought it was hilarious. But it hurt." I let go of Mikey to reach up and hold her hand.

Natalie chimed in. "Finally, Danielle was strong enough to escape. I don't know if divorcing a police officer in England is like divorcing one here can be, but Danielle could have lost everything – home, kids, everything. They sometimes join together like a band of brothers and defeat anything that threatens one of their own, and they aren't always very careful about the truth. At least, in this town...No, I guess it isn't true of the other three police officers in this town, just the Spruce Bruce and Jim."

"Fortunately, I have Natalie and Shea and several other good friends," I sniffed and wiped my eyes with my pajama sleeve. "They helped me find a divorce attorney from the next county over who wasn't scared of facing down the police. And I was able to get away from Jim." I sighed. "It's been wonderful living free from abuse, although he has what seems like half of the town convinced I had no cause, and they don't let me forget it." I shrugged in defeat. "What can I say? Jim is very convincing when he wants to be."

Shelly said darkly, "And now he sits at some desk in England, living the life, while you sit at his desk here." Then she smiled. "And we're glad you are."

Detective Hawksworth looked at me in surprise. "My American counterpart is your ex-husband?"

"He's a terrible husband and father, but when it isn't personal, he's actually a very good detective," I answered.

"But you just said that he mocked victims of crime. Especially victims of sexual crime," he protested.

I nodded. "When the case isn't his. But when it is his case, he rarely talks about it, and he always does his best to ensure justice is meted out."

He shook his head. "Blimey. You take 'fair' to another level, don't you?"

I shrugged. "I try to be honest." I smiled up at my kids. "You are absolutely wonderful." I gathered them in a group hug and kissed each of them on the forehead. "Thank you for taking care of me. We make a good team, don't we?" They giggled and nodded in relief.

"Now," I became brisk, wiping the tears from their cheeks. "It's my turn to take care of you, and I'm going to do that by telling you to get back into bed. Shelly, you don't have to go to school tomorrow. You can sleep in. That goes for you two, too. Okay?" They all nodded. "Great, off to bed everyone."

I watched them go, but Shelly, as she so often does, turned at the door. "You will tell us what he says, right?"

"Of course, sweetie." I smiled my reassurance.

Only after they were gone did I turn nervously to Detective Hawksworth. Shame, that most degrading of all emotions, was washing over me in waves. Would he side with his colleagues or with a woman and her children? In my experience, police officers band together against a threat, whatever the threat may be, even a wife. And with all they see in their line of work, they often become hardened, sometimes even blaming the victim, like Jim and Bruce did. And still do, I'm sure. But this officer came from another place, half a world away. Maybe that made a difference. *Or maybe he has a different attitude than Jim and his friends.* I thought. *Maybe it's simply that I'd gotten to know the wrong police officers.*

Chapter 13
I Don't Believe It, Either

"I'm so sorry, Mrs. Baker," he said softly. "No one should ever have to live in fear of a loved one. No one."

I released my pent-up breath. "Thank you," I said.

He smiled gently, his dimples only shallow grooves. "You must be a very strong woman to have escaped as you have – your home and your family intact. Well done."

Natalie sighed, too. "And I thank you, Detective. You are just and kind. That's a novelty in my experience, and I like it. I like it a lot.

"Now, I must get myself back to bed. Good night Danielle. Good night, Detective." She dragged herself up and slowly left the room.

I went with her to the door, and watched her walk toward home. At the edge of my lawn, Shea reached for her and enveloped her in a hug. I was touched by his sensitivity to what might be happening. Instead of shouldering in, all manly curiosity, he waited patiently for Natalie to finish inside so he could walk her home. What a great man. I stood on my porch for a moment, breathing the night air. There were seven or eight neighbors still standing at the edge of my yard. As I stood there, they all went home, calling good nights and supportive words to me. I answered with thanks in my words and my heart.

Back in the kitchen, I found Detective Hawksworth rinsing out his mug at the sink. He turned with a smile when I entered.

"Thank you, Detective," I said before he could speak. "I appreciate you listening and being kind."

Officer Smythe spoke up from the table. "The recorder is off, sir. May I speak freely?"

Detective Hawksworth turned quickly. "Yes, always."

"Thank you, sir." She turned to me. "Mrs. Baker, you don't know what went on down at the station. Jim used to tell us the different things he had done to you, bragging, you know? We couldn't help you while you were married, until you asked for help, and you didn't."

"It took a long time to get strong," I said.

Officer Smythe nodded. "It always does. But we did our best during your divorce to protect you and the kids. We recommended a lawyer to Jim who, he didn't know this, but that particular lawyer is sympathetic to abused spouses. And we took shifts, keeping an eye on Jim when he was off-duty, in case he thought of coming over here and harassing you. I've enjoyed knowing we were able to help you, behind the scenes, as it were. And I thought it was time you knew. We're not all like Jim and Bruce."

I stared at her. "Wow. I really didn't know. Thank you." I walked over to her, and she stood. "I'm going to hug you, now," I warned her and matched words to actions. She was surprised, but she smiled and hugged me back.

Then she gathered up her notebook and pen, said, "Good night," and disappeared into the dark morning.

Detective Hawksworth smiled also. "I must go now, Mrs. Baker, unless you are afraid to stay here alone? I could ask a woman police constable to – a woman police officer, pardon me, to stay here with you and the children, if you like."

Slowly I shook my head no. "Thank you," I said, "but I'm okay now. This does have to do with Jamie's death, doesn't it? I mean, it has to, with the two phone calls. I just can't figure out why they would threaten *me*. I don't even know all the gossip."

We walked toward the front door. Detective Hawksworth answered carefully, "It could do so, and I'm inclined to think it does. However, it could just be mischievous youths venting their frustration over her death."

I looked at him sideways.

"No, I don't believe it, either," he smiled. "However, I have called here several times in the last few days, so the neighbors may think you have much to tell me. All I can say is, be careful, and call me if you need anything."

I grinned up at him. "Are you always this available to the people involved in a crime you're investigating?"

My inner voice was horrified. *You're flirting!*

Shut up, I told it back. *I think it's just the relief of opening up.*

Detective Hawksworth smiled back. "Yes, I try to be available, Mrs. Baker. But I must say it's a distinct pleasure in this instance."

See? I told my own critic. *It's okay.*

"Oh, I remember what I was going to ask yesterday. Who found Jamie's body?"

Detective Hawksworth said, "Her mother found her in the morning when she didn't get up in time for school. Why do you ask?"

I shrugged. "It seemed important, and I didn't even think of it. Her poor mom."

We said good night, and the detective left. After closing the front door, I gazed at my once-beautiful living room, a room I had spent years lovingly restoring, now a shambles. The bookshelf that I had assembled myself was lying on the floor, books scattered everywhere.

The couch cushions were in shreds. I remembered the summer I had painstakingly recovered the couch. It had taken me sixteen months to find just the perfect fabric, and I knew I wouldn't be able to match it. The center cushion was gone, taken to whatever they call CSI in real life.

One antique wingback chair was on its side, and the other stood backward. The coffee table my parents had given me years ago was still in one piece, although it had a long scratch on it. An end table was scratched, also.

Two lamps lay shattered on the floor, but I wouldn't miss them. They had been gifts from my mother-in-law, my *ex*-mother-in-law. They'd been ugly new, and were even uglier now.

And there was a hole in one window. The police had covered it with plywood.

I sat down in the doorway to my no-longer-beautiful living room and began to cry. The tears rolled down my cheeks, and I swiped at them angrily. Rocking back and forth, I beat my fists against my knees, and yelled at God, "Jim should have been here. He should have been the husband he promised to be. I shouldn't be facing this alone.

"*You promised* to provide for my every need, so provide already! Oh, God, please."

There was a quiet tap on the front door. I knuckled my eyes and leaped to answer it. "Who's there?" I demanded.

"Detective Hawksworth, Mrs. Baker."

I opened the door, and he stepped in, pulling me into his arms as he had earlier. The floodgates burst, and I sobbed with abandon. The trauma of the last few hours mixed with the remembered trauma of my marriage had undone me, and I babbled as I sobbed, pouring out many years'-worth of fears and hurts and crushed dreams. Without my realizing it, Detective Hawksworth pulled us both into the house and got the door closed. We stood in the entryway for what seemed a very long time, until the tears slowed and finally ceased.

I pulled away just a little. I felt safe and comforted in his hug.

"Thank you," I didn't dare let him see the mess of my face. "I feel much better, now." He handed me a couple of tissues, and I lay my head on his shoulder for another moment as I mopped up the mess. I was comforted again when he lay his head on mine. We stood there another minute or two.

"Are you alright, now?" He asked gently. I nodded and thanked him again. The tissues had disintegrated, so I rubbed at my face with my sleeve. "I'm here if you want to talk some more."

I shook my head. "Thank you, but I think I've talked enough for one night." I gave him a watery smile. "And I feel at peace, now. God really does provide for my needs, doesn't He?"

Detective Hawksworth smiled gently. "He certainly does. I had no intention of coming back, but I'm glad I did."

"Thank you, Detective." I looked at him out of red, swollen eyes, but I didn't care. God had given me what I needed, a friend with a strong hug.

"Fine, then," he said more briskly. "You'll be safe from more break-ins, especially tonight. I came back to tell you that there are extra patrols scheduled on this street until this case is solved."

I glanced at his face and was nearly undone again by the gentleness I saw there. I assured him I was better, now, and that I would be going to bed. So he wished me good night and left.

How nice, I thought as I climbed the stairs. *I feel safe. The police will patrol, and it won't be the Spruce Bruce. You really do provide, God. Thank you.*

I thought I would have trouble sleeping, but I slept deeply and dreamlessly.

Chapter 14
Likely Story, Young Lady

For a few days, life was quiet and almost normal with school, and baseball, and exercise, and walks with Natalie. I decided to give myself a rest from writing until next week. My neighbors and several friends in town stopped by with food and hugs; they wanted to hear what had happened. I made a lot of coffee and shared it with people whose concern made me feel loved.

Pastor Ted and his wife, Wendy, stopped by to check on us. They helped me duct tape the remaining sofa cushions and turn them over. I would replace them some day, when I could afford the fabric.

Peggy Sue stopped by, too, with her grandson, LeRoy. Mikey took him out back to play catch (with Ramon the Wonder Dog's hilarious hindrance), and Peggy Sue helped me replace the hundred or so books on the book case.

"I would cheerfully kill *anyone* who tried to hurt my babies," she assured me. "Especially now that I have babies to protect. My daughter and grandson are my greatest treasures."

I agreed that my children are my greatest treasures, also, and I protected them as well as I could. She said she understood but that I must have a really long fuse. She wasn't sure she wouldn't have stomped downstairs and introduced "that stinkin' creep" to her baseball bat. I had to smile. Peggy Sue talks big, but I doubted she would actually hit someone before she had just cause.

"And these are just things, Peggy Sue," I reminded her as I waved at my living room. She agreed, half-heartedly, saying she would rather the creeps stayed outside. I couldn't agree more.

The kids helped me buff the coffee and end tables, returning them to their previously beautiful condition, almost. Shelly went to school on Friday and said she was the most popular girl for the day.

And Natalie stopped by to replace the sofa cushion that the police had borrowed. Where she found one sofa cushion – one that actually fit – was a mystery she refused to solve for me. (Shelly told me later that the print on the cushion was the same as the couch in the games room at Abe's house, but she didn't say anything, because Natalie was so proud of herself.)

About noon on Friday, my mother called. I do love my mom, but she can be a bit protective, even from New Jersey where she and dad moved when they retired. Hannah happened to answer the phone, and I listened to her side of the conversation.

"Oh, hi, Gramma G. How are you?" I heard some squawks from the receiver. "No, we're good." Squawk, squawk. "No, really, Gramma. Everything's fine. Do you want to talk to Mom?"

She sent a pleading look my way, and I took pity on her. Hannah handed me the phone, and I gave her a quick hug. "Hi, Mom. How are you doing?"

"Danielle Grace, what is this I hear about a murder in your town? Do you not have a phone with which to call your dad and me when something important happens? Of course you do. So why is it I have to read about it on facebook? Huh?"

"I'm glad you're doing well. Yes, I'm just fine, too." I answered.

She made a "pfft" sound, and I could imagine her waving the niceties away with a well-manicured hand. "Yes, I'm fine. Now, answer my questions. By the way, your father is here, too, and he wants to know just as much as I do."

"Oh. Hi, Dad."

"Danielle says hello, Raymond." Obviously, my dad would know what's going on, but he would have to hear it second-hand. As usual.

I continued, "We've been pretty busy, and with you being three hours ahead of us, I was finding it difficult to call when you weren't in bed."

Mom grunted. "Likely story, young lady. Don't you know I'm worried about you and my grandchildren? And you didn't call me? I feel like you don't even care.

"All right, fine, yes, and your father is worried, too, he says."

I rolled my eyes at the blatant manipulation. "So, what do you want to hear about?"

"Everything," she breathed. "I know who was murdered, that girl Jamie, right? The one whose mom drinks? But I don't know why. Do the police have suspects?

"Oh, no," she exclaimed. "Who's investigating? Our dearly unbeloved ex-son-in-law sleaze-bag jerk face . . . I really need to come up with a good name for him . . . isn't investigating, is he?"

I laughed. "No, he's not in town right now," I answered. "And you know —"

"Yes, I know you don't like me to talk about him like that in front of the kids, but I'm not in front of the kids right now, am I?"

I sighed. "Nope, you're not."

She continued, "So, who is investigating? Surely not the Spruce Bruce."

"There's a new detective who seems to be very good," I told her. "He did a pretty good job interviewing the kids . . ."

"You let someone interview my grandchildren? How could you? Raymond, she let some stranger interview our grandchildren. Don't you think we should fly out there and protect her? I really think we should. Get the credit card bill, find out how many air miles we have saved up."

I took a deep breath and asked the kids to clean the kitchen. *You could intervene about now, Lord. You really could.*

I told Mom as much as I was allowed to say about the murder, which really brought home to me all that I didn't actually know. And I convinced her and Dad that I didn't need them to fly out and hold my hand. I may have indicated that the police were close to an arrest. Not exactly a lie, more of a prevarication. Or possibly faith.

A few minutes later, I had brought her up to date and was avoiding being set up with yet another "nice young man" of my mother's choice, when God answered my prayer.

Hannah loudly and clearly announced, "Mom, Mikey and I are ready for your help with our science experiment."

I grinned my thanks and said, "Hey, I have to go. Hannah and Mikey need my help with school."

"I heard, dear," my mom answered sweetly. "And Hannah's timing is perfect. I must rush off so I'm not late for my mani/pedi. You remember my manicurist, right?" She continued without waiting for an answer. "Well. She couldn't do my nails last week, because someone had broken into her house and trashed it. Whoever it was left fingerprints behind, and they caught him the next day. But the police never did find everything he stole. It seems he had had a duplicate key made, somehow." She made that 'tsking" noise she so likes. "And my nails are just a *mess* because I missed last week."

I thought about that for a moment. "Can someone do that?"

"Do what, dear?" she asked absently.

"Get a duplicate key made to someone else's house."

"Obviously," she answered. "Because someone did. I'm so glad *you've* never had a break-in, my dear. Anyway, gotta go! Give the children hugs for me. Yes, Raymond, okay. And give them hugs from their grandfather, too."

I laughed and answered, "Will do. And I love you both."

I sighed in relief, hugged Hannah and Mikey, and thanked them for rescuing me. I told them they deserved a treat.

So we enjoyed a vinegar-and-baking soda rocket experiment in the back yard. Ramon the Wonder Dog thought it was great fun to chase the rocket (an old two-liter bottle), and the kids laughed themselves silly. They laughed even harder when we spied the cats sitting in the kitchen window watching us race around the yard after the dog and the rocket.

Chapter 15
Pertinent Background Information

Late that afternoon, I walked in the sunshine to Dari Mart for a gallon of their excellent milk. They advertise that their milk goes from cow to store within forty-eight hours. It works; it's the best milk around. And I had managed to run completely out. I was full of plans for Sunday's dinner, humming a tune, so I mindlessly grabbed the milk, sailed past the colorful rows of ice cream, and turned toward the counter where I ran full tilt into a tall, thin man.

"Oh. Excuse me," I apologized as I staggered back. The milk nearly flew from my grasp, and I took a moment to make sure I didn't drop it.

He turned and smiled oddly at me. He had two teeth missing, and his nose was crooked from an old break. "Oh, no problem. You're Danielle Baker." It was a statement, not a question.

I looked more closely at him. "Yes? Oh. You're Jamie's dad. I'm so sorry for your loss." He didn't answer me, and I didn't know what else to say, so I stared awkwardly around the store. The cashier rang up an order of fried chicken and potato wedges as she chatted about her upcoming wedding. I wished she'd hurry. He was making me nervous.

Jamie's dad continued to smile at me as the next person in line put down a can of chewing tobacco and a case of beer. His smile was eerie, and I started to fidget. Finally, I couldn't stand it anymore. "Can I do something for you?"

Still smiling oddly, he said, "I heard you had a break-in recently. I hope no one was hurt."

"Yes, we did," I answered uncomfortably. "And we're fine, praise the Lord."

He rocked back and forth on his heels. "You might consider taking a vacation, you and your kids. You know, just until this case is solved and the person who did my baby girl in is caught."

I stared up at him. Was he serious?

He raised up to his fullest height and stepped in toward me. I took an involuntary step back as he towered over me. "Knowing police officers, and being the girlfriend of one, and knowing police procedure, what with you having a cop ex-husband, might not be good for someone."

"Like the killer, you mean?" I asked sarcastically. He didn't move or change expression. "Are you threatening me? Do you know something about the break-in?"

Still smiling oddly, he whirled around, threw a ten dollar bill onto the counter and walked out with his own milk.

Girlfriend of a police officer? Are you kidding me? I've known the man for less than a week. Dude, he is not *my boyfriend,* I called silently to his back.

"Hey," the cashier called out. "You want your change?" She stared at the six dollars and coins in her hand. "Best tip I've had in a long time," she grinned at me.

I stared at the door he'd gone through as I put my milk on the counter, wondering what that was all about. It was downright creepy. I determined to put it out of my mind, though. I had a dinner to look forward to, and grieving parents sometimes say weird things.

Maybe I should mention it to Natalie, though, I thought as I trudged home with the milk, my good mood all but gone.

On Saturday we did a big house cleaning in preparation for Detective Hawksworth's social (as opposed to police) visit. We were glad we'd worked so assiduously on the living room in the days before, so we wouldn't have to spend the time on it on Saturday. Judging by their cheerful willingness to actually clean, the children approved of him. Jim had been gone for more than four years. Maybe it was time for me to start thinking of dating again.

Anyone but a policeman, that is.

I asked Natalie what she thought when we got together again Saturday afternoon to talk about Jamie's death. Shea was in his workshop finishing up a beautiful but complicated breakfront cabinet for one of the wealthy farmers in our town. It was to be a birthday present for his wife. Farming must pay well, judging from the amount of work being put into – and therefore the price of – the cabinet.

Abe was playing video games with a couple of friends upstairs; we could occasionally hear the thumps and yells. Natalie's daughter, Tabitha, was shopping with a friend, and Danny was at my house with Mikey, shooting hoops. We had the house to ourselves, so we sat in the living room with mugs of coffee and a plate of brownies.

"Yes, you should date again," Natalie said. "It's been way long enough...You might even date that gorgeous detective." She grinned wickedly. "Hmm. I'm sure I could get him to ask you out."

"No, you don't," I commanded. "You will keep out of it. He's coming for Sunday dinner. If he wants to ask me out, he will. We are *so* not in junior high anymore. Besides, it was a question of should I, not an announcement that I would. I'm still not sure I'm ready."

"You are," Natalie announced. "It's totally obvious."

I blew a razzberry, and we went back to discussing Jamie.

Natalie said, "I had a conversation with Father Bingham about Jamie's family."

"You did? Why?" I blew on my coffee.

"They're members of the Catholic Church, and I thought he might be able to tell me something."

"Was he?"

She sighed in exasperation. "No, he wasn't. They may have been members, but they never set foot in the church."

I rolled my eyes. "So why are you telling me?"

"Because one of us needs to be actively doing something to find answers," she pointed at me. "You seem to be in the middle of excitement –"

"Not my idea of a good time." I interrupted.

"So, I thought I should actually do something before you and the kids get hurt."

Brilliant. I let the police handle it, yet all the excitement comes my way. Natalie questions people, and no one even looks at her cross-eyed. "Have you talked to anyone else?" I sighed.

She hesitated. "Well, no. I've been busy working and cleaning up the mess at your house."

We stared at each other. Finally, I said, "We're not any good at this, are we? Gossip, or as you term it, 'caring and sharing' is just fine, but actually asking questions is hard to do. And I still think the police should handle it."

"Maybe they should, but are you comfortable with that? That break-in the other night was pretty scary."

I sighed. "Okay, who do you think we should put on a suspect list?"

Natalie thought we should take another look at little Kelly Green, because she had argued with Jamie. And I thought we should talk to Jamie's boyfriend, Forrest. The only point we really agreed on was that we didn't know enough. Natalie would have to talk to some more people.

"Except we know this," Natalie shifted to her other hip. "Either two separate people are out to get you, one to harass and one to harm you, or the person who broke in the other night wanted to scare you, not hurt you."

I stared at her. "I hadn't thought of that." I grabbed another brownie for comfort. "I assumed it was one person. I hope it is."

"I really think it is," she assured me. "I mean, in a town this small, surely there aren't two people out for your blood. Even during the divorce, people mostly left you alone, only glaring at you from across the street."

I snorted. "True, but divorce and murder are very different."

"So, let's assume it's one person. Why would he call just before he broke into your house?"

"Presumably so I would be totally freaked out. As I was."

"Right. He wanted you awake for the whole performance," Natalie grinned triumphantly. "If you had been asleep, you wouldn't have been as afraid."

That reminded me of my encounter with Jamie's dad at Dari Mart. I leaned forward and told her all that I remembered.

"That's really creepy," she said. "Was he trying to warn you away, or did he think he was being helpful?

"Trust me, his attitude was *not* reassuring." I shuddered as the scene flashed through my mind.

"So if he wasn't trying to help you, then maybe he was trying to tell you not to investigate," Natalie ventured.

"Why would he do that?" I wondered. "I'm *not* investigating! I've hardly talked to anyone recently, except you. Besides, he said something about Detective Hawksworth being my boyfriend." I rolled my eyes. "As if."

Natalie laughed. "You're being a bit dramatic, aren't you?"

"But he's only been here a few days." I protested. "If I'm being dramatic, anyone who thinks we're dating is being precipitate."

Natalie grinned at me. "Of course they are. Have you ever known this town not to be precipitate? I often know what I've done before I do it; all I have to do is listen to other people talking."

I growled in frustration, so Natalie changed our focus and started suggesting various reasons why Jamie's dad might want to kill his own daughter – or try to scare me, but we couldn't come up with anything reasonable.

"Not that murder is ever reasonable, but it usually makes sense to the murderer," Natalie said. "We just need to think like him or her, and it might make a twisted kind of sense to us, too."

I sighed and stood up. "What we really need is more knowledge. I'm going to go home and take a nap."

Natalie grinned. "That's how you're going to get more knowledge?"

I laughed. "No, but I do think more clearly when I've had some sleep."

SATURDAY EVENING, MIKEY and I did a grocery run. I always take one of the kids with me to help with the lifting and to teach them how to shop. Homeschooling doesn't only happen during school hours. One day, they would be shopping for themselves, and this is a perfect opportunity for them to learn grocery store math, frugality, and the joys of eating store brands.

Just before we left, Natalie called. When he heard who was on the line, Mikey rolled his eyes, grinned, and walked back upstairs.

"I talked to Uncle Leo," she told me.

"Well, that's nice, dear. And how is Uncle Leo?"

She laughed. "He's fine. Remember when he was involved in that suspicious death a few years ago?"

"Oh, right. He was a witness, if I remember correctly."

"You do," she sighed. "I had no idea what that entailed." I made a 'pshht' noise in agreement. "I told him about our murder and asked for any counsel he might have for us. I also told him how much you hate what you call "gossip" and how hard it is for you, because you want to help, but you don't like talking about other people."

"Yes?" I prompted as she paused.

"He said something interesting," she continued absently. "I wrote it down, because I didn't want to get it wrong. . . Here it is.

"He said," she cleared her throat, "and this is something the police officer told him. You know how close-mouthed he is about his clients and their families."

"Aren't all morticians?" I asked.

Natalie gave a lady-like snort. "Yes, but he is even more so. I can barely get him to tell me the names of the people who died."

I laughed. "Why would you want to know the names of the people who have died in San Francisco?"

I could practically hear the grin over the phone line. "To give him a bad time."

"Oh, Natalie," I laughed again. "You must drive him nuts."

"No, I think he likes it," she answered. "Anyway, what the police officer said when Uncle Leo didn't want to *gossip* about his clients and neighbors. He said, 'Once someone is murdered, whatever you know about them is no longer gossip; it becomes pertinent background information.'"

I pondered that for about a minute while Natalie waited patiently. Finally, she asked, "Well? What do you think?"

"I think he has a point. I may not like talking about people, but knowing it is – what did he call it? – 'pertinent background information' will help."

"I thought it might. Glad I could help." I grinned, said I'd talk to her tomorrow, and yelled for Mikey. It was time to get groceries.

As I drove down Coburg Road into Eugene, I pondered Jamie's death, the upcoming prom, Natalie's Uncle Leo's new definition of gossip . . . 'pertinent background information' as it applies to a murder investigation, Detective Hawksworth's advent into our lives, his dimples, his eyes, his accent. "Stop that!" I commanded myself. I glanced over to Mikey in the passenger's seat to see if he had noticed me talking to myself. He was engrossed in a book on mummification, so I looked at the saddleback on the Coburg hills – my favorite part of the whole range - and slowed down as I entered Coburg.

Coburg is a beautiful little town well known for its antiques and "old town" atmosphere. I like the corn field that in the summertime nestles up next to Main Street, the gazebo in the park, and the cute storefronts. However, everyone knows you don't want to exceed the speed limit in Coburg. I spend as much time looking at my speedometer as I do looking at the road when I drive through.

On the other side of town, I increased my speed and thought some more about Jamie and the impact her murder was having on the community. Did my kids or I have any more 'pertinent background information' to give to the police? I prayed for an answer to this mystery. And soon.

Chapter 16
Have You Heard Something New?

During worship on Sunday, we were singing one of my favorite songs when I noticed a new voice behind me, a rich baritone. The voice was attractive, and the vowels took me back to my college choir days. Then I realized the person singing wasn't American.

Good gracious. Is he here? It took a lot of self-control not to turn around.

Pastor Ted spoke on The Thief in the Night. My kids giggled and looked at each other with that "I wonder where he got *that* idea" look. I shushed them and whispered, "It's not all about us." They thought about that a moment, and realization that I meant Jamie's death and not our break-in sobered them. But the sermon was good; we were exhorted to keep a guard on our lives and to stay alert, because you never know when the enemy might try to steal your life – physical, spiritual, or emotional. My kids exchanged sober looks several times.

When church was over, I turned to find Detective Hawksworth sitting just a couple of pews behind us. The smirk on his face made it plain he'd sat there intentionally. Several people moved between us, introducing themselves to him. With his looks and that accent, he was very popular with the ladies especially.

Don't be catty, I told myself as I watched the group of women around him. Within moments, insecurity and self-doubt were overwhelming me; there are so many pretty women in our town.

And he's a very attractive man. I was sure any woman would be happy to go out with him, so why would he choose mommy-of-three me? I sighed and reminded myself I don't like policemen. *What's happening to my defenses? Why would I even entertain these ideas? Where are they coming from?* I needed to talk to Natalie.

Pastor Ted approached right then, distracting me from my thoughts. He asked after us and reiterated his assurance that all we had to do was call if we needed anything. I thanked him and turned back to the spectacle. Pastor Ted watched with us for a few moments.

Woman after woman shook Detective Hawksworth's hand or gave him a welcoming hug, asking him questions and inviting him to different church functions. Finally, Pastor Ted looked at Mikey and said, "You know, if someone doesn't rescue him soon, he may just be eaten alive." He winked in our general direction before walking away, and Mikey waded in.

"Excuse me," he announced loudly. "He's coming home with me, and my mom has to finish dinner. Excuse me."

The ladies good naturedly let them through, Detective Hawksworth laughing as he finally reached us.

"Do all Americans give hugs as freely as the people here in this village do?" He asked. "Even in Salem, people were hugging me all the time."

I shrugged. I wasn't about to tell him just how good-looking he is. "I think it's a Pacific Northwest thing. I don't notice it in other parts of the country."

"Well, I think I like it. I feel like a celebrity," he declared.

Shelly looked at the ladies still watching us. "You look like one, too," she grinned at him. "And you're going home with us. I feel like the entourage to a celebrity." She hooked her arm in his and walked with exaggerated stately grace to the parking lot. "Did you bring your car, Detective?"

"Yes, it's right over there. Where did you park?" We all rolled our eyes at him and laughed.

"We only live five blocks away," I answered. "Don't people in England walk?"

He grinned. "All the time. But not in the middle of a case. We never know when we will be summoned to an emergency."

Duh. I remembered my ex-husband's lectures on the subject. Shelly assured him, "Dad never walked, either. How about you and I go home in your car, and I'll let you into the house while Mom, and Hannah, and Mikey walk home."

Quickly I said, "No, honey, I think it should be Mikey. He deserves the privilege after not being allowed to follow the police around our house and watch them work the other night."

Detective Hawksworth looked his thanks as Mikey jumped up and down. "Yeah!" he shouted and ran toward the detective's little blue compact.

As they drove off, I explained, "A sixteen-year-old girl and a police officer do not belong in a house alone. Or in a car."

"Oh, right," Shelly exclaimed. "Dad told me about that. I forgot...Do you think I should apologize?"

I pondered that a moment. "No, I think it was taken care of just fine." We finished our walk in companionable conversation. I know several people who don't seem to enjoy their kids, but I like mine. And they usually like me. I think home schooling has helped strengthen our relationships.

As I finished preparing lunch, Natalie stopped by. Detective Hawksworth and the kids were in the living room talking. Well, the kids were asking questions about England, and the detective was answering them the best he could. I could hear their voices and an occasional word. There were bursts of laughter at times, too. I smiled and hummed.

"It sounds comfortable," Natalie echoed my thoughts as she leaned against the sink. I nodded contentedly. "So, has he asked you out, yet?"

"No, and I'm not counting on it, either. And neither are you," I said firmly. As Natalie took a chip with salsa from the tray on the counter top, I slapped her hand good-naturedly, grabbed the tray, and took it into the living room.

"Chips and salsa for an appetizer," I announced, placing it on the coffee table. I looked at the children one by one. "Don't –"

As a chorus, they chanted, "Don't make a mess, and if you do, clean it up." They all laughed, and I joined in. As I left the room, I called, "Please don't feed the animals."

Natalie had set the kitchen table before I returned. "I wasn't sure if you were going to eat here or in the dining room, but this is where you always eat, now, and I didn't think you wanted to change anything."

I nodded. "Thanks, this is perfect. You know how Jim would punish the kids if they spoke during a meal in the dining room."

"Yeah, I remember. Sometimes he flipped their forks out of their hands or tossed their plates against the wall to keep them controlled. We were here for a couple of those dinners."

I leaned against the counter. "I hate the dining room. I wish I could do something, erase all the memories in there."

Natalie slipped a napkin under a fork. "Home schooling in there doesn't seem to be a problem. Maybe you could make it more School Room and less Dining Room."

"That's a good idea, actually." I shrugged. "Today, though, I'm hoping for a casual, happy meal. And thanks to your help with the table, we're almost ready."

She grinned. "My pleasure. Have you learned any more about Jamie?"

I laughed. "Detective Hawksworth only just got here. Have you heard something new?" I pulled the enchiladas out of the oven. They were perfect, with crispy cheese around the edges.

Natalie sniffed. "Mmm. Smells wonderful. No," she continued as she headed to the fridge, "I don't know anything new. It's been a few days. You'd think we'd know something by now.

"I did ask my kids which exchange students Jamie knew. They said she was friendly with the boy Lars, from Norway. Lemonade or water?" She held a pitcher of each.

I spooned the Spanish rice into a bowl. "Lemonade, thanks. Did she know anyone else?"

Natalie placed the pitcher on the table. "Well, Abe thought she spent time with Karl from Germany. And he's seen her with Daniel from Israel."

We smiled at each other, and I rolled my eyes. "I don't suppose she was friendly with any of the girls?"

"Abe didn't think so. I'll talk to those three tomorrow, if I can catch them."

I sighed. "The whole case seems to have come to a halt."

Natalie nodded morosely. "Frustrating, isn't it?"

As I placed the food on the table, Natalie sneaked out the front door, whispering, "Have fun."

I announced dinner, and we all filed into the kitchen. Detective Hawksworth didn't look frazzled, so he must have enjoyed the question and answer time with the kids.

We prayed and passed food around to a buzz of conversation. One bite, and Detective Hawksworth announced, "These are delicious. What do you call them?"

"Enchiladas," Shelly told him. "They're a Spanish dish...well, Mexican, really."

"I love them," he declared. "We have Spanish foods in England, but I don't often have them. These, however, I would eat."

Thank you, God. I did a little mental jig, and conversation continued in a casual, friendly way. This dinner was turning out to be a very good idea.

I was visiting with Shelly about plans she and her friends were making for Prom when the word, "shit" floated on the air. Mid-sentence, I turned to find the source. Mikey was explaining to Detective Hawksworth the origin of this cuss word.

"—Briton was conquered by William of Normandy in 1066, when he earned the name William the Conqueror," he said.

"Mikey, Detective Hawksworth knows his own history," I gently remonstrated with a smile.

"I know, Mom, but I was going into the history just a bit so I could explain." I nodded, and he continued.

"You see, when William of Normandy conquered Briton, he gave lands to the men who helped him in the invasion. Britons who were landowners who pledged their allegiance to William were allowed to keep some of their land. But with the rule of the Normans came a new language, you know? And because the Normans were land owners, they were the upper class, and everyone wants to be like the upper class."

Detective Hawksworth nodded solemnly, a twinkle in his eye. I hid a smile at his careful attention to what my son obviously thought was new and exciting information.

Mikey continued earnestly. "So instead of cow, now we have beef. And instead of pig, now we have pork. And instead of shit, now we have feces. And so on."

"At the table, Mike?" Shelly rolled her eyes.

"It's just a word, Shelly. Anyway, as the Angles and Saxons learned the language of the Normans, many Celtic words went out of use except by the lowest classes - the serfs, swineherds, people like that.

"A few generations later, the upper class boys would go 'slumming'. I think that's what the English call it when an upper class boy wants to date a lower class girl, right?"

The detective nodded again. He seemed genuinely interested now. "Actually (I just loved his "acshully"), they used to call it that, but not anymore."

Mikey nodded. "So, they would use words that the lowest classes would use, so they would seem like they were in the same class as the girls, or closer to their class anyway, okay?

"And then, they decided to be really daring and use the words in front of their friends. Gasps and giggles met this daring use of lower class words at first," I smiled as Mikey quoted me directly. "So when that was accepted, and many of the upper class boys were using these 'naughty' words, they started saying them in front of their parents and other adults. It was a way of being rebellious. 'Look at me. You can't control me.' Eventually, the words were considered 'cuss words' and everyone who used them was considered rebellious and a problem child...or something like that. Right, Mom?"

I nodded. "Yes, Mikey, you did a pretty good job of explaining it to Detective Hawksworth. Well done." I smiled at him. He was certainly having fun.

Hannah said, "It's interesting, though, about those words that aren't curses or blasphemy. They're just words. But their use comes from rebellion, and the people who use them are usually rebellious, even now."

"And they don't bother to improve their vocabulary beyond those words," Shelly contributed. "Those types of words seem to preclude a large vocabulary. Initially, they say them to get a reaction, but because they use them repeatedly, the words themselves lose their power. Eventually, the person and his or her words end up seeming pathetic."

"Where did you learn all of this?" Detective Hawksworth laid down his fork, fully engaged.

"Oh, Mom has a whole classroom lecture on the subject," Mikey informed him.

"Three years ago," Hannah interrupted, ignoring Mikey's scowl, "there was a huge outbreak of foul language at the school. Some of my friends were disgusted by it, but the more it surrounds you, the harder it is to resist using those words. My friends called them 'tapeworm words'; it was like they just got inside and began to suck the intelligence out of their minds. We talked quite a lot about what they could do about it."

"I had spoken to the kids about foul language," I contributed. "So Hannah asked me to do something."

Detective Hawksworth looked confused. "I thought you were homeschooled, yet you talk of friends at school?"

"Yes," I answered, "we homeschool, but the kids are in band and sports, and they have a lot of friends at the school."

"Ah, yes, of course. You told me that. Please continue." He smiled at me.

Distracted for a moment by his dimples and blue eyes, I lost the thread of the conversation. "Oh, yes. While I was praying about the situation, Hannah had a conversation with her band teacher about what we here at home call 'The Etymology of Naughty Words'. He was impressed."

"He asked Mom to talk to the school." Hannah said proudly.

I smiled. "I spoke to the principal about it. She, too, wanted me to talk to the school. I told her I would lose the kids if I spoke to too large a group; with the first 'shit', I would lose the boys."

The kids giggled and nodded. "We decided I should speak to the fifth and sixth graders, class by class. By about a week after the lectures, the language problem was pretty well cleared up. I taught them what each word means, why it has the stigma it has, and what people think of others who use these words."

"She does it every year, now." Shelly, too, looked proud of me. "And the cussing problem –"

"It isn't solved," Hannah cut in.

Shelly smiled at her. "No, but it is way down from what it used to be. And all because of Mom."

I was touched by their obvious pride in my ability to teach something important to their friends. I smiled around at them, a silent thank you. Finally, my gaze fell on Detective Hawksworth. He still wasn't eating. He seemed to be thinking hard.

Chapter 17
At Sixes and Sevens

"Is everything okay?" I asked him.

He started out of a reverie. "Oh, yes, everything is fabulous. I was just thinking of Jamie." He grimaced and glanced around the table. "I'm sorry. Everything I do and talk about seems to reflect back onto the case."

We assured him we weren't offended by his comment or his thinking, and he relapsed back into a reverie. Shelly quietly said, "I'll bet I know what you're thinking."

Detective Hawksworth raised his eyebrows as he finally lifted his fork to take another bite of enchilada. "Do tell," he answered with a twinkle in his eye.

"Well, I'll bet you were wondering if Jamie and other kids like her would have turned out differently if her mom was more like ours."

Hannah breathed, "Ah, yes. Because Mom gives us a lot of time, and she teaches us so much."

I felt my face go hot. "Oh, come on," I started, but Shelly interrupted me.

"No, seriously, Mom, you homeschool us, give us time, and boundaries, and love. And there are a lot of kids here who don't have that."

I smiled sadly. "You're right, hon, and I feel so badly for them. And for the moms who wish they could stay home but can't afford to. But don't try to make me out to be 'Super Mom', because I'm not."

Mikey rolled his eyes. "No joke there."

The others laughed as I said, "Mikey."

"Actually," Hannah's gentle voice floated through the laughter, "Mom being imperfect helps, too. At least it does me. I know I don't have to be perfect to be a great mom."

It was time to change the subject, before I got teary-eyed. "Well then, does anyone have room for dessert?"

"Dessert?" Mikey shouted. "You bet!"

I pulled out a plate of Jumbles cookies – chocolate chips, dried cherries, coconut, and pecans – and placed them on the table. A cheer went up from my children. Shelly immediately grabbed the plate and took three cookies, passing it on to Hannah.

"Don't be greedy," I called from the kitchen. "Detective Hawksworth, would you care for coffee? It's decaf," I apologized.

"I'd love some to go with these...*cookies,*" he mischievously showed me his dimples.

I placed two mugs on the table and sat down. Dinner had been a success, and I was feeling cozy. I sighed contentedly.

When we were done, I asked the kids to clean the kitchen. Detective Hawksworth sat quietly, seemingly enjoying the family atmosphere while the domestic work was divided. Then, we took our coffees to the living room where I closed the door on the noise – clanking plates, laughter, and conversation.

"I like your children, Mrs. Baker," he said as we sat in comparative peace.

I smiled. "I like my children, too, Detective."

He listened for a moment. "Do they always enjoy clearing up after a meal?"

"No one enjoys 'clearing up' after a meal," I answered drily, and he laughed. "But they're happy today. Thanks, in part, to you."

We talked about life in England, and how different America is in comparison. He told me that the Willamette Valley is similar to his beloved home. It was pleasant visiting about nothing in particular. I think he enjoyed it, too.

At one point in the conversation, Detective Hawksworth asked, "May I ask where you found your information on the excellent...er...lecture your children shared with me?"

I smiled. "You liked it that much?" He nodded. "Well, that's gratifying. I looked through the online etymology dictionary site. It gives the date the word was first used in print and defines it according to its original language. Then, I researched the history of that particular time period and subsequent periods. I combined the research and came up with a logical explanation of that word's use throughout time. It's the best I can do without a doctorate in either etymology or the History of the Middle Ages." I shrugged, apology and defense vying for expression.

"Fascinating," he exclaimed. "I was thinking my colleagues back home might like to do something similar. Foul language, as you Yanks call it, isn't considered such a big deal back in England, but I'm thinking it should be."

He sat thoughtfully for a moment. "Would you be willing to share your notes?"

I blinked at him. "Wow. Thank you. Yes, I would be willing." We shared a smile. *Wait until Natalie hears this.* I danced a little inside.

The noises in the kitchen subsided. Shelly asked if Amy could come over to work on homework. Mikey was right behind her. He wanted to go to Danny's. Hannah came in a couple of minutes later and asked if she could Google forensic science.

Detective Hawksworth chuckled as I answered, "Of course, hon. No need to ask permission for something like that."

Then he sighed. “I really must go,” he said. “I don’t normally work on a Sunday, but this death has the town at sixes and sevens. See,” he announced proudly, “I’m even beginning to talk like an American. I called this little village a town.” He grinned at me.

I grinned back. “Perhaps, but what does it mean, ‘sixes and sevens’? I know some English phrases but not that one.”

He threw his head back and laughed. It’s a pleasant, baritone laugh. “I should have known I couldn’t get it right, yet. That means confused, upset at something not anticipated...”

“Discombobulated,” I said mischievously, and laughed at the look on his face.

“I will never be able to use that word in a sentence.”

I relented. “It means turned upside down, confused.”

“Ah. Well. ‘Sixes and sevens’ is easier to pronounce.”

I hesitated as he stood. I knew it was time to tell him about my adventure at Dari Mart yesterday, but I didn’t want to. When I didn’t stand with him, he looked at me sharply and sat back down.

“I need to tell you about something that happened yesterday,” I told him. “It isn’t anything, really, which is why I’m hesitating, but it was weird and a bit scary, and anything weird and scary should be reported, I’m sure, but I’m not sure today is a good time to tell you, but you’re going back to work anyway, and . . .”

“And we’re having fun, and you don’t want murder interrupting,” he broke in. “I understand, but you’re right that you need to report everything . . . what did you say? ‘Weird and a bit scary’? You know I’m willing to listen, so please tell me.”

I took a deep breath to curb the babbling and told him about Jamie’s dad at Dari Mart, about the strange smile and the insinuations. Detective Hawksworth listened closely the first time, then he asked me to repeat the experience. He asked several questions the second time, then he repeated to me what I had said, using slightly different words. He asked me to agree or disagree with his word choices.

Finally, he said, "So, taking away the words describing atmosphere, there was a man who stared at you while you both were in line at the store. He smiled for too long, stood too closely to you, and suggested you should take your children out of town until Jamie's killer is found. Then he intimated strongly that you may not be safe, as you are the ex-wife of a policeman and the girlfriend of another."

I blushed at his last sentence but merely nodded. "Yes. Stripped of all 'atmospheric descriptions' that is what happened."

He sat in thought for about a minute. I asked, "What do you think?"

He smiled and swiveled his eyes around to mine. "I think that village life in the U.S. is just as full of gossip as it is back home." I groaned in agreement. "I also think grieving parents say some strange things, but I will look into it and see if he meant anything by it."

I thanked him heartily, relieved to place this uncomfortable situation in his hands.

We took our mugs into the kitchen. As I turned from the sink, he was there, close behind me. I looked up into his face, my heart racing, my stomach doing pleasurable flip flops. I forgot to remind myself that I don't like policemen.

"Mrs. Baker," he said quietly, "we haven't known each other long, but I feel as if we've gone beyond the formal address. Would I be out of line if I asked you to call me by my given name, Nigel? At least, when I'm off duty."

I was short of breath, being this close to him. "I would like that very much, Nigel."

"What do I call you?" he asked with a deepening of his dimples.

"Most people call me Danielle. Natalie sometimes calls me Danny," I told him. "It's up to you what you want to call me."

"Danielle is a more feminine name." He placed his hands on my shoulders. "I may be old-fashioned, but I like feminine."

I could only nod. He kissed me lightly on the cheek, said, "Thank you for lunch," and we walked to the door.

"Please come again, Nigel," I said as we stood at the door.

He smiled down at me. "I'd like that." And then he was gone.

I closed the door and sighed like a teen aged girl.

"Hey, Mom, Amy and I . . ." Shelly walked into the hall and stopped. "What's wrong?"

I smiled at her. "He wants me to call him Nigel," I answered. I couldn't stop the grin that spread across my face.

Shelly hugged me. "Cool. Does that mean he wants to come back and visit us again, like, be friends?" She jumped up and down a couple of times, reminding me of Mikey.

I nodded. "I think so." She and I giggled together. I mused, "It's nice, isn't it, knowing Uncle Shea isn't the only good man in town."

Shelly ran upstairs. "Where are you going?"

She turned at the top. "I have to tell Amy. She'll want to know."

"Know what?" I shouted as Shelly's legs disappeared into her bedroom. I shook my head, and Natalie's face peaked around the door.

"Can I come in?" she asked as she came in. I laughed.

"I think there might be a few cookies left," I told her as we walked back to the kitchen where Ramon the Wonder Dog was vacuuming under the table. He saves me so much work. "I would have come to your house."

"Don't reprove me for standing – *glued* – to the front window for the last three hours," she said. "I need to know *now*. Every detail."

I grinned. "At least you waited until he was gone."

"Hey, be proud of me. I figured he was gone when Mikey showed up at our house, but I waited until his car turned the corner before coming over."

We took our coffees and cookies out to the front porch, and I told her about lunch, the 'shit' conversation, everything, saving the friend part for last. Well, it happened last. Natalie rolled her eyes and sighed.

"It's like an Edwardian romance," she said. "First, you have to overcome the formal name problem."

"It's not a problem."

"Not anymore," she grinned. I grinned back and removed a cat from the vicinity of the cookies. I wondered where Tom (or was it Jerry?) was still hiding. "Second, you have to overcome the impropriety of dating outside of your class."

I lifted an eyebrow at her. She can't do this, so she hates it. "What class?"

"Well, he's a policeman," she scowled. "Therefore, you're a higher class than he is."

I shook my head. "Doesn't work. I was married to a policeman before. Besides, he isn't a patrolman or a meter reader or anything. He's a detective. Much higher on the ranking scale."

"And pay scale, too," she mused. "Okay, second, you have to overcome –"

"Nothing," I said firmly. "Get it out of your head this is an *anything* romance. We're friends. Which, considering his profession, is a miracle by itself. If it moves on to something else, then it does. If not, which is more likely, then it doesn't. I'm not going to anticipate anything...and neither are you. Do you understand me?"

She grinned. "I love it when you get all 'homeschool mommy' on me. You can be very firm when you choose to be."

I huffed. Then I smiled. "Okay, Aunty-Mommy, now you know everything I know."

Natalie looked at the little table I keep between the wicker chairs, picking up cookie crumbs with her forefinger. "What do you think he was pondering?"

I thought back to the dinner conversation. "Oh, you mean when he was lost in thought for a minute during dinner...I don't know." We were quiet, considering what he might have been thinking about.

"You should have asked," Natalie finally said, leaning back in her chair.

I made a face at her. "How could I ask? We were in the middle of dinner."

"You could have asked later."

I shook my head. "It never crossed my mind."

Briskly, Natalie stood. "Let's take a walk. This murder is wreaking havoc on my weight. I've had two cookies already today, and I had two yesterday, and they seem to travel from tongue to hips in zero point two five seconds."

Chapter 18
But People Are Talkin'

I rolled my eyes in agreement and looked at the overcast sky...it didn't smell like rain, so we were good. It was now a few minutes after seven, and I calculated that we had about an hour and a half before sunset. Plenty of time. I went inside for a change of clothes. Natalie came upstairs, too, and opened Shelly's door.

"—and they were standing by the front door...Hi, Aunty-Mommy," she called cheerfully.

"Hi, Mrs. Shalligan," Amy echoed.

Shelly continued, "You should have seen Mom and Detective Hawksworth. You would have loved it."

Natalie laughed. "I heard all about it. Your mom and I are going on a walk. Let the dog out if we're not back before dark."

Shelly nodded cheerfully. "Take the pepper spray," she said, and Natalie closed the door on Shelly gracefully sitting on the floor, surrounded by clothes, books, and discarded food containers, cheerfully telling her best friend Amy all about her mom's 'new friend'.

We left the house at warm-up speed. The loop from my house crosses Main Street, goes through the *old* new development, built ten years ago, and back to the old part of town where my house is. It's fun to go from old to new and back to old again, tracing the history of our little town.

Although Natalie's house is only a couple of blocks away, it sits so that we miss the old part of town walking instead through the *new* new development, built only five years ago. Our little town is growing.

As we walked, we discussed the case, tossing different possibilities back and forth but getting nowhere. Crossing Amethyst Street, we stopped to visit with Peggy Sue who was taking groceries out of her car.

"Hey, girls, I'm glad you stopped by. I hear you're gettin' real friendly with the new detective," she said to me, shifting a bag from one arm to the other.

I shrugged. "He's nice, and I think he might be a little lonely being so far from home."

"Sure, honey," Peggy Sue chuckled. "I'll just bet he's lonely."

I rolled my eyes and smiled patiently.

She continued, "I also hear you're helpin' him with his investigation, asking questions and offering suspects. Be careful you don't get hurt doing that."

Natalie and I looked at each other in consternation. "What are you talking about, Peggy Sue?" I asked. "Where did you hear that?"

Peggy Sue's smile widened. "Well, you know how it is. I can't quite remember who said it, but she was a real reliable source."

"Oh, no," I groaned. "It isn't true."

Natalie nodded. "She isn't helping him at all, Peggy Sue, and you can tell everyone you know. He's asked Danielle's kids some questions, but that's all."

"And he had to be there for Sunday dinner, so the kids would feel more relaxed, right?"

I blushed. "No, I invited a refugee from another country over for a home cooked meal and a visit. I've done it for years with the high school exchange students, and you know it.

"And we didn't discuss the case at all. In fact, we gave him our 'shit' lecture."

"I like that lecture," she said, momentarily distracted. "LeRoy, my grandson," her face lit up as it always does at the thought of him, "didn't come to town until too late to catch it, but I'm hopin' he'll hear it next year."

"Yeah, Mikey really enjoyed telling Detective Hawksworth all about it." *Stay distracted*, I thought. Not a chance.

"So, who have you questioned? And who did you tell *him* to question?"

"No one." I growled.

"Then what were you doing at the school?" she asked. "And why was that little Kelly Green crying when he was done questioning her?"

Natalie put on her Boardroom Face. "We don't know anything about what he said to Kelly Green -"

I cut in softly, "And he had to question Shelly at school because he tried to talk to her at Natalie's." I looked up at the clouds that suddenly seemed to mimic my mood. "She fell apart."

Peggy Sue looked chagrined. "I'm sorry, Danielle, I never thought about that. I'm sure it was too much like Jim – *you mean he yelled at her?* I'm gonna wring that scrawny puke-head's neck!"

"No," I exclaimed, laughing and blinking away tears. I gave her a quick hug. "No, he did a great job of being gentle, and he was careful not to push Shelly. It was just, I don't know, too much like home. Talking at school, on her turf, so to speak, was much better."

I had to smile in spite of myself; Peggy Sue threatening someone on my daughter's behalf. In a tangle, Peggy Sue comes out on top every time. Well, sometimes Natalie wins.

"But I still want you to tell everyone you know that Danielle isn't helping in any way," Natalie told her. "Danielle's house was broken into and the living room trashed. It's going to take a lot of money to fix it all, not to mention everyone was – and still is - scared spitless!"

"Yeah, I know, I helped put away all those books." She looked at us funny. "Are you sure you aren't helping him in any way?"

I lifted an eyebrow. "What are you hinting at?"

"Well," she said slowly, "what with Jim being a police officer – and *everyone* knows how wonderful *he* was," she rolled her eyes, "and now you're going out with this detective guy –"

"I am *not* going out with him. We have never been on a date." I declared. "And you can tell everyone that, too."

"Okay, okay," she answered, shifting the bag back to her other arm. "I didn't mean to rile you up, but people are talkin'."

"People talk too much in this town. They always have. You'd think they'd watch TV or something. But no, they just keep on talking.

"This conversation is over. Come on, Natalie, I need to walk." I turned and left quickly. Natalie stayed a moment to tell Peggy Sue not to worry, I'd get over it, and she jogged to catch up with me.

"Relax," she panted, "you know how people are in this town."

"Yeah, a lot of gossips."

"And a lot of gossips get it wrong a lot of the time," she reassured me.

"Why isn't Jamie's murder overshadowing me?" I demanded. "I'm a lot less important than Jamie."

Natalie shook her head. "Maybe you want to think so, but a lot of people like you."

"Can't tell, can I?"

"Besides, you are connected to Jamie's murder, if only because Detective Hawksworth has been at your house more often than at other people's houses."

I was walking quickly to stay ahead of my anger. Natalie finally grabbed my arm to slow me down. "Hey, we're going to get shin splints if you keep this up. Slow down; we can talk at a slower pace, okay?"

I sighed. "All right, I'll slow down." I looked over to the old grain mill that still operates, right there in the middle of town.

"Who are they?" I asked. Natalie slowed to a stop beside me.

"It looks like Kelly Green and . . . Jamie's dad?" she asked.

"I don't know," I answered. "It kind of looks like Jamie's dad...but a little different. You know what I mean?"

"Wow, you're right." We moved closer, trying not to be seen, but we were in the middle of a parking lot. I had a fleeting mental image of the Keystone Cops, when they would try to hide behind each other or look like a car. I wanted to laugh. Yeah, we were brilliant.

"What are they doing?"

"It looks like they're arguing."

But their body language shouted something different. Kelly's head was tilted up, her hip jutted out. She looked like she was flirting with the man.

Or boy. It was either Jamie's father or someone who looked remarkably like him. From that distance, we couldn't tell. He was standing over her, anger in his face – obvious even from that distance – yet his arms and chest were poised like a boy who was trying to impress a teen aged girl.

"It's confusing," Natalie squinted into the half-light. I nodded.

Suddenly the two noticed us. I pantomimed surprised as I knelt and tied my shoelace. Did I say we were brilliant? They turned and walked away.

"Very interesting," said Natalie as we walked on thoughtfully.

Turning a corner, we ran into Papa Jong, literally. Max Jong is a small widower, a fourth-generation Chinese-American who runs the town's one pharmacy. He has four boys, all excellent athletes. He's coached several sports, and he tells all of his student athletes to call him Papa Jong. The whole town has taken up the honorary title. He was carrying cartons of sunglasses into his shop, and our collision caused the boxes to fall. We apologized and helped him pick them up. I was glad they'd been well-taped shut.

"I'm sorry, Papa Jong," I said.

"No problem, Mrs. Baker," he said cheerfully. "Nowadays, they make sunglasses to withstand a nuclear war."

"But they put a curse on them so you'll lose them after the first week," Natalie joked.

Papa Jong laughed. "I wouldn't be surprised. Where are you ladies going in such a hurry?"

"We're taking an exercise walk," I answered. "Or, we've been trying to, anyway. This seems to be the day for running into friends."

"Yes, I've seen many friends today, too," he sobered. "In fact, I saw poor Mrs. Sneider. She was looking for someone to sell her a fifth of vodka." He shook his head sadly. "She was already too far gone, so no one would sell to her. I offered to take her home."

He placed his box on the counter as we entered the shop after him. Papa Jong's shop looks a little like a pharmacy, and a little like a tourist's dream with postcards, sunglasses, umbrellas, and locally made crafts scattered around. It's very inviting and conveniently placed next door to the Chamber of Commerce.

"She made a funny comment," he continued, his elbow resting on the box.

We set our boxes on the counter so we could hear better.

"She said that it wasn't fair. People were hinting that she was responsible for Jamie's death, and all she ever wanted for her girl was to have a happy home life here in this small town. Then she said," he paused for emphasis, "'there's one person who could tell all about Jamie's death if only...that person...would talk.'" He lifted the boxes and went around to the back of the counter.

"Don't you think that's a funny comment?" he asked.

Natalie and I looked at each other. "That sounds like a dangerous comment to make in public," I answered thoughtfully. "If it got back to the right person – or the wrong person – she could get hurt."

Papa Jong looked at me long and hard. "Then, perhaps you should make sure the *right* person hears about it before it's too late."

Then he smiled, dispelling the somber mood. "And I will now set up the sunglasses display. After all, Oregon does get sun sometimes." He started whistling as we left the store.

We walked slowly toward home, discussing what we'd seen and heard.

"I think he wants you to talk to Detective Hawksworth," Natalie nudged me.

"Don't poke me with your elbow," I said absentmindedly. Natalie laughed softly and waved to the mayor as I continued, "No, really, do you think he meant that?"

"He was as subtle as a sledge hammer."

I smiled. "Yeah, he was, wasn't he? Should I call him tonight or wait until morning?"

"Why not call him tonight?"

"Well, he's been working all afternoon. I'm sure he won't want to work late into the night."

"Then again, he won't want another body to take to the morgue," Natalie's logic was unimpeachable.

I sighed. Maybe some day I'd be able to call...*Nigel* about something other than this case.

But I didn't need to call him after all. As we turned the corner toward home, his car pulled into my driveway. I was glad I was wearing the little jogging suit Natalie had made me buy. It never hurts to look attractive.

We discussed his car as we finished our walk. "I like little two-seaters," Natalie commented.

"I like my minivan," I answered.

"But...*Nigel* seems to like the four door compact," Natalie smiled. "I guess you can get more oomph for your money with something like that."

"Yeah, like gas mileage."

"Right, like gas mileage." She rolled her eyes, and I laughed.

"Good evening, Detective," I called. The breeze ruffled his hair as he leaned against the car, hands in pockets. I exercised utmost self-control to keep a goofy grin off my face. This man was seriously good looking.

"What were you ladies discussing?" he asked with a smile. "You looked very much like a couple of teenaged girls giggling over something naughty." (So cool. It almost sounded like, "no-tee"!)

We smiled. "We were discussing your choice of vehicle," I answered. "Natalie thinks there's something about a four-door compact that you like. Something..." I paused.

Natalie joined in. "Danielle thinks it's all about gas mileage." We waited expectantly.

"Sorry to disappoint you," he said with a grin. "It's a 'company' car, nothing to do with me." We all laughed, and I invited them into the house. Natalie hesitated.

"Is this official?" she asked.

Detective Hawksworth – *I need to get used to calling him Nigel,* I thought – assured her she was welcome to join the discussion, and we all went straight to the kitchen. I grabbed a glass of water. Natalie took iced tea from the fridge; it's her favorite, so I always have some there. Nigel wanted coffee, so I started some in the coffee maker.

Finally, we settled down at the table. Shelly, Hannah, and Mikey all came running downstairs at the sound of Nigel's voice. There was confused conversation for a few minutes. Eventually, I asked the children to give us some time to talk, and they reluctantly agreed.

Except Mikey, who was on a mission. "You have to come see my latest science project before you go. It's a clock radio that's hooked up to a potato." Mikey extracted a good-natured promise from Nigel before he left.

I brought the coffee to Nigel after pouring myself a cup. As I set them on the table, Natalie decided she wanted some, too. Since we were having a coffee session, I decided to add the cookies from the freezer; we'd eaten all of the cookies from lunch.

"What brings you here again, Nigel?" I asked cheerfully. I was afraid he was here to give me bad news, but I wasn't going to let it show. Natalie glanced at me. She knows me so well.

Nigel chewed on a cookie for a moment. "It seems there are rumors going round that you're helping me with the investigation."

I nodded. "We just heard."

"So I think it may be better if I distance myself a bit. The break-in may be tied to our friendship, and if it continues, there may be another attempt. I didn't want to just disappear, though. So," he turned his hand over, "here I am."

Chapter 19
Officer Nichols . . .

I stared at the surface of the table for a few moments. The tension was thick in the room. Although I knew Natalie wanted to intervene on my behalf, she did what all excellent friends do and waited for me to make a decision before telling me I was wrong. "You're trying to be considerate of my safety and reputation," I said slowly, "and I'm grateful."

"But?"

I sighed. "Do you see this table?" He nodded and looked at the table top. "It's seen many years of use, as you can tell by all the scratches and the occasional nick in the surface." I glanced at him to make sure he was following me. Natalie's shoulders dropped as she relaxed and nibbled on her cookie. She had a good idea where this was going.

"Although the surface is scratched and nicked, it's still a nice table, sturdy and attractive. The general use it's seen, even the occasional ill use, hasn't changed it from good to bad. And it still serves this family three generations after it was created." I glanced at Nigel again. He was listening intently.

I took a deep breath. "People are talking...okay. People do talk in small towns. You know that. I'm sure they talk in England, too." He grunted in agreement. "Well, so what? Distancing yourself now won't make the break-in not happen. That's already over with. And it won't make another break-in not happen, because people will just think I've given you some information that's taken you off somewhere. And when you've dealt with it, you'll come back. That's how people in small towns think.

"And if you think my reputation will suffer because you're coming around, well, I'm like this table – scratched, gouged even, but still . . . somewhat attractive, and just as useful as I was many years ago. More useful, I think, because I know I can withstand the trials of life." I smiled at the table top. "Age does have one advantage – I'm not worried anymore that I'm not good enough.

"Besides," I smiled at him. "The kids really like having you come around. You are just the person to give them hope that the police are actually worthy of respect. So don't distance yourself from us, please...unless you want to."

He seemed to study me for a moment. I caught a movement out of the corner of my eye and saw Shelly, Hannah, and Mikey listening carefully. When my eyes came back to him, he was smiling.

"Right, then. I shall continue to 'come around', as you call it. Thank you. I didn't relish the thought of losing our friendship." The children cheered and ran into the room. Once again, there was confused conversation, hugs, and general chaos. Natalie left for home, and Mikey brought his potato clock radio downstairs for Nigel to admire.

After Nigel left, we sat around the table discussing our new friend and his job, his attitude – so different from Jim's - and Jamie's death. Mostly, though, we just talked about life. Shelly told us she had asked David Kingston to Prom, a good-looking senior and a good friend.

Hannah asked if she could go on the youth group day trip to the coast. I said she could, if she could pay for it. She groaned. Hannah hates to pay for anything. Mikey said he wanted to try out for summer soccer. It would mean driving to Albany three days a week, but I could work while he practiced.

Glancing at the clock, I announced, "Bedtime, folks," and Mikey rushed to be the first to brush his teeth.

As the girls stood to go up, Shelly said, "Someone's been leaving flowers at Mrs. Sneider's house. Like, every other morning there's a new bouquet."

"Really?" I wondered what that meant.

"Yeah," Shelly continued, her browed wrinkled, "and no one knows who it is."

Hannah said, "It's Officer Nichols."

Shelly looked surprised. "How do you know that?"

Hannah blushed, and I wondered if she knew how cute that makes her. "One of the boys in band lives next door, and he saw him."

We were all thoughtful for a moment. I was pretty sure Shelly and I were pondering the flowers, but I wondered if Hannah might be pondering the boy in band. I was sure of it when Shelly asked, "How old is he?"

And Hannah answered, "Fourteen."

Shelly and I laughed and Hannah blushed again, this time because she had misunderstood the question and gotten caught thinking about a boy. I hugged her and told her not to worry about it, I'd done the same thing before. I answered Shelly's question, "I think Officer Nichols is in his thirties."

"Isn't Mrs. Sneider too old for him, then?" Shelly asked.

I smiled. "Not everything is done for romantic purposes, Shelly."

She snorted. "No, sometimes we do things out of guilt." And her face went white. "Mom, you don't think . . ."

I shook my head. "No, I don't think Officer Nichols had anything to do with Jamie's death. I think he might just feel a deep compassion for Mrs. Sneider."

Shelly's breath came out in a whoosh. "Oh, good. 'Cause he reminds me of Detective Hawksworth. You know? Like, he's compassionate and seems to have a lot of integrity."

I nodded and prayed my reassurance was right, that Officer Nichols was, indeed, just a compassionate man.

* * *

Monday morning dawned bright, with blue skies and fluffy white clouds. "It's a miracle," I exclaimed happily and then laughed when I remembered Papa Jong and the sunglasses. *He* had seen the weather report, anyway.

"Mikey, Hannah, Shelly, it's time to get up," I called. I filled the kettle with water for tea and oatmeal and left for Natalie's house to exercise. When I came home, all three kids were sitting at the table eating breakfast.

"How are you all this fine morning?" I asked cheerfully. They just looked at me and continued eating. "Don't tell me you aren't in a good mood on this fine day."

Shelly rolled her eyes. "Mom, even the sun isn't cheerful, yet; it's too early."

"For your information, sweetheart," I retorted, "the sun is even more cheerful than I am. It's shining away, playing with little fluffy white clouds up in an azure sky."

"The sky isn't azure until July," Mikey informed me sullenly.

I laughed. "Okay, you go on being grumpy. I'm going to take a shower and decide what kind of field trip we can take on a nearly dry, sunny day in April." I had the satisfaction of hearing Hannah and Mikey debate where they wanted to go today. Shelly complained loudly that she wanted to go back to homeschooling. Super Mom had woken them up.

We spent several hours at the Science Bin in Eugene. It's one of our favorite field trip destinations. Afterward, we went to Alton Baker park, ate a picnic lunch, and declared the day a success.

There was a message on the answering machine when we got home, and I realized I'd forgotten to take my cell phone with me. I hoped it wasn't Shelly.

It was Natalie.

"Danielle, where are you? I've called three times already. Call me as soon as you get this message."

I called her immediately. "What's up?" I asked.

"Why didn't you answer your cell phone?" she complained. "People carry them so they can be reached in case of emergency."

"Is there an emergency?" I asked anxiously.

"No, but that's beside the point."

"Natalie, you're not making sense," I chuckled in relief.

Natalie took a deep breath. "Okay, I called because Jamie's mom was found unconscious outside her trailer this morning."

Chapter 20
We're Not Going That Far, Mom

I gasped. "Oh, no. I forgot to tell Nigel what Papa Jong said. What happened?"

"She'd been hit on the back of the head. She's in a coma, and they don't know if she's going to make it."

I groaned. "Poor Linda. What if she dies? It'll be my fault."

"Be careful what you say," Natalie hissed. "Someone might hear you and think you're confessing to murder."

"Good grief, I'm not doing that," I answered. "I feel like an idiot, though."

"Look, stop beating yourself up, and call your detective –"

"He isn't my detective," I said absently.

"Well, call him anyway, and tell him what Papa Jong said, okay?"

I sighed. "Okay, I will. You don't want to do it for me, do you?"

"Don't be a coward, Danielle. Besides, I have to cook dinner."

"You don't cook." But I was talking to dead air. I groaned again.

The front door slammed, and Shelly called, "I'm home."

"I'm in the kitchen," I answered absently. The phone was still in my hand.

Shelly was excited. "Hey, Mom, guess what? Jamie's mom was found this morning next to her trailer. She'd been hit on the head, and no one knows how long she'd been there. One of the volunteer firefighters found her on his way to a call."

Shelly chattered on about school, the newest rumors concerning Jamie's death, and plans for Prom. Finally, she said, "Mom, I don't think you're listening."

"Hmm?" I pulled myself out of my reverie and hung up the phone.

"I just said we're going to rent a limo, and all you did was grunt. What's wrong?"

"A limo?" I perked up. "That sounds like fun. How many are sharing the rental, and how much will it cost each of you?"

"Well, the guys are going to rent it. It seats twenty, so they're looking for ten guys to go in on it, which would be about $25 each." Shelly was excited again.

"That seems a bit spendy," I said.

"Well, we'll be going nearly a hundred miles, round trip, so it costs extra."

"A hundred miles? Where does that boy think he's going to take my little girl?"

Shelly said patiently, "Mom, we live twenty-three miles from the dance, and the limo will take us to dinner, then the dance, and home again. That's at least seventy-five miles. And if we go anywhere else, like maybe dessert after the dance, that makes it about a hundred miles."

I smiled. "You're right, of course. I'm just not paying attention. Are you sure you can't have the dance at the resort outside Harrisburg? That's only, what, about seven miles from here?" There's a new resort right on the Willamette River just north of Harrisburg. We all wondered how it would do, out in farm country, but they seem to be booked through summer.

Shelly rolled her eyes. "Gag. Prom that close to home? Every parent and little brother or sister would be there, peeking in the windows, laughing at us. Or worse," she said as she headed for the stairs, "telling naked baby stories. I'm gonna get started on my homework." Suddenly, she turned around, walked across the room, hugged and kissed me, and left. I stared after her, wearing a silly grin. It feels so good when my kiddos spontaneously hug me!

Then I groaned. I would now have to call Nigel, and I dreaded doing it. *Don't be a coward,* I told myself. *Too late,* I answered myself. I giggled and dialed his number.

He answered on the first ring. "Detective Hawkswuth!"

I was taken aback at his gruff greeting. Gathering my wits, I answered, "Hello, Detective, this is Danielle Baker."

"Danielle," I was cheered by his warmth. "What can I do for you?"

I took a calming breath. "I have some information about Jamie's mom. I was supposed to tell you last night, and I forgot in the, umm, other matter. I'm so sorry."

"Don't feel badly," he answered. "You couldn't have known."

"That's just the thing. I could have guessed, and I didn't." I was feeling bad all over again.

"I tell you what," he answered. "I don't think I've eaten all day. How about we meet at Cecily's Café?" I noticed he pronounced Cecily with a short 'e', Cessily. "I'll buy dinner, and you can tell me all about it."

"I'm tempted," I hesitated, and he waited patiently. I sighed. "I'm afraid you're going to be disappointed in me when you hear what I have to say. Besides, I think you're going to want to interview Papa Jong; he gave me the information."

"I doubt that I'll be angry," he assured me. "But why don't you tell me in the car park, and if I have to do something about it, we'll not have gone into the café and wasted a good meal. How does that suit you?"

I smiled. "You really want to eat, don't you?"

"Yes, I'm way beyond peckish and have moved into famished."

I laughed. "Okay, I'll meet you there. When?" We settled on fifteen minutes, and I rushed upstairs to check my hair.

"Oh, good gracious, look at me, Lord. My jeans have grass stains, I spilled mustard on my shirt. I look like one of my kids." I changed quickly, spraying water on my hair. Everyone with curly hair knows you don't comb it when it's dry, that water and finger scrunching are the best way to tame the wild mop. I brushed my teeth, told the kids they were on their own for dinner, and headed out.

Shelly rushed to her bedroom door. "Where are you going, young lady?" she asked in mock seriousness, a frown between her eyes.

"I'm going out to dinner with a really cute boy," I answered coyly.

"What's his name, where are you going, and when will you be home?" She grinned at me.

"We're not going *that* far, Mom." I rolled my eyes. We laughed and I hugged her. "I have my cell phone if you need me."

"We'll be fine," Shelly assured me. Hannah and Mikey came from their rooms, and they all said good-bye.

"I'm only going to dinner." They laughed and were chatting happily when I let myself out. *I love my family,* I sighed contentedly.

Nigel's little blue compact was already there. I parked beside him and transferred to his car to tell him what Papa Jong had told me.

"You look great," he said.

"I must have looked really bad last night for there to be such a difference today." I teased.

He blinked and smiled. "You're feeling sassy today." He grinned. "And that isn't at all what I meant. But what did you need to tell me?"

I sobered instantly and told him. With a sigh, he pulled out his phone and left himself a message to interview Papa Jong. I told him I didn't know his address.

"You were absolutely right," he shook his head. "You should have told me last night."

"I know. She might not be hurt right now if I'd remembered to say something to you."

He continued, "Then again, Papa Jong needn't have told me through you. If he had spoken to me directly, Ms. Sneider probably wouldn't be injured."

I brightened at the thought of the shared guilt. Nigel chuckled. "Come on, luv, let's get us some dinner."

My hand jerked to a halt over the door handle, and I stared at him. He stared back a moment, then laughed. "Sorry. It's a term of endearment between friends and family."

"So it means nothing at all?" I asked as we walked across the parking lot.

His face turned red. "Not nothing, really. But it does mean you're my friend." He cleared his throat, and I felt my face redden in response.

Unfortunately, we entered the café at that moment, and our matching red faces drew a lot of attention. *Life in a small town,* I mentally shrugged. There was nothing I could do about it.

As we waited for our meal, I asked him for details on how Jamie's mom was hurt, and when.

He picked up his butter knife and made patterns in the table cloth. (Cecily's Café is the only eatery in town with table cloths; pretty high class for a small farm town.) I glanced around the café while waiting for him to answer and noticed several people looking at us sideways. Perhaps coming to a restaurant in town wasn't such a good idea.

"She was hit on the back of the head with a clay flower pot," he answered somberly. Then his lips quirked.

I bit my lip but couldn't hold in the giggle. "Sorry," I said, sobering quickly.

He grimaced. "Sounds like a comedy film, doesn't it? I don't know of anyone else ever being hit with a clay flower pot. Even when I walked the beat."

"Was it empty?"

He raised his eyebrows. "Good question. It was about half full of dirt and rocks, quite heavy enough to do the damage it did."

I thought for a moment. "It sounds like something a man would think a woman would use. Or maybe a woman did do it, because it was handy and she could actually lift it. What do you think?"

He shrugged. "Dunno. Either way, it was effective. If the pot had been plastic, it would have bounced off her head and hit the assailant on the back swing. As it was, he or she chose well.

"Unless the goal was to kill her," he continued, "which I doubt, because the assailant would have had plenty of time to finish the job."

"Oh, no," I whispered. "How long did she lie there?"

He cleared his throat. "She lay unconscious for about seven hours."

I gasped. "So I really could have saved her from being hurt?"

"No, I don't think so," he assured me. "The medical guru placed the time of injury at between six and seven p.m. You said Papa Jong . . . Papa Jong?" I nodded. "What a name – passed on his information after seven o'clock."

I nodded, relieved. If I could have helped her avoid injury, and did nothing, I would have borne the guilt for a very long time.

Then again, if I had spoken last night, she wouldn't have lay on the ground for so long. I didn't mention that uncomfortable thought, and neither did Nigel.

I remembered what Shelly said last night. "Did you know that Officer Nichols takes flowers to Linda Sneider every other morning?"

He nodded. "We thought she needed the encouragement. Nick works the night shift, so he grabs a bouquet just before he goes home."

"We? Nick?"

"Down at the station. Nichols's nickname is Nick." We grinned at that.

I sobered. "You are a kind man." For some reason he blushed.

Just as a loud rumble announced Nigel's great hunger, our food arrived. Cecily specializes in all the foods the farmers love best: steak, lamb, chicken, and very few vegetables. Nigel ate as if he'd been fasting for several days.

"Nigel, slow down," I laughed. "No one is going to steal the food off your plate."

He grinned at me. "Right. It's been a while since I last ate with humans, so I'll try to be civilized."

I laughed again, and we enjoyed our meal.

Chapter 21

We Aren't Trying to Help the Police

I stopped by Natalie's on my way home. I knew she'd be waiting for me to call, and a visit in person would be a nice surprise. She was ironing her work clothes for the week.

"I hate clothes that need ironing," she declared as I walked through the door.

"There's an easy solution for that," I grinned.

"Don't buy clothes that need ironing," she threw a wet hand towel at me. It missed by about three feet. I picked it up and placed it back on the ironing board.

"How was dinner?" she asked.

"Did you call my house? Or is it around town already?"

Natalie's face contorted into the Cheshire grin, sneaky, silly, and goofy-looking. "I shall tell you nothing."

I chuckled. "It was pretty good. Cecily has added two vegetarian dishes."

"No way. The farmers must be having conniption fits."

I grinned and nodded. "I ordered the lentil and carrot garden burger. It was delicious and huge, so I brought the rest home for lunch tomorrow."

Natalie grimaced. "Lentils and carrots, and you paid for it?" We laughed together. Natalie adores lentils and carrots. I knew she'd be down at Cecily's Café the next day to try the dish herself.

She hung up a blouse and lay a skirt on the ironing board. "Did you find out anything new?"

I nodded and plunked down into a high-backed dining chair. "Yeah, Jamie's mom was hit on the head with a clay flower pot. It knocked her out, and she lay unconscious outside her trailer from somewhere around six or seven in the evening until 2:00 am when a firefighter found her."

Natalie put the iron down. "A clay flower pot? I don't know whether to laugh or cry for her." I nodded again. "Is she going to be okay?"

"Well, she's in the hospital right now. Nigel hopes she'll be conscious soon, so the rumor that she might not make it seems to be wrong."

"I'm glad of that. Who found her?" I shrugged. I didn't know. "You didn't ask?"

"I thought I had," I defended myself, "but I got distracted by the clay flower pot."

Natalie thought a moment and picked up the iron again. "It seems to point to a woman, doesn't it?"

"Or it's supposed to," I countered.

"True. It could be a man trying to seem like a woman."

I put my feet on a chair. "Shelly told me that someone has been leaving flowers outside at Linda Sneider's house. Every other morning."

"No kidding? Who?" Natalie was almost done with the skirt.

"Hannah said that a boy in band told her that it was Officer Nichols."

Natalie stopped rubbing the iron over a wrinkle and shook her head. "No way. That man is not involved in Jamie's death. Is he?"

I smiled. "I asked Nigel."

"Oh, you asked Nigel. You remembered to ask Nigel about the flowers but not about who discovered Linda?"

"I don't have counsel for the defense, so just let me tell my story, okay, smart aleck?"

She grinned. "Tell on, Scheherazade, tell on."

I stuck my tongue out at her. "I thought there might be something in it, you know, some special reason why he would do that."

Natalie nodded. "And is there?"

I smiled. "Yeah. Nigel said everyone at the station thought Linda could use the encouragement. That she should know that she isn't going through this alone."

"Crap." Natalie plonked the iron down and stared at her skirt.

"You didn't burn the skirt, did you?" I started to stand up.

Natalie rolled her eyes. "Of course not." I sat down again. "I just mean, every time we think we have a lead," I snorted. "I don't know what else to call it. Every time we think we have a lead, it seems to go nowhere."

She picked up the iron, started to use it on the skirt, and slammed it down on the board. "Okay. We need to figure this out. It's about time we look at who our suspects are."

"Natalie," I sighed. "We aren't trying to help the police in their investigation."

"Oh, no?" She moved from behind the ironing board and sat across from me.

"No. They have a job, and I have a job, and you have a job, and they aren't the same jobs." She just looked at me. I avoided her eyes; my brain was whirling.

"You're thinking," she sang.

Finally, I looked at her. "We have several people who could be guilty," I said.

Natalie jumped up and grabbed a pen and paper from a small notebook she keeps next to the phone. She handed it to me and plopped herself back into her chair.

"Write," she commanded.

I barked once, grinned, and started writing.

"Okay, first, we have Jamie's dad." I wrote: Larry Sneider.

"Motive?"

I shrugged. "I'm a writer, Natalie. I could come up with several motives, and most of them would make a great book. Let's see, he wanted her to move in with him and she wouldn't, so he got mad and strangled her. Or she was planning to run away with her boyfriend, and he didn't like the idea, so he told her not to, they argued, he got mad and strangled her. Or she was pregnant and got an abortion, he found out, argued with her about it, got mad and strangled her. Or..."

Natalie rolled her eyes. "Okay, let's skip motive for now unless one jumps out at us."

"Second," I continued, "we have Jamie's mom."

"No, that won't work." Natalie jumped up to pace. "She was injured, and that knocks her out of the running."

"Not necessarily, Natalie. Her injury could be totally unrelated to Jamie's death."

"Or it could be completely related," Natalie argued.

"I'm leaving her on there," I said firmly. "Because I can come up with . . . four scenarios right now that would explain why she was hit with that flower pot."

"Spare me the writing prompts," Natalie grimaced and sighed. "Fine, leave her on the list. For now."

"Number three: Kelly Green."

"What on earth for?" Natalie settled back into her chair.

"Well, she was fighting for Jamie's boyfriend. You know how emotionally unstable teens are."

Natalie pounced on that one. "All right, then we need to add Jamie's boyfriend to the list. Does he have a name?"

"Forrest Pearson."

"Oh, right. I think Shelly told us that a few days ago. A few days that feel like a few weeks."

I nodded in heartfelt agreement. "Number four on our list needs to be –"

"Forrest is number four, Danielle."

"Oh, right. Then number five is...do we have any more suspects?"

We stared into space for a few minutes. Natalie shifted her position. I often wonder if she knows she does this before saying something important, but I've never asked. There's no reason to get rid of that moment of preparation for those poor people in the boardroom.

"She was pretty promiscuous. You don't think there might be someone out there, a cast-off, who got mad enough to harm her, do you?"

I pondered this. "I don't want to throw it out completely, but we don't have any way of knowing who that might be. And we'd have to put down, 'X – the unknown factor.'"

"I think that's a given," Natalie sighed.

"And look at this list," I tossed the paper across the table. It read:

Larry Sneider
Linda Sneider
Kelly Green
Forrest Pearson
X

"Every time we talk about this, our list gets longer, but we have no answers, no evidence, nothing. It gets more and more confusing instead of less so. Not to mention, it's a pretty pathetic list, only four people on it."

"And someone named, 'X.'"

I groaned. "We should be letting the police handle this."

"Well," Natalie shifted again, and I waited for it. "It might be time for a party at your house." She looked at me carefully. "You know how the kids talk more freely around you than they would around any other adult."

I smiled. "You're buttering me up." I thought about it. "But it's working; I'm going to seriously consider your idea."

Natalie grinned triumphantly. "I knew you'd do it."

"I said I'd think about it." I rose from the hard dining room chair. "Don't you think it's time to get cushions for these things?"

"How else can I get rid of company without being rude?" she countered. With that, I went home, already planning the party - who to invite, what to offer for food, where to put the cats who hate company. And Ramon the Wonder Dog would have to go to his dog house early. And back again to the food issue. Teenagers can put away an awful lot of food.

Chapter 22
We'll Prop You Up and Drink a Toast

Thursday evening, as the first of the teens arrived, I was wondering if this was such a good idea. Oh, the party was a great idea; it had been several weeks since the kids and I had thrown one, but using a party to pry information out of teens? I didn't know...

They came in groups of twos, threes, and fives, depending on how many could be crammed into a car, van, or pick-up. Because my parties are tame, the police look the other way when the kids go home, cars stuffed to overflowing. They're just happy to know the teens are having a good time *without* sex, drugs, and alcohol. The Christian music and PG movies are an added benefit, and the whole town loves that I give parties every so often. They'd like me to give more, but parties cost money and energy. Bring-your-own-snack helps with the money aspect, but I do have a limited supply of energy.

Edgar slammed through the front door, announcing, "Yeah! Mrs. B, you're the awesomest! No school tomorrow, party tonight, and I can stay as late as I want," He's a nice kid with an overwhelming voice, a bass that can blow out eardrums.

I hugged him. "Edgar, you can stay until I fall over, but that may only be about eleven o'clock."

"That's okay," he answered. "If you fall over, we'll just prop you up and drink a toast to your memory."

I raised an eyebrow.

"You know, like in the old west, in the mining and timber towns. When someone would die, his buddies would bring his coffin into the local tavern, open it up, and prop him against the bar. Then everyone would drink a toast to him. It was cool."

I laughed. "Gruesome, but you're right. Go on in," I told him and several others. I watched as they filed into the living room, a couple of them breaking off to go into the kitchen. I followed.

"Lenny, Bill, what's up?" I asked. They were leaning against the counter, not talking.

Lenny's a tall, skinny boy who looks like he never gets enough to eat. But I've seen him put away a giant pizza and a two-liter of soda pop and return an hour later for more. "Mrs. Baker, can we talk to you?"

I called to Shelly to man the front door and walked over to the boys. "Are you okay?"

"Mrs. B," Bill cleared his throat. "Mrs. B, we know you had your house broken into the other night."

I nodded. "It was, but no one was hurt."

"Yeah, we heard. But we were wondering if you wanted a couple of us guys to stay here with you for a while, in case they come back. We could sleep on the couch downstairs."

He looked at Lenny, who continued. "We're really worried about you. We don't want anything to happen to you or Shelly or the kids."

My heart and eyes overflowed just a little as I smiled at the boys. "You guys are wonderful, both of you." I hugged them, bringing the blood rushing to their faces. "Thank you for the offer. I'm not sure your parents would approve of your offer, but I do. And of your bravery and kindness.

"I don't think we need you to stay here, though. At least, not right now. If things get really bad, either I'll call you, or – if it gets really scary – we will move out until this is over, okay?"

They nodded, glanced at each other, and shifted a little.

"Is there something else?" I asked.

Bill nodded to Lenny who answered, "People have been talking -"

"Ah, the rumor mill," I smiled. "Perhaps you've heard that I am investigating Jamie's death?" Both boys nodded. "And that the new policeman is now my boyfriend?" Blushing, both boys nodded. "And that I keep telling the police new information?" Again, they nodded. "Yes, I've heard the rumors, too."

"You don't always," Lenny said.

I nodded. "You're right, I don't. In fact, I often miss the gossip going around town. But several friends have made sure I am hearing what is being said about me this time, because they don't want me to get hurt." I looked at both boys. "Like these two friends of mine."

We smiled at each other. Lenny's ears were pink, and Bill puffed out his chest. A little praise - and friendship - can mean so much!

"And as far as those stupid rumors go," I continued, "all I can say is, don't believe what you hear, unless you hear it from the source. And then, don't believe it unless you see it for yourself. And then, don't believe *that* until you've prayed about it."

They both laughed in relief. After they assured me they would be available if I ever needed anything, we returned to the party. I looked around the living room. *These are great kids,* I thought.

There were about twenty teens in our living room, a tight squeeze. The music wasn't very loud, but the conversation was. It centered around Prom – who was taking whom – and Jamie's death. I gathered that Jamie's mom was conscious but couldn't name her attacker. And a couple of groups glanced my way, so I knew they were talking about me – and probably the new English detective. Food was disappearing quickly.

We visited for a while. Then we opened the breakfront that by a miracle was unscathed after the break-in and put in an old movie. We like to use old movies so the kids can visit through it. Conversation stops at the good parts (usually action sequences) and gets going again until the next good part.

After the movie, I asked, "Have you all been talking about Jamie's death much?"

They shrugged, teen speak for, "Don't ask, don't tell."

I smiled at them. "Oh, come on, I'm not the Gestapo. I'm not even your mom." They laughed and someone called, "You're better!" More laughter went around the room. I joined in with a dramatized, "Thank you," but comments like that concern me. I always look for whoever makes comments like that, so I can check in, make sure everything is okay at home.

One of the teens, a small, pimply boy named John, said, "We have an idea who we think may have done it, but it's like thinking a family member's guilty, so we don't say anything."

"Yeah," Tessa, a junior, said. "I mean, everyone is related to everyone, or knows someone who's related to whoever you think may have done it."

"Stupid small town," Cindy, a freshman, muttered. An older girl sitting next to her nudged Cindy's elbow and smiled kindly. Cindy sat up straighter, a smile lighting her face.

"I know what you mean. It makes it hard to talk about, or even think about. But I also know you've been talking anyway," I looked around the room. "What do you know about Jamie's dad? Is anyone here related to him?"

No answer.

"Then he should be safe enough to talk about, right?" Several of the kids grinned, so I continued. "Could he have done something like that to Jamie if he got mad enough?"

"Hey now, you're talking about my mom's boss's sister's ex-husband's nephew's best friend's cousin's former roommate!"

Edgar boomed from across the room. Everyone laughed and joined in the conversation. *God, bless Edgar!*

"I think it could have been anyone," said a pretty redhead. I couldn't remember her name.

"How could it be anyone?" countered a good-looking senior named Roy. "Could it have been you?"

"Of course not. But Jamie knew so many people and got into so much trouble....I just think it could have been a lot of people."

Several heads nodded.

"Like who?" I asked. *Ungrammatical wench.* I told my writing self to shut up.

"Forrest was looking to get rid of her," a boy suggested. Several people shushed him.

"That's okay," Forrest said quietly into the uncomfortable silence.

"No, it is not okay," I firmly asserted. "In this house you are innocent until proven guilty, right, Shelly?"

"Oh, yeah," Shelly grinned. "And when you *are* guilty, Mom's love drives like a knife." Forrest grimaced.

"Shelly's not saying you're guilty, Forrest." My heart nearly broke for him. "Relax, hon. In this house, you're just another one of the guys, always welcome, always loved."

Shelly's best friend, Amy, came to the rescue this time, "Well, what *about* Jamie's dad? Does anyone know him?"

Several people shrugged or shook their heads. A hand went up, another freshman. Everyone chuckled, and the tension was broken once again.

"His name is Larry, and he works at the Rock-n-Roll Tavern. He knows my dad...not very well."

"What's he like?" I asked.

"Well," the boy shifted, uncomfortable at being the center of attention. "He's real thin and balding on top with a few strings of hair combed over."

"Ugh. A comb-over," someone said. Everyone laughed and nodded.

The boy continued. "He's got a big Adam's apple. Oh, and he laughs like a donkey." He tried to imitate the laugh, which set the kids off again. The description matched what I remembered about him.

"I've heard his laugh. It's . . . what word did Mr. Long use in English today? Atrocious. That's it. It's atrocious," a senior said. Several of the kids nodded.

"Do we know where he was the night Jamie was killed?" I asked.

Nearly twenty heads shook from side to side.

"I don't think he's so bad, actually," contributed a sophomore named Luis. "He helps at the food pantry, and I sometimes see him working on one of the local charity houses."

The teens looked surprised. "I didn't know that," said Shelly.

Luis giggled. "He does have a pretty awful laugh, though."

There were chuckles all around, and the teens waited expectantly for me to ask another question.

"Well, what about Jamie's mom? Any ideas?"

"I feel really sorry for her," Pamela, a junior, spoke up. "She and my mom grew up together, and she had a pretty terrible childhood. And then her marriage lasted, like, just a few months, and she's done her best for Jamie, but she doesn't . . . didn't really know how to be a good mom."

Edgar moved over and put his arm around her. "There's always something breaking your heart, isn't there, Pam?"

Pamela smiled and shrugged.

"I'm sorry she's had a rough life," Amy said, "but Jamie did, too, and part of the reason was because her mom's an alcoholic."

There was general nodding.

I asked, "Does anyone know anything about the night Mrs. Sneider was injured?"

The teens looked at each other. Roy, the senior, spoke up again, "Only what everyone is saying, that she was hit with a clay flower pot," snickers rippled around the room, "and that she lay on the ground for several hours before someone found her." All faces sobered again.

"Well, do we know anything else? I'm not asking you to investigate or anything, but it is a big deal in our town right now."

Several heads nodded, and kids began talking amongst themselves again. After a minute or two, someone called to another group, and a general discussion began. Ideas and gossip passed quickly around the room, some whispered, some shouted. Paper was produced, and the senior girl with the best handwriting, Cherry Harkin, wrote down what everyone knew about different people who had anything to do with Jamie. It was a jumble on the paper, but I kept an eye on it so I could confiscate it later. Eventually, ideas tended toward the silly and slid into the downright ridiculous.

"I know," Edgar's bass sounded above the chatter, "Jamie was really Mother Teresa reincarnated, and her alter ego. Friar Tuck came back from the grave and killed her to keep her from going to hell." Laughter exploded, kids falling all over the place in their hilarity. It was obviously time to bring the discussion – and the party – to a close.

"All right, everyone," I shouted. "It's eleven-thirty, and I need my beauty rest." Good naturedly, they all stood and started clearing up the mess, something they'd done from the very first party. Didn't I say they were good kids?

Before the piece of paper could be slid into the garbage, or someone's pocket, I snagged it and hid it under the flour bin in the pantry. Cliché, I know, but it was the largest container in there. Twenty minutes later, after loud good-byes and many hugs, I told Shelly she had a great group of friends. She agreed, and we sat at the kitchen table for a while, rehashing the evening. She finally went to bed, tired and happy. I checked on Ramon, asleep in his dog house, and let the cats out of my bathroom. They had shredded the toilet paper but left the rest of the room intact. The bird had already been covered for the night. With a weary sigh, I sat back down at the kitchen table.

I called Natalie to let her know Hannah and Mikey could come home. She knew already, because Abe would have made it home, but it's a courtesy that I think is important.

"They're watching a horror movie and don't want to leave," she said. I could hear the movie in the background.

I was aghast. "You're letting them watch a horror flick?"

She laughed. "They're watching some home movies of ours that feature them as little kids. They're laughing uproariously at the hair dos on some of us."

I smiled. "I wish I'd joined you all for that," I said wistfully.

"Well, Jim's in a lot of them, so I thought you'd want to skip this group of videos." I nodded and told her to send them home soon. I knew she'd have Abe walk them the two blocks to our house.

While waiting for the kids, I went into the pantry for the piece of paper with the notes on it. I'd been a little concerned that someone would have taken it, but it was still there. I sat at the kitchen table and worked on deciphering what it said. I was still working on it thirty minutes later when Hannah and Mikey walked in with Natalie.

Chapter 23
Black Is the Color

"I guess you couldn't wait until tomorrow, could you?" I teased Natalie. I kissed Hannah and Mikey, listened to their excited story of the videos they'd watched, and sent them to bed. They were still laughing as they went up the stairs. Shelly met them on the upper landing and asked what was so funny. They all went into Shelly's room.

"Fifteen minutes, guys," I called up the stairs. "Okay?"

A chorus of, "Yeeees," floated down.

Natalie and I sat at the table, the paper between us.

"What does it say?" Natalie asked. "Is it even English?"

I laughed. "Yes, but the talk was moving so quickly, she didn't have time to write nicely or even in complete thoughts.

"This one says 'L. S.' – Larry Sneider? That's Jamie's dad – and says...something about child support."

"Oh, I wouldn't think that would be an issue at this point, would it?" Natalie asked. "I mean, he only has a couple – had a couple of more years before he wouldn't have to pay anymore."

"Unless she went to college," I countered. "But you're right. You'd think he'd have gotten fed up with paying child support years ago if he was going to." Natalie nodded.

I pointed at a group of hieroglyphics. "Oh, but here it says...'girlfriend'. Maybe he's gotten a girlfriend and doesn't want to spend money on Jamie when he could spend it on her."

"Why would a woman want to go out with him?" Natalie asked.

I shrugged. "This says, 'Forrest'. Oh, I thought they'd stopped talking about him. He was at the party."

"He was? Wow. I would have thought he'd stay away, what with all the gossip going around."

"That's how much you know about teens," I told her. "A recluse will go to a party, if he's lonely enough. I imagine he's pretty lonely right now."

Natalie thought about it. "Yeah, he's really being scrutinized, poor kid."

I nodded. "It says something about Kelly next to his name, and...does that say, 'abortion'? I wonder if it was his child that was aborted."

"Which would mean Jamie wasn't 'not pregnant' in the traditional sense. What she told your kids, remember?" I nodded again. "What else does it say?"

I tried to make out more. "Oh. This is new. This says 'Mr. Jacobs'. That must be the French teacher. Next to it is something...I can't quite make it out." Natalie moved around the table to help read.

"Is that an 'a' or an 'o'?" she asked.

"Well, it might be an 'a', because next to it looks like two 'f's." We looked at each other.

"Does that mean 'affair'?" Natalie asked me.

"No way," I answered. "Mr. Jacobs has been here for almost twenty years." We studied the paper some more.

"I don't know. The more I look at it, the more it looks like 'affair'." Natalie said. She sat down again. "This is getting icky. I don't like it anymore."

I looked at her sternly. "Either we settle this problem, or we live the rest of our lives knowing there's an unsolved murder in our town, our wonderful small town where we've chosen to raise our children."

She nodded and sighed. "You're right, of course. But I still don't like it."

"Yeah," I agreed. "It's icky." Some lettering caught my eye.

"Hey, look at this. It says, 'O. Nichols', and right next to it is a heart crossed out." We looked at each other. "Does that mean they were seeing each other?"

"You mean Officer Nichols?" Natalie was amazed. "He's got to be nearly ten years older than she is."

"And that means statutory rape charges, if caught," I thought out loud.

"Wow, that would really be a reason for shutting her up, wouldn't it?" Natalie, too, was thinking fast. "Especially if she was talking baby...or marriage...or said something about telling her mom. It would ruin his career at the very least. And he's the one taking flowers to Linda, remember?"

I nodded but didn't want to get sidetracked into speculating about an officer I liked, if only because he was nice to me. I continued to look at the paper.

"This says...it looks like, 'Dad' and 'friendship.'"

"Maybe whoever wrote this was saying her dad didn't like her friendship with Jamie," Natalie suggested.

I shook my head. "I don't think so. Cherry Harkin wrote it, and she and Jamie only had a passing acquaintance. I asked her. But someone else might have written it."

Natalie came around the table again to look at the paper. "Does it look like different handwriting?" she asked.

"I can't tell," I scoffed. "It's so messy, several different hands could have written this."

"Maybe someone told Cherry to write it," she suggested, "and then asked her not to put her name."

"—or his name." Natalie nodded and sat down again. It might have been easier if she'd sat next to me, but she would have gotten less exercise.

Finally, I rubbed my eyes. "It's nearly one in the morning. I need to go to bed."

"Me, too," she sighed. I walked her to the front door, glad to see she'd brought her Mercedes. I noticed my minivan looked much dingier than her car, even in the dim porch light. I decided not to envy her.

It didn't work.

I tucked the paper into my underwear drawer and went straight to bed. I dreamed all night long that different people in town were chasing me. Once, the mayor was after me and he fell with a bang. Another time it was Mr. Jacobs. He ran into a truck, and the resounding noise jarred my teeth. I ran for several hours in my sleep and awoke exhausted.

I rolled over to look at the time, and there was a long-stemmed black rose next to the clock. I picked it up. It was fresh. The clock said 7:30, so it wasn't the kids. I'd never known them to get up early if they didn't have to. I checked their rooms, just in case. They were all asleep.

I checked the front and back doors. They were locked, deadbolts in place. I looked at the rose in my hand. "How did you get here?" I wondered. "Are you a warning or an expression of affection? You aren't from Nigel. There's no way he would break into my house just to give me a rose . . . yeah, that's silly. He wouldn't do that.

"Besides, you're black, the color of threat. Of death."

I scolded myself and reined in my imagination. I put it back on the nightstand next to the clock and waited impatiently until nine to call Nigel, just in case he was able to sleep in this morning.

"Good morning," I said to him with as much cheer as I could muster.

"You sound tired," he answered warmly. "Did the youths keep you awake until all hours?" I knew he and the deputies had been prowling last night, and they would have known exactly what time the party ended.

"Yes, they did," I answered with a sigh. "Even after they left, they and their parents chased me in my dreams all night."

"Oh, I hate dreams like that." he answered. "You're probably knackered. And sore."

"Yes, I am," I answered. I didn't know what 'knackered' meant, but I was definitely sore. "Do you have those kinds of dreams often?"

He chuckled. "Only when my super has me on the carpet for not solving a case quickly enough," he answered good-naturedly. "Then he runs after me with the overtime worksheets in his hands all night."

I chuckled. "I'm so sorry. The way I feel this morning, I can imagine what you go through."

"What can I do for you, Danielle?" he asked. "Or is this a social call?"

"No, I wish it were," I said and immediately blushed. I heard a colleague approach him and ask a question. He lowered the phone and answered.

"Sorry," he said. "What did you say?"

I wasn't going to repeat myself, so I plunged right in. "Someone came into my house while we were sleeping and left a black rose next to my bed." I sounded as confused as I felt. "It's still fresh, so it wasn't left last night during the party. Besides, I would have noticed it then."

"I'll be right there," he said quickly and hung up.

I realized he really would be right here, and I rushed to clean up my room a little bit. As I was throwing clothes onto the chair, I thought of the piece of paper. I looked in my underwear drawer but couldn't find it immediately and frantically pawed through my underwear.

Ah. Here it was. Relieved at finding the paper intact, I didn't hear the first knock on the door. As Detective Hawksworth banged the lion's head knocker the second time, I quickly checked myself in the mirror, shoved the paper back under my panties, and ran down the stairs.

He looked harried. "I thought something may have happened to you when you didn't answer," he said, taking long, calming breaths.

I let him in. "I'm sorry, I didn't hear you the first time. I sometimes don't if I'm upstairs."

"You haven't been clearing up, have you?" he asked.

I blushed. "I didn't want you to see how sloppy I am at night," I answered candidly.

He smiled grimly. "While I appreciate the compliment, you may have destroyed some evidence."

I blinked at him. "Oh, I guess it is a compliment, isn't it?" I smiled up at him. "Come on up."

We climbed the stairs and entered my bedroom. "I picked up the rose, wondering if it was from my kids, but they were still asleep, so I put it back where I found it."

Nigel took a couple of pictures of the rose and clock, standing in different spots.

"You didn't hear anything?" I shook my head. My face must have gone blank, because he said, "You've thought of something."

"Well, I told you I was having dreams all night long of people chasing me," he nodded. I sat on the bed, and he leaned against the dresser. "Well, I was dreaming they were chasing me for a piece of paper. In my dream, the mayor fell with a bang, and later, Mr. Jacobs ran into a truck with another loud noise. It may have been outside noises seeping into my dream."

He had me tell him all the dreams I could remember, the noises I heard in my dreams, and anything else that came to mind. He had me repeat it all. Then he asked questions that helped me remember even more dream details. I was amazed at what I could remember when questioned the right way.

"Are you always a heavy sleeper?" he asked.

"No, usually, I wake up to the smallest sound here in the house. Which is why the dog sleeps outside." I sighed. "But last night was the party, and afterward, I looked at the paper..." My voice petered out.

"What's this about a piece of paper?" he asked. Reluctantly, I reached into my underwear drawer to retrieve it. He watched me, amused.

"Well, I had to put it somewhere," I defended myself. "And I didn't want to put it back under the flour bin in the pantry."

"That's where you hid it originally?" His dimples deepened, and I felt myself grow hot. This was a morning for blushes.

In my embarrassment, I failed at first to notice he was holding the paper by the corners. He studied it for two or three minutes.

"It seems to say that Forrest Pearson may have been responsible for the abortion," he mused.

"You can read it that easily? I worked on deciphering that thing for thirty minutes last night before even *beginning* to figure out how to read it. And Natalie thought it wasn't even English."

Nigel smiled at me. Oh, those dimples. "I'm trained to detect things, Danielle, but I do enjoy your admiration." I reddened again, and he chuckled.

Shelly and Hannah appeared at my bedroom door. "Mom," Shelly said, hands on hips, "you told me not to have boys in my room, but what do I find you doing? What will Hannah think?"

I smiled, patted the bed, and they piled beside me. "Do you see the 'gift' someone left me in the middle of the night?" I pointed to the rose. "You didn't happen to leave it there, did you?"

Shelly and Hannah both shook their heads. "Did Mikey?" They shook their heads again, eyes wide.

"Are you saying someone came into our house in the middle of the night, while we were sleeping? Came into your room and left this rose for you, then left again? We could have been killed." Shelly hugged herself.

Hannah was more concerned about my safety. "Mom, you were completely unaware of him being here? You slept through the whole thing? He could have hurt you, and you wouldn't even have known who it was." I nodded somberly.

The girls exchanged a glance and looked at me. Shelly said, "You always wake up right away when there's a noise in the house. Why didn't you this time?"

I shrugged. "I don't know, honey."

"Were you drugged or something?" Hannah asked.

"No, sweetheart." I rubbed her arm. "I was very tired after preparing for the party, hosting the party, cleaning up *after* the party, studying this paper, and then going straight to bed. You know how my mind works. If I don't read the Bible before bed, I tend to have very loud dreams, and I was so tired, I just turned out the light, and everything I'd been thinking about just rushed at me all night long."

The girls looked relieved. Hannah said, "That makes sense. I suppose."

I suggested they get some breakfast, and asked Detective – Nigel – if he would like to go down to the living room to talk. "The girls are right. I need to show by example what I teach with words."

Nigel looked around the room. "I'd like to check which windows are locked and which might be accessible from outside. It's possible someone unlocked a window in order to come back later."

I nodded. "I'll show you the only four that open."

His eyebrows rose. "Four?" (It sounded like, 'Foh'. Oh, goodness, would I ever get over his cute accent?)

I smiled and looked around my room with pride. "The house is well over a hundred years old, Nigel. We've spent almost fifteen years making it beautiful again, but windows have to be replaced one at a time. They're custom made and expensive. The two kitchen windows, the new one in the living room, and Mikey's window all open; the others are original to the house and painted shut."

"Well, that will make my job easier, then," he said good-naturedly as he walked out of the bedroom. He made the mistake of going into Mikey's room first. An eleven-year-old's dream is to work with a detective, and Mikey is no exception. He was out of bed and hopping as soon as Nigel's tread in his room woke him. I stood in the doorway and watched Nigel work it out on his own. I thought, *it's good for him*. Then I realized he'd probably had training in dealing with eleven-year-olds, like he'd had training in deciphering illegible handwriting. I shrugged and went down to the kitchen.

Chapter 24
An Insufflator

When Nigel and Mikey joined us, it was a scene of peaceful domesticity that must have wrung his heart. I offered him some coffee.

"Decaf, of course," he said with dimples.

"I'll buy some of the caffeinated kind, if you plan to visit us on a regular basis," I offered.

He shook his head. "I don't mind decaf in the least." He took his mug to the table. "All doors and windows accounted for," he said cheerfully. "Every last one is locked."

"So how did whoever it was get in?" I asked.

He shrugged. "Dunno. There aren't any jimmy marks at the windows, and the doors have bolts. By the way, I noticed only two exterior doors. Are there others?"

I shook my head. "They let in too much cold air. The original owners decided to limit drafts by putting doors front and back only."

Nigel nodded.

Suddenly, he stood and left the room. Mikey raced after him. When he returned, there was a grim look on his face.

"What's wrong?" I asked. Shelly and Hannah froze.

"Someone carefully cut all the paint round the window in the downstairs bath," he looked angry. "I should have thought of it straight off, it being on the ground floor and available to anyone here at the party. I must be going senile. I'll dust it for prints as soon as

I've finished this coffee. No one goes in there until I've finished with it." We all agreed, Mikey loudest of all.

A few minutes later, he took his fingerprint apparatus from the car and, followed by an eager Mikey, dusted the window frame for prints. He asked, "Who cleans this bathroom, Michael?"

Mikey was in heaven; he was helping the police. "We all do, or we kids do, anyway. Why?"

Nigel looked at him. "Because this window frame has never been washed by the look of it," he said. "I can't tell who touched it last, because there are at least fifteen different finger marks on it."

Mikey looked crestfallen. "I didn't know I needed to," he said.

"Normally, you wouldn't need to, not every time. But for an investigation such as this, it's vital that surfaces be clean so that if there's another break in, we'll have a clear set of prints to work with." Mikey nodded soberly, scrutinizing everything Nigel did.

I stood in the bathroom doorway. I knew I would need to buy Mikey an insufflator, a camel's hair brush, and gray powder so he could practice taking fingerprints. (What is an insufflator, anyway? Why is it called 'an insufflator'? Who invented it? Ah, the questions we homeschool mommies think to ask.) Hero worship shone from Mikey's eyes. *Oh, Lord,* I prayed, *please don't let him be hurt.*

I left them to get on with cleaning up the powder marks on the window, and by the time I'd brushed the coffee off my breath, they were back in the kitchen.

I asked, "Will you please clean up the kitchen, kids?" and invited Nigel into the living room. "Step into my parlor, said the spider to the fly," I grinned at him. My line was ruined by Ramon and the cats following him in, and we laughed.

"So someone entered the house through the bathroom window, left a rose beside my bed, and left again," I said as we sat down.

"No," he answered with a grin. "I thought Michael needed something exciting to happen. His doleful eyes followed my every sip of coffee, and I took pity on him."

"You *lied* to him?"

Nigel shook his head. "No, someone did try to cut the paint away from the window, probably many years ago, but it didn't work; it's still painted shut, as you said it would be. However, Michael got a bit of excitement, and he will do a better job of cleaning from now on."

I smiled at him. "All right, I see what you did. Thank you - for giving him excitement *and* for not lying to him. How did someone get in?"

"I don't know," he answered, "unless someone has a key. Do you think your ex-husband would have given his key to someone here before he left?"

I shook my head. "I changed the locks."

Nigel said, "Hmm, well, someone seems to have a key. I strongly recommend you change the locks again. Today."

I groaned. "Do you know how much that costs?"

"Do you not have the money?" he asked. "As an officer of the law, I believe everyone deserves to be safe in their own home. Oh, bother, now I sound pompous."

I grinned. "No, I don't have the money to buy two new doorknobs, Nigel. And you didn't sound pompous; you sounded...caring. I'll figure it out somehow, but it may take a few days. In the meantime, the kids can bed down at Natalie's."

"Not you?" he asked sharply.

I shook my head. "No, not me. I don't sleep over with anyone who's married. I'll be fine," I assured him. "I'll lock my bedroom door and keep both phones next to me."

He didn't like it, but we weren't close enough friends for him to say anything more. I was glad, because although we have enough to live on, we don't have enough to do more than buy the essentials, and I'd scrimped in order to send Shelly to Prom. I really needed this next book to sell well in order to set us up for a little more luxury.

And then he asked the dreaded question. "Why do you have this paper?"

"Well, we were visiting at the party last night, and I asked the kids what they thought about Jamie's death." His face tightened. Oh, boy. I took a deep breath and continued. "We sort of talked about different aspects of Jamie's life...kind of trying out different scenarios...of people who would maybe wish to hurt her. The kids got excited about it, and as they talked, one of the girls wrote it all down. She wrote really fast, because there were about twenty kids here, and they were all talking pretty much at once." I looked at my hands, feeling guilty. *Dog-gone-it, Natalie,* I thought. *You suggested it.*

Nigel's face was a thundercloud. I waited for the roar, experienced as I was with Jim's tantrums.

"Danielle," Nigel said quietly. It was more ominous than thunder. "A murder investigation isn't a game. It can be dangerous to anyone who has access to the wrong information, and you just blithely dragged in twenty teen-agers, putting them in potential danger."

"But it's like a game to them," I protested. "They haven't seen the body, and while they'll think of Jamie every so often, they won't really miss her. It's almost like living in a detective story."

"This isn't a game," he continued patiently. "And in detective books, someone gets killed, then another, then another. The hero or heroine usually survives by the skin of his or her teeth. Do you really want to be one of those statistics? You do not," he answered himself. "And as I said, murder and murder investigations are dangerous to many people, not least of all friends of the police. Do you understand me?" I nodded. "Good. Then you know that you can't meddle in it at all. So far, you've had two break-ins, and you aren't even involved – except that I now find out you deliberately invited comment on the situation, even to the point of having a young girl write down what was said." He looked at me.

"Are you listening?" he asked.

Somewhere in his speech, I realized he wasn't scary at all and had lost track of what he was saying and began listening to his beautiful accent, gazing at his handsome face, dark brown hair, and piercing blue eyes. *He's even more handsome when he's angry*, I thought.

"Danielle," he rapped out.

I answered, "I don't know what you said, but it sounded beautiful," and smiled fatuously at him.

He stared at me a moment, and then his head flew back, and his laugh rang out through the house. I snapped out of my trance completely at that moment.

"What's so funny?" I asked.

He wiped the tears from his eyes. "I daren't tell you," he gasped, still laughing.

"Why not?" But he didn't answer me. I tried to remember what I'd said as Nigel stood to leave. I was sorry to see him go, but I knew he had a lot of work to do before this case was solved. I was beginning to wonder if I *wanted* the case solved if it meant he would leave the area for good. I enjoyed his friendship.

Admit it, you also like his handsome face, my inner voice teased me. I had to agree. I realized I was overcoming the embarrassment of being attracted to this man, and the fear of his being a policeman.

"I need to take the rose with me and do some research, find out where it came from, okay?" he asked before he left.

I nodded and wondered, *Where does someone buy a black rose? And why didn't I think of that sooner?*

As Nigel opened the door, he said softly, "Please stay safe."

My stomach turned over pleasurably as I nodded. And he was gone.

ON SATURDAY MORNING, we did our weekly house cleaning. I was finishing up the kitchen, singing and dancing along to a song on the radio. The kids and I often sing and dance together, but it's a family thing only. I sang,

"Let's be naugh – ty,

Not nice, but naugh – ty.

Rouge and lipstick and dress cut way down low.

Let's be naugh-teeeeee.....tonight!"

I saw movement out of the corner of my eye. Turning, I was aghast to find my children and George Graham, the owner of the hardware store, standing in the doorway watching the performance, grins on every face. My own face turned red, and I stood there in humiliation.

"Bravo, Mom," shouted Mikey. He rushed over to hug me.

"Loved it, Mom," Shelly, also, gave me a hug. "Oh, by the way, Mr. Graham is here." I mumbled a sarcastic thank you.

Hannah, always more compassionate, hugged me and whispered, "You looked really good dancing, Mom."

As the children returned to their cleaning jobs, George Graham said briskly, "I have an order here to change the front and back locks. Okay if I get started?"

I stared at him. "I didn't send in an order."

"It was that English dude. He said it was a Sherriff's department job." He shrugged his shoulders. "So, do you want me to get started, or what?"

The lion's head knocker banged three times. I said, "Just a moment," and opened the door to find Nigel standing there.

Glancing at the van, he said, "I see your Mr. Graham is here to change the locks."

"I didn't order the locks changed, Nigel," I said, quietly fuming.

He reassured me, "They won't be billed to you. The Sherriff's department has a fund for situations such as this where someone needs protection and can't afford it."

I'd never heard of such a fund and said so. "I won't take charity, and I don't want your financial help." I hissed at him, conscious of George Graham nearby, arguably the town's leading gossip.

Nigel pulled me outside and closed the door, telling Mr. Graham, "Won't be a moment, sir."

He cheerfully answered, "Don't worry about me, I'll be fine."

"Danielle, the Sherriff's department really does have a fund for situations such as this. There are times when a victim needs a window replaced immediately and insurance takes too long, or when a person needs a can of pepper spray, or – like you – their locks changed. It even has a guard dog for hire. The fund covers the expense, and if and when the person is able to pay it back, the money is used for the next one who needs it."

I felt my face grow hot. "I really had no idea." I blinked back tears.

"Will you allow Mr. Graham to change your locks?" I nodded, and Nigel opened the door, suggesting Mr. Graham start on the back door. Then he led me to the wicker chairs on the porch, and we sat.

"Danielle, I wouldn't dare help you financially. It wouldn't be appropriate. Besides," he smiled to soften the blow, "you're so independent, trying to help would be the quickest way of ending our friendship."

I was struck in the face with his correct assessment, ashamed of my attitude of intense, proud independence. I looked at the hills peeking over rooftops. "I'm an idiot, aren't I?"

Nigel shook his head. "You're a beautiful, talented woman," he said gently, "fighting to regain - and retain - your self-respect." He surprised me by taking my hand, and I turned to look at him. "May I tell you more?"

I gulped and nodded.

"In this village," he continued, "there are two types of people in your life: those you let in, and those you don't. Those you don't let in are usually past friends of your ex-husband. Most of them have seen the truth, but they don't know how to tell you that they don't believe you to be the fool your ex-husband would like them - and you - to believe you are."

Tears welled up. How I wanted that to be true! I blinked quickly as Nigel continued. "I see a woman who is trying to make her way in a complicated situation." He smiled as he looked into my eyes. "You are a mother of three wonderful children. You are an accomplished author. And you are a good friend to many. But you are still trying to prove yourself to the town and to yourself. And you're doing that by getting involved in this case, and I'm concerned you're going to be injured.

"Please stop helping."

Chapter 25
Please Stop Helping

I stared into his beautiful eyes. Slowly, I withdrew my hand, and just as carefully as he had spoken, I answered, "Thank you. For saying what you did. For being honest. I promise you I'll think about it."

I sighed. "But, I can't stop helping, you know. At first, I didn't want to get involved at all. Investigation is the police's job."

"Yes, it is."

"But then you talked to Shelly, and to Hannah and Mikey. And then Kelly Green, and several other friends. And I realized something: this is my town. Even the people who don't like me are part of my town. And I love this town. And these kids, all of them. Many of them come over here and find a safe haven."

I glared at the hills. "Do you know, we often have a teen or two for Easter or Thanksgiving dinner, or even Christmas? Can you believe there are parents who leave their kids at Christmas? They go on a cruise or something and seem to believe a fifteen- or sixteen-year-old will be fine staying home alone – at Christmas!"

I shook my head and looked Nigel in the eye. "It's a messed up world we live in, and I can only do my part, and my part right now is to do everything I can to make this town safe. And I can do that by helping you."

"No," Nigel said, quietly urgent. "I don't need your help."

"Yes, you do," I answered calmly. "This is my town, these are my people. I can get answers that you can't get. I can talk to people who would regard you as a wonderful example of some British novel they've read, or reality Brit Com, but they wouldn't necessarily tell you the things you need to know, because they would feel that you might not understand – you're not American."

Nigel sighed in frustration. "I won't admit I need your help. I think I could get round most of the problems you're suggesting."

He pondered a moment. "You're not going to stop trying to help, are you?"

"I can't."

Shaking his head, he sighed. "Right, then. I won't ask you to stop helping if you'll do your utmost to remain safe, you and your children. *And* you will tell me everything - and I mean *everything* - that you learn. *And* you will take direction from me, whether I tell you to change your locks, or move out of your home, take a short holiday, or stay away from a certain person, whatever I know needs doing. Deal?"

I smiled and nodded. "Deal."

Mr. Graham stuck his head out the front door. "You done arguin', yet? I'd like to get this other door done. I left George Jr. alone in the shop, and he's likely to give away the deed if I don't get back soon."

I laughed and told him to go ahead and change the lock, explaining to Nigel that George Jr. hates charging people money for the things they need.

Before Nigel could stand up, I said briskly, "Since we now have a deal, I have some questions for you."

"I said I wouldn't ask you to stop helping. I didn't say I would give you information."

"I only want to know if anyone has an alibi, so I can stop wasting my time on them," I argued.

He groaned. "All right. Jamie's mum was in bed, alone. She heard nothing all night, but there were several empty vodka bottles in her bedroom, so it's possible she was passed out, not just sleeping."

"*Several* empty bottle? Would she be able to drink even one whole fifth of vodka in one day? I wonder what that would do to her."

Nigel grimaced. "She may have. We don't know when she started, but witnesses saw her drinking in the late afternoon, so we don't know if she was capable of doing harm to Jamie, even if she didn't drink an entire bottle in one day. It depends on how much alcohol she can handle. I've known people who could drink more than that and still be semi-functional."

"Poor woman." My eyes followed the ridge of the Coburg Hills for a moment. Just looking at them calmed my aching heart. "I wish I could do more for her."

"Do you want me to stop?" I shook my head no, so Nigel continued. "Jamie's dad was in bed alone, also. He has no roommate, so we have no means of verifying his alibi."

"He's a strange man."

Nigel chuckled. "Can't arrest a man for being strange."

I smiled. "Certainly not. There aren't enough prisons for that kind of thing . . . Sorry, that was in poor taste. What about Jamie's boyfriend? Does he have an alibi?"

Nigel shrugged. "No one really has an alibi, because it was the middle of the night. And I could say the teens have their parents to vouch for them, but every bedroom has a window, so I can't rule anyone out."

I thought about that. "Okay, I accept that. But what about Bruce Carey?"

"What about him?"

"Does he have an alibi?"

Nigel stared at me. "Why would he need one?"

I leaned forward. "Nigel, he is a chauvinist who loves the power the uniform gives him. He enjoys intimidating the town, and he obviously has a lack of self-control - just look at how his partner had to physically drag him away from my house when I refused to let him intimidate me during questioning. And Jamie was well known as a smart-aleck rebel. If those two tangled, it could be ugly."

"Oh . . ." He looked around the front yard and asked plaintively, "Can I use one of those 'naughty words' from your lecture right now?"

I smiled stiffly. "I'm sorry, Nigel. I assumed you would look at everyone, regardless of their profession."

"Good Lord, woman, do you think I would set a police officer above the law? You have much to learn about me."

He pondered a sudden thought. "And may I ask another question? Are there many officers here in the States like Bruce Carey? Is the entire police force a full barrel of 'bad apples', so to speak?"

I opened my mouth to answer, but he continued, "No, I retract the question. I have met many dedicated, honorable police since I've been here. And even the British police have a few bad apples on the force. But this one . . ."

He sighed and shook his head.

I smiled as he left a few minutes later, satisfied that I had at least nudged him into looking at *everyone*, regardless of their occupation.

LATER THAT EVENING, I sat at Natalie's dining room table and asked, "What does a strangled girl look like?"

Shelly and Hannah were busy with friends, and Mikey was upstairs with Danny. He had brought his 'engineer box' of broken small appliances to tinker with. I'd snagged the opportunity to have a cup of tea with Natalie and re-hash the case. Nigel may not want my help, but he needed it, and he was getting it.

Natalie looked startled. "What?"

"What does a girl who has been strangled look like?" I repeated. "Nigel chewed me out for asking the kids for help, and I told him it was like a game for them because they hadn't seen her. I got to thinking: It's kind of like a game for me, too. I didn't see her, and I wondered if it would be more real to me if I knew what she'd looked like after being strangled. It probably doesn't look like what we see on TV, and I would *never* have asked Jim for a description." I shuddered at the thought.

Natalie shook her head. "No, nothing at all like what we see on TV," she agreed. "If I remember correctly – from reading detective novels, not from experience..."

"Of course."

"The face turns bluish black and swells, and the tongue protrudes between the teeth, and it's a dark color – black-ish red. I think something happens to the eyes, too, like they bleed a little, maybe. It's nasty," she concluded.

"The poor girl," I said softly. Natalie nodded. "This isn't a game, is it?"

She shook her head. "No, and we need to find out who's done this before he does it again."

"You think it's a man...or a boy."

Natalie nodded grimly. We sat silently a few moments.

I swished my tea around and around. "We know that Jamie had had an abortion, right?"

"I think so. Maybe."

"Nigel kind of confirmed it, actually," I sat up straight. "When he stopped by after that weird rose was left in my room."

"What did he say?"

"He was looking at that piece of paper. He was really mad about that."

"I know, you told me. Twice."

I grimaced. "Yeah, well, he said . . . hang on." I racked my memory. "He said, 'It seems to say that Forrest Pearson may have been responsible for the abortion.'"

"Like he already knew there had been one?" Natalie asked.

I nodded as we pondered that a moment.

I continued, "We also know Jamie and Kelly were both fighting over Forrest Pearson...Why?"

Natalie blinked. "Why what?"

"Why were the two girls fighting over Forrest? He seems like a nice enough kid and everything, but he isn't Hollywood gorgeous. How could he be with his gangling body and big Adam's apple? He isn't an athlete or a musician or even into theater. So why were they fighting over a kid who doesn't do anything spectacular or even interesting, who doesn't have a car or a job, who isn't even very good-looking? What does he have that would make two girls fight over him?"

"Wow, that's a great question, Danielle. I have no idea." Natalie thought a moment. "Do you think he may be dealing drugs?"

"Here?" I was skeptical. "Natalie, we're a town full of farmers and people who work for farmers. We do have a small drug problem, as every town in America does, but it isn't so big that we don't know who's dealing. That salmon-colored house by the river, the green trailer in the trailer court, and that little pink house on Sapphire Avenue. They're the only places in town that you can get weed, even though it's legal now. I'm not sure anyone here even goes for the harder stuff."

"They probably do," she said. "And we wouldn't have a clue, because we and our kids are completely naïve about drugs."

I sighed. "All right, then, let's leave it for a minute. Supposing Forrest doesn't deal drugs. What does he have that would make two pretty teen-agers fight over him?"

"I wonder if he's just *nice*, you know?" Natalie suggested. "Maybe there just isn't a lot of kindness in their lives."

I was doubtful, but said, "I suppose it's possible. I know I'm responding to Nigel's kindness."

Natalie snorted into her tea. "Yeah, you are."

I flipped my teaspoon and hit her between the eyes.

"Hey!" She yelped. We laughed and mopped up the spilled tea.

"Anyway," Natalie continued, "we're looking at more than just Forrest as a possible suspect."

"Right," I agreed. "But it's a question I want answered. Maybe I'll ask Shelly. Did you talk to the exchange students? Who were the three you mentioned knew Jamie?"

She ticked them off on her fingers. "Lars from Norway, Karl from Germany, and Daniel from Israel. I did talk with them."

"And?" I asked hopefully.

She sighed with frustration. "All three said they hardly knew her. Maybe they didn't, but I wasn't sure if they just didn't want to get involved in a police investigation."

I nodded thoughtfully. Frustration was building, and I tamped it down.

"So, I just visited with them," Natalie continued. "I don't know if I got anything useful, but Lars says Daniel hangs out on the edge of Jamie's crowd, Daniel says Karl has a crush on Shelly –"

"He does?"

"That's what Daniel says. And Karl says Jamie had started smoking recently. That's all they knew."

"She did? That girl," I shook my head. "She was really walking down a messed-up road. I wish I could have done more for her."

Natalie patted my hand. "You did all she would let you do, hon."

I nodded. "We need to talk to Daniel again, though. Or tell Nigel to."

Natalie agreed, and we sat quietly for a while and sipped our teas. Finally, I roused myself. "And now, let's look at the least possible suspect."

Natalie smiled. "On the basis that that's the one most often guilty in books?"

"Of course. If I were writing this story, I'd make the guilty one Papa Jong...or Officer Nichols. Then again," I continued, "if there were any justice in the world, it would be Officer Carey – a.k.a. the Spruce Bruce – who was guilty."

Natalie snatched up the idea. "Yeah, we could cast him in the role of dirty old man."

"But she turned him down because he's too fat," I laughed. "I could write this book."

Natalie frowned and rubbed the red spot on her forehead. "But it isn't a book. And we don't know they even knew each other."

I bounced in my chair. "Yes, we do." Natalie's head snapped up. "Remember? We saw him take her home one night after curfew. We were walking late, and she'd been at a party. She was weaving her way home, and he stopped and offered her a ride. He even had her sit in the front seat instead of the back."

Natalie said slowly, "That was before he had this new partner, then."

Chapter 26
It Was A Story Idea

My eyes widened. "Wow, we just put him in an unethical position for a Sherriff's deputy, with an unaccompanied female minor in his car without a witness. Why didn't we say or do anything about it at the time?"

"Remind me. When was it?"

I sighed. "About two years ago, wasn't it?"

Natalie placed her hand on mine. "That was when you were fighting Jim for child support, and you wanted him to have to have supervised visitation, remember? We spent most of those walks in prayer."

I nodded, remembering. "Then how come I remember it now?"

Natalie shrugged and took another drink of her tea. "The memory is a crazy thing," she answered, setting down her mug. "But it does mean he knows her...or knew her two years ago."

We looked at each other. "Do you suppose we should tell Nigel?" I asked.

Natalie made a scoffing noise. "Absolutely. Maybe he didn't kill her, but he isn't safe to have around anyone's daughter, if he's going to bend or break laws like that."

I walked to the phone, feeling like a sleepwalker. For the first time, I felt as though I were going to seriously point a finger at someone who might have actually committed murder. Everyone else just seemed like guessing, just playing a game, and as much as I disliked the Spruce Bruce, I didn't like the thought of turning him in as a possible murderer. What if I was wrong? On the other hand, Natalie was right. He shouldn't be in uniform.

"I liked it better when it was a story idea," I said.

Natalie nodded soberly.

Nigel's voice mail picked up when I called. After the beep I said, "Nigel? This is Danielle. Are you aware that Officer Carey knew Jamie; at least he did a couple of years ago? He gave her a ride home in his police car one night after curfew. I know it doesn't sound like much," it sounded like less and less as I talked, "but Natalie and I thought you should know."

I hung up the phone and looked at Natalie. We were still staring at each other when Natalie's oldest, Abe, walked into the room.

"What's up, Ladies?" he asked jauntily. "You look as if you've just turned your mother in for murder."

We laughed, and the tension was broken as twin mental images flashed of our mothers being led away in handcuffs.

"Never in the world would I do that to the police," I assured him. We all laughed, and Natalie agreed.

I continued. "Actually, we were wondering if you knew whether or not Officer Carey knew Jamie."

"Oh, sure," he sobered instantly. "They went out a couple of times a month or so, usually when he was off duty, but sometimes in his patrol car. Of course, when his new partner came to town, they had to be more careful." He grimaced. "He used to be sure to tell us kids that he was taking her to look at some police exhibit or something like that, but we all knew he was screwing her –"

"Abe!"

"Sorry, Mom. Anyway, we all knew they were 'seeing each other'." He sketched air quotes. "It's wrong, but what can you do when it's the police? There's really no one above them in authority, so we just let it slide. I mean, if we tell someone, he might come after us. He's pretty scary." He shrugged, reached into the fridge, and took the entire jug of milk with him back to his room.

I stared after him. My mind shrank from considering the Spruce Bruce and Jamie, so I concentrated on the more benign subject of Motherhood. "He's going to drink the whole gallon?"

Natalie answered absently. "That or he dumps it out the window. He's been doing it for about three months, now, and he's two inches taller. Growing seems to make him thirsty."

I shook my head and pulled my mind back to where we were. I asked, "But what do we do about the Spruce Bruce and Jamie? Do I call Nigel back?"

"Well, what did you say? I can't remember; I'm so tired." She rubbed her eyes.

I sighed. "I can't remember, either. I guess we'll just have to wait for him to call, if he does. He may be so angry with me for interfering he doesn't want to be my friend anymore."

Natalie chuckled. "Don't be so pessimistic, honey. Of course he'll call back. Didn't you say you told him something that made him laugh? You'll see. He'll call. You're irresistible to him."

I wished I could remember what I'd said to make him laugh so hard. I stood. "In that case, I should head home. If he calls, he'll probably call there. You want to come?"

Natalie shook her head. "I've got to get ready for work in the morning."

"You never work on Sundays."

She gave vent to a sigh of frustration. "Some *idiot* plugged the wrong cable into the wrong slot and blew out the entire sound board yesterday. Not only that, the microphones were still plugged in, and they're fried, too. So I have to wrestle with the insurance company...on a Sunday. Grr."

"No kidding? I'd want to ream the guy. Who did it?"

She looked sheepish. "I did."

I laughed all the way home. Mikey didn't want to leave, and he was really miffed that I wouldn't tell him what was so funny. When we reached the house, he stomped up the stairs.

I sat at the computer with a mug of hot cocoa and tried to work on my book, something I hadn't had a lot of time for lately. Every few paragraphs, I'd read over it and have to erase it all. My mind just wasn't on make-believe. Finally, I sighed and turned it off. I needed this murder solved, so I could get back to earning a living.

Shelly came into my office. "Oh, Mom, I didn't know you were home. I thought it was just Mikey. Detective Hawksworth called a few minutes ago. He said you left him a message."

"Shelly, did you know Officer Carey was in a relationship with Jamie?"

She shifted from foot to foot a few times. "Yeah. They used to go places after school. He usually tried to make it sound like police business, but it was obviously something else."

I felt my temper rise. "Why didn't you say something? Why didn't you talk to the teachers? They're trained to help students in abusive situations."

"They're trained to call the police, if someone is in danger." She corrected me. "But Officer Carey *is* the police." Shelly's brows drew down over her nose. "I knew you wouldn't like it, Mom, and that you couldn't do anything about it, so I didn't say anything. No one did."

"Shelly –"

"And he's a police officer. Who's going to believe me? Or you, for that matter? I mean, Detective Hawksworth is a great guy and all that, and I trust him to do his best for us, and I hope he asks you out," that surprised me, "but how do I know how he's going to react if I accuse his colleague of inappropriate behavior with a minor?"

"But Shelly, you're a child."

"*Mom.*"

"Well, you are. Especially in this situation." She rolled her eyes. "Look, do you know what to do for someone who is caught in an abusive relationship?"

"Call the police," she muttered mutinously.

"What if you can't?" I countered. "What do you do then? Do you talk to a teacher? Do you talk to the principal? Or maybe you could call Child Protective Services directly. You might even call the public prosecutor. Or *maybe* your mom knows to do those things, and you should talk to her.

"This is so stupid!" I almost shouted.

"Of course it's stupid, but why are you yelling at me?" Shelly countered.

"Because I'm angry, Shelly," I answered with quiet intensity. "Angry that the kids in my town have been placed in this situation; angry with Bruce Cary, the child molester; and yes, I'm a little bit angry with you for trying to carry this on your own."

Her eyes filled with tears, and she answered, "I never thought of those things."

I stood and pulled her into a hug. "I know, honey. That's why you have me, to help you think of them."

Shelly sniffed and pulled away. "What are you going to do?"

"You mean, other than pull out my favorite butcher knife and go after him?"

Shelly snorted and nodded.

"I'm going to report him, of course, to the one police officer who has, so far, shown not only integrity but authority."

Still wiping her eyes, Shelly grimaced. "I don't know how he's going to take that."

I answered grimly, "We're about to find out."

She followed me into the kitchen. "Will I have to be interviewed by him again?" she asked as I punched numbers into the phone.

I shook my head. "Abe told his mom and me the same thing." Shelly sighed in relief, and I wrapped my arm around her.

Nigel answered on the third ring. "You sound tired," I said.

"Well, this case is beginning to get me down. What was it you wanted to tell me?"

I let out a calming breath. "Natalie's son, Abe, told me, and Shelly confirms, that Officer Carey had an ongoing intimate relationship with Jamie Sneider. He often picked her up after school in both his personal car and his police car."

He was silent for a few seconds. "Hold up a moment. I want to make sure I've heard you correctly. Officer Carey was known to have an intimate, sexual relationship with a minor. He often picked her up in either his personal car or a county Sherriff's Deputy car, and he drove her from school property to destinations unknown. Is this what you are telling me?"

Slowly, I nodded. "Yes."

He took a deep breath. "And Abe Shalligan told you this, and Shelly confirmed it?"

"Yes." His anger came through the phone wires and made the receiver hot.

"When did this 'relationship' start?"

I looked at Shelly. "How long had it been going on?"

She shrugged. "At least all of this school year. I don't know if it started in the summer or if it was going on last spring, too."

"Shelly is there?" Nigel barked, "Let me talk to her."

"She doesn't want to talk to you when you're angry," I answered decisively.

"All right, fair enough," he breathed deeply. "But tell me this: are they the only ones who know of this, or is it common knowledge amongst the youth?"

"My understanding is that it's common knowledge."

He exploded, "And why did they not tell us this before, like when it first happened? Are there no teachers they could report this to? No parents?"

"As they said, who would believe them, a bunch of teen-agers, against a police officer? He is the authority in this town, and they didn't know who would have more authority than he. So, they just quietly raged and said nothing." I began to tremble. Shelly stood straighter and placed her arm around me, a comforting role reversal.

Using great control, Nigel answered quietly, "Thank you, Mrs. Baker, for coming forward with this information." He spaced his words evenly. "I promise you there will be a careful investigation into this situation. Is there anything else I can do for you?"

"No, thank you, that's all," I said quietly and hung up.

Chapter 27

There's a Storm Brewing In Albany

Shelly stared gravely at me. I grimaced and said, "I have a feeling he's going to turn that place upside down, and every cop who's ever even *thought* of doing something wrong will be sweating." I wiped my hand on my pants. "I'm sweating, and I don't even work for him. Whew! I think there's a storm brewing in Albany."

Shelly's shoulders dropped, and she grinned. "It's about time. Mom, I think I like that man. He might even be a keeper." She hopped and skipped her way up the stairs, in her relief singing a song about sunshine and lollipops. I followed her up. It was time for me to hit the pillow.

I wondered, just before sleep came, what Nigel was doing at that moment, and if it had anything to do with the information I gave him tonight. Was he turning desks upside down? Or maybe he was physically throwing miscreants against the wall, like the Spruce Bruce? I sank into pleasant dreams of an angry Nigel doing great feats for my benefit.

SUNDAY DAWNED BRIGHT and sunny but a bit windy. The Willamette Valley is long and narrow, a perfect combination for wind, and we were getting our fair share of it that morning. Hannah was at a sleep-over, so Mikey, Shelly and I walked to church without her.

Nigel was absent from service, and I wondered if it was because he was trying a different church, was mad at me, or was wreaking havoc in Albany. Whatever the reason, it was easier to concentrate on the service with him gone. *Huh. I wonder why that is.* I told myself to hush and listen to Pastor Ted.

After lunch I took a wonderfully invigorating nap. About three o'clock, I was straightening my bedroom when someone banged on the front door. I ran down and looked through the living room window. The Spruce Bruce was standing there in civilian clothes. He looked angry and rumpled.

"Uh, oh," I whispered to the Lord. "What do I do?"

Right on cue, like in a bad horror flick, Hannah's friend's mom pulled into the driveway to drop her off. I saw Hannah's face in the windshield and motioned her to go away. She spoke to her friend's mom, but then slowly got out of the car. I couldn't believe it. Now I *had* to answer the door.

The Spruce Bruce was looking at Hannah as I opened the door. He turned back to me. "What's the big idea, telling that jerk detective I was having an inappropriate relationship with a minor, *Mrs.* Baker?" he loudly demanded.

I said, "Hannah, come on in." I stepped back to let her in, and the Spruce Bruce moved as if to come in before her. I quickly stepped back.

"You aren't coming in, Bruce," I told him quietly. "This is Hannah's home, and she's welcome here. You are not."

Feet planted firmly in the doorway, Bruce wouldn't let Hannah pass. "You and me got to talk," he said.

"Hannah, please run to Aunty-Mommy and ask her to call the police for me?" Hannah dropped her backpack and ran like the wind. I looked at the Spruce Bruce and knew this was going to be a big battle. I'd let Jim abuse me, and I'd escaped him; I wasn't about to let another man do the same.

"Bruce, you need to leave. I have nothing to say to you."

"I'm not leaving, Bitch. You turned me in, and we're gonna *talk* about it."

"No, you may talk all you like, but not to me. Now, step back so I can close the door without injuring you."

He glared at me a moment and stepped forward, closer to me. I looked up at him, a mountain of a man, and prayed for deliverance. Several self-defense moves flashed through my mind, but I wasn't sure there was enough room in the hallway.

From up the street, I could hear the tune of a popular rock song. Several teen-agers were in a pick-up going way too fast. Just as they reached my house, one of them shouted. More quickly than I thought possible, there was a screech of brakes, and the pick-up emptied into my yard. Two teens grabbed the Spruce Bruce's left arm, and two grabbed his right. Two more wiggled through the door, their hands on his chest. I blinked, and Bruce was on his back, seven teens sitting on him as he bellowed profanity to the heavens. It took me a moment to realize the seventh teen had knelt behind and tripped him up as the two in front pushed.

The relief overwhelmed me, I began to laugh. After a moment, the teens laughed, too. They high-fived and fist-bumped each other while I laughed until tears streamed down my face and my stomach hurt. And still, the Spruce Bruce bellowed. A few minutes later, as we were regaining control of our laughter, a patrol car followed by Nigel in his little blue compact pulled up.

"Well, Ma'am," said Officer Nicholls, "it seems you have it all under control." He grinned at me.

"Not I, Officer," I answered, wiping tears from my face. "God has it under control. At the moment I thought he was going to physically attack me, these angels arrived." I smiled at Edgar, Lenny, Bill, Forrest, and their friends. "Thank you, men, you did a fabulous job."

They looked embarrassed and pleased. "Aw, shucks, Ma'am," Edgar's bass boomed, "it weren't nothin'." They all laughed as they stood.

Officer Nicholls took the Spruce Bruce with him, stuffing him into the back of the patrol car. He protested the entire time. "It's all a misunderstanding. You don't get it. She was threatening me. You can't do this to me; I'm a police officer. You're ruining my good reputation around here." Finally the car door closed, and we all sighed in relief.

I turned to the boys. "How did you happen to be here at just the right time?"

Bill said, "Hannah was running like the devil himself was after her. She was crying, too, so we stopped to help. She told us what was up, and we came as fast as we could." He looked at the others. "Like we said, we're here any time you need us."

"Perfect timing, guys, thank you. I'd ask you in, but I know Detective Hawksworth wants to take a statement. I'll be making another batch of those jumbles cookies you like so much this evening, though, if you want to stop by for a few." Their smiles were their acceptance, and they turned toward the truck.

I looked at Nigel. "Shall we go in?"

As he sank wearily onto the sofa, he asked, "May I tour your home some time?"

"Of course."

"I've seen the lounge here," he patted the sofa, "and your kitchen. But except for checking windows, I haven't really *looked* at your house. And what I see is attractive. The house, of course." He shook his head and rubbed his eyes. "Don't mind me; I'm knackered. And not talking straight."

He sat back wearily. "I don't normally tell that to people who are part of a murder investigation. You won't turn me in, will you?"

I smiled. "Of course not, if you'll translate 'knackered' for me."

He chuckled. "It means completely worn out, exhausted."

"Ah. Thank you. And one day soon, I'll take you on a tour of the house."

He sighed. "Thank you Now, shall we start with the phone call I received from a hysterical Hannah?"

I jumped up. "I should call her and let her know I'm okay." I rushed to the kitchen and called Natalie's house. She answered on the first ring.

"I'm okay," I said quickly. "I'll tell you all about it after I've given Nigel my statement." She agreed to wait and hung up.

I quickly made coffee, thinking even decaf might help Nigel stay awake and returned to the living room, the 'lounge' as he had called it. Two steps inside, I realized he was asleep. I sat down in the chair across from him and took a sip of the coffee that was supposed to be for him. I figured, with a Detective's training, he wouldn't nap long. And while he slept, I could study him. He was worth studying.

I was right about both. Twenty minutes later, he woke up, turned red, and began to apologize, wiping his chin in case he'd drooled. He hadn't.

Chapter 28
The Hawk Circles

"Don't apologize," I told him. "If I had had enough sense to wait until this morning to give you the information about the Spruce Bruce, you would have gotten more sleep."

He nodded. "But then I would have had to work all night tonight, instead of last night." I handed over the rest of the coffee, lukewarm but drinkable. He gulped it quickly and rubbed his hand over his face. "Where were we before my gross dereliction of duty?"

I smiled. "I believe I was going to tell you all about the confrontation with Officer Carey."

He frowned a moment. Then his face cleared. "Why do you call him the 'Spruce Bruce'?"

I grinned, then scowled. "He's a dandy. He's so careful about his appearance, everything ironed to perfection, no stains, hair perfect at all times. But that belly of his is so fat it's almost obscene. And I know his parents; that stomach isn't genetic, it comes from life choices. And while he takes such care of his external self, he obviously cares nothing at all for anyone else. It makes the rest of him, all that careful grooming, a joke. A poor joke, I grant you, but a joke nonetheless."

Nigel nodded, and his dimples appeared in a sad smile.

He took me through the confrontation moment by moment. When I told him about Edgar and his friends and how they had tackled the Spruce Bruce, he chuckled, shook his head, and wrote it down. "I like Americans," he said. "Your ingenuity is appealing."

"Thank you, Detective," I bowed in my chair and he chuckled again. "But how did he find out I turned him in?"

Nigel's eyebrows contracted. "I don't know. But I guarantee I will find out."

I gave him a lopsided smile. "Sometimes accidents do happen, and they really are accidents, Nigel. I'm not sure that's true this time, but I don't imagine the Spruce Bruce has too many friends. So, if I were investigating this, I'd start there. If his friends aren't guilty, then I'd assume it was a genuine accident, and not lop off anyone's head. Not that I'm telling you how to do your job; just thinking out loud."

He looked at me in consternation. "*If you were investigating this?* Please don't interfere in something else."

I laughed and assured him I wouldn't – *in this,* I amended silently.

He continued, "Do you plan to prefer charges against Officer Carey?"

"For what?" I asked. "I don't think it's against the law to prove yourself a fool."

Nigel smiled. "No, perhaps not, but he did threaten you."

I shook my head. "No, he said no words that could be used against him; it was all body posture, facial expression, and tone of voice. Except that he called me a bitch, he did nothing indictable."

Nigel sighed. "So you don't wish to prefer charges against him."

Again, I explained. "He did nothing that would hold up in a court of law. Nigel, he didn't physically touch me. He tried to come into my house ahead of Hannah. I told him he wasn't welcome, and he didn't go away, but he didn't do more than intimidate me, for the most part.

"Maybe you can attach a complaint to his file for behavior unbecoming..." I paused.

Nigel nodded as he wrote in his little notebook, "...an officer."

"Is it?" I pondered.

He slowly raised his head. "Is it what?"

"Is it 'unbecoming *an* officer'? Or is it 'unbecoming *of* an officer'? Or maybe it's 'unbecoming *to* an officer?"

He stared at me, his mouth open. "Does it matter?"

"Of course it matters! If I wrote that phrase into a book, half my readers would write to tell me it was wrong, and if I didn't know for sure, I'd wonder about it, and my publisher would want a re-print – probably at my cost – and the readers of my blog would get into fights about it, and eventually they'd draw blood through the computer screens."

Nigel stared. "It can't be that bad."

"What can't be that bad?"

"Writing. People care enough about how something is phrased to argue over it to the point of drawing blood?"

I smiled and nodded. "If you're good enough to draw a large audience. Although I may be exaggerating about the blood."

Nigel shook his head. "I shall research the exact American phraseology and let you know, shall I?"

I laughed and thanked him. The information wasn't important. Yet. But I never know what my next story is going to be about.

A few more minutes, and I walked him out. "This is the part of the investigation that gets me," he spoke softly as we stood outside. "I've put in hours and hours of work and find I've not got what I need for an arrest."

I poked him in the arm. "First of all, it's only been, what, two weeks?"

He shrugged. "It isn't the length of time, it's the amount of information that matters. And we have a lot of information."

I thought about that and nodded. "Okay, I accept that. Do you know who's guilty, though?" I asked.

He sighed. "Normally, I would at this point at least know who to concentrate on, but in this case, there are at least four people with motive and opportunity. I feel as if I'm circling over this town, waiting to find –"

"- The guilty one, your prey. Detective 'The Hawk' circles." I grinned at him. "I like it. If I were writing a book about this..."

"Don't."

I continued to smile playfully at him. "Okay, I won't, Detective."

Nigel smiled but turned serious almost immediately. "And now I must deal with 'the Spruce Bruce' as you call him. I hate it when an officer goes bad."

"At least you know exactly what he's capable of, so it shouldn't take too long."

I wasn't sure he was encouraged, but he attempted a smile with his farewell.

As soon as he drove down the street, I called Natalie and asked her to bring Hannah home. They finally arrived as I was placing the first cookie sheet in the oven.

"Mom!" Hannah ran and held me tight. I rubbed her back and her soft, curly brown hair.

"It's okay, sweetie," I cooed. "It's all right. I'm okay, and Officer Carey is gone, now. You did a great job helping me out today."

She pulled away and studied my face. "I was scared," she said. "He looked and sounded just like Dad."

I nodded. "I know, Hannah. I was scared, too."

"You were? You sounded so calm, like it was no big deal. I thought maybe you didn't understand that he might hurt you." She started to cry.

I led her to a kitchen chair, and stood over her, rubbing her hair some more, her face planted against my stomach. She wrapped her arms around me as I assured her, "I understood, baby. My heart was racing, my legs felt like jelly, and I was breathing really fast.

"But, Hannah? Sweetie? I had absolute faith that God had it under *His* control, no matter what happened. We've been through a lot, and we've gotten strong because of it. I wasn't about to let him know he was scaring me; it would have made him feel even more powerful.

"But you." I tilted her face up. "You were fantastic. You didn't fall to pieces or stand petrified, although it's probably what you wanted to do." She nodded and sniffed. "You responded immediately and ran when I told you to. And you stopped to tell Edgar and the boys what was happening. That's what really saved me."

Her face lit up. "It did?" She has a soft spot for Edgar.

I nodded. "Yes, just when Officer Carey was looking the scariest, that pick-up full of boys screeched to a stop in front of our house, and they jumped out and knocked him onto his back, right there on the porch. It was awesome. You should have seen him with seven teen-agers sitting on him. He was squirming and yelling, but he couldn't get up. And it looked so funny, we just laughed and laughed until Officer Nicholls and Detective Hawksworth came. That made him even madder." We were all laughing now.

"I wish I'd seen it," Hannah said, but I knew she'd take the image with her. It would help her overcome the fear of the last hour. The beeper went off, and I took the cookies out of the oven – one dozen down, only six to go.

When Hannah went upstairs, Natalie asked, "Where were Shelly and Mikey all this time?"

"Mikey's with the youth group cleaning up the community garden. And Shelly's at Amy's – again – looking at Prom hairstyles. I don't know, Natalie, I'm just about ready to have this Prom thing over with so we can get back to normal."

Natalie nodded. "Yeah. You're sure you're okay, though?"

I assured her I was fine, now.

She nodded and grinned. "Because I wanted to tell you that a junior girl asked Abe to the Prom yesterday."

I stared at her. "And you didn't tell me?"

She did a little dance step and giggled. "I didn't know until a couple of hours ago."

"Who is she?" I placed the next tray in the oven and sat down across from her. Natalie looked at her fingernails, judging whether or not it was time to re-paint them. "Come on, tell me!"

She grinned. "Okay," she leaned forward confidentially. "You know Elizabeth Jayde?"

"The red-headed cheerleader?" An image of the party, the pretty red-head, and Abe sitting next to her flashed through my mind.

She nodded. "I guess she and Abe have been friendly this year, and she asked him to be her date."

"I can't believe it," I said. "Well, I can believe it, actually. They're going to be the best-looking couple there." I looked around quickly, making sure none of the kids could hear me and tell Shelly. *Oh, right. Only Hannah's home.*

Natalie sat back smugly. "Uh-huh. I guess I do have a pretty good-lookin' son."

I reached back for a cookie and threw it at her. It landed on her chest.

"Hey," she yelped and took a bite.

"Don't look so smug. Shelly's beautiful, and her date's good-looking."

"I never said she isn't," Natalie was quick to assure me. "Besides, beauty is only defined by the standards applied by society....and that standard comes from a culture that is killing itself."

"Uh-huh. But it still feels good to have beautiful kids."

Natalie grinned. "Yeah, it does."

Chapter 29
I Have No Idea What You're Talking About

Monday evening, Natalie and I were walking the loop when Peggy Sue tooted her horn and pulled up just ahead of us. She hopped out of her car and demanded, "Where did y'all get the idea that I was with Jamie and Linda Sneider the night Jamie died?"

We blinked at her. I glanced at Natalie and said, "I have no idea what you're talking about, Peggy Sue."

"Are you sure? 'Cause that detective of yours questioned me for over an hour, saying he'd been told I was at their house the night Jamie was killed, and he didn't seem to believe me when I told him I was at home, in my own bed, alone. And the only people I know who willingly talk to him about Jamie are you two."

"Peggy Sue," Natalie began, "we have not told Detective Hawksworth anything about you –"

"—because you're too old to be interested in men," I continued.

"So you'll have to believe us when we tell you –"

"That if you want to get him alone somewhere –"

"—you'll have to do it on your own –"

"Not with our help." I finished.

She burst out laughing. "You two are like a comedy routine. You really didn't tell him anything about me?"

"I'm sorry, Peggy Sue," I said sweetly. "But if you really want to spend some time with him, and he's worth spending time with –"

"Those dimples," Natalie cooed dreamily.

"I'll tell him you confessed." I smiled. "It's the best I can offer."

"On the other hand," Natalie continued, "If you want us to talk to him *for* you –"

"You're going to have to tell us where you were –"

"The night Jamie died."

We looked goofily expectant.

"I'm not telling you," Peggy Sue answered as she did a little hop. "You two are nuts." Climbing back into her car, she shouted as she drove away, "I forgive you!"

"Hey, we're pretty good at that," Natalie said.

"Yeah, girl." We fist bumped and laughed.

As we continued our walk, we discussed Peggy Sue's accusation.

"Do you really think he pulled her in for questioning?" I asked. "I wouldn't want to think she's under suspicion."

Natalie shook her head and waved at someone on a lawn mower, "I doubt she is, now. Detective Hawksworth seems to like to eliminate people from his list. Like you." She grinned.

Playfully, I shoved her, and she weaved into the path of Gramma Gertie, a cranky old woman who walks back and forth in front of her house every evening. She wears brightly colored muumuus and slippers, and she scrapes grooves into the sidewalk with her walker. Gramma Gertie growled at Natalie who skipped nimbly away. We said good evening, just to be nice.

"Stinkin' teen-age girls, always runnin' in front o' law abidin' people," she grumbled to herself as we passed. "Think they own the world." She turned and glared after us as we grinned at each other.

As soon as we were out of earshot, I exclaimed, "I love Gramma Gertie."

Natalie snorted a laugh. "I haven't been called a teen-aged girl in years. I think I'm beginning to like the old coot."

We passed the school grounds and counted seven middle-schoolers playing wall ball. You'd think they'd be doing homework on a school night...or taking a shower, please.

As we entered the old new development, we spotted Forrest Pearson.

"Isn't that Elizabeth Jayde over there talking to Forrest?" I asked. Natalie slowed her pace and peered into the half-light.

"Looks like it," she said. "I hope they aren't going to start dating and ruin the Prom plans she's already made with Abe."

I lifted an eyebrow. "Seriously? They're talking. That's it. Maybe they both live down here."

Natalie shrugged and continued to stare. "Maybe."

I nudged her. "Stop staring. Besides, Prom's this weekend. Do you really think she would make plans on Saturday and break them on Monday?"

Natalie sighed in relief. "You're right. I won't worry about it." She continued to stare. "I will tell Abe to find out what they were talking about, though."

I laughed. "Natalie, you can't ask him to do that. It isn't any of his business. Or ours."

"It's all our business, Danielle. Jamie's dead, and your detective isn't getting anywhere very fast..."

"He isn't *my* detective!"

"So we need to find out what's going on. Forrest is a person of interest right now," she hissed, "and I want to know what he's up to."

"I like Forrest. He's just a nerdy, gangly kid who has his whole life ahead of him. I just want him to be an innocent bystander."

"You may want that, but is he? He's dating one girl, flirting with another, and now we find him in close conversation with yet another girl."

I stared at her. "Natalie, listen to yourself. You're saying he may be guilty of *murder* because Jamie and Kelly were fighting over him.

We have no idea if there was any basis for a fight. And now you find his guilt even more possible because . . . How many men do you talk to in a day?"

Natalie looked uncomfortable. "That's different. It's mostly work-related."

"Ha! Different. Right," I scoffed. "For all we know, they're discussing their World History assignment, or their next Spanish test. Or maybe she's asking him how he's doing, after the violent death of his girlfriend. Or maybe they share a similar home life, and he's asking her how things are going. Then again, maybe he's noticing she's an attractive girl – he wouldn't be the first boy to notice that." I shook my head. "You can't automatically assume he has something to hide just because he talks to more than one girl a week."

Natalie smiled. "Okay, I'll admit your argument has some merit. But why did they turn away from us when we saw them?"

"Let's ask." I veered toward the two teens. "Hey, Forrest. Hi, Elizabeth."

They turned toward me as Natalie caught up. Two quiet hellos drifted through the dusk, and my heart melted. They looked so sad.

"How are you two doing?" I asked quietly. "Are you all right?"

Forrest searched my face and glanced at Elizabeth before answering, "I'm okay, I guess. It's a little hard right now. I'm not quite sure who my friends are."

I heard a little sigh escape Natalie as she moved forward and enveloped Forrest in a long, tight hug. Elizabeth smiled at me. "I told him you two were his friends. He wasn't sure."

I returned her smile. "I remember that feeling." I looked at Forrest as memories flashed through my mind of what I call the 'divorce years'. Turning back to Elizabeth, I said, "I'm glad he has a friend in you."

Natalie stepped back, and Forrest wiped his eyes. "Besides," I continued, "this young man is one of my angels."

Forrest snorted a laugh and asked for a tissue. We all laughed as Natalie handed him one, saying, "Mix tears and laughter, and you get a mess."

As he finished wiping his face, Forrest said, "Mrs. Baker, I didn't kill Jamie. You know that, right?"

How do I answer this one, God? I smiled and said, "I trust that if you had, you would have been showing different signs than you're showing right now, hon. But if you know anything, anything at all, you need to tell Detective Hawksworth."

It was almost dark, now, so I couldn't see faces very well. Still, I thought Forrest wanted to say more, but he only nodded.

"We have to get going," I said. "You are both welcome at my house, any time, okay?"

They thanked me, and we continued our walk.

Natalie sighed. "Okay, you're right, he's just a nerdy, gangly kid, and he needs love and support right now."

"I think he knows something," I said quietly.

"Tell Detective Hawksworth." Natalie threw up her hands. "I just want this case solved, over with, gone away before Prom."

My head whipped around. "Are you serious? Prom is this Saturday. How do you think this is going to be solved by then?"

I tripped over an uneven patch of concrete, and Natalie grabbed my elbow. "I don't know, but it needs to be, so that boy and every other kid can enjoy their Prom knowing they don't have a murderer on the loose, maybe at the dance itself.

"Besides, I don't think Detective Hawksworth really wants to go to Prom, not at his age."

I began to laugh, visualizing Nigel in a tux, complete with flower, standing around watching a couple of hundred kids jerking their arms and legs – what they call dancing – to some kind of tribal beat with screaming guitars – what they call music. I described the scene to Natalie, and she started laughing. We were still giggling when we parted for the night.

"Are you going to Prom?" I asked Nigel on the phone later. It wasn't official police business, but I couldn't help it. I had to know.

In a surprised voice, he asked, "Are you asking me to escort you?"

I was dumbfounded. Was he serious? His chuckle reassured me, and I expelled my breath. "I can imagine Shelly's face if I showed up in a formal gown with a flower on my shoulder to her Prom," I laughed. "No, Natalie mentioned that she thought you'd go to Prom if you haven't made an arrest by Saturday night."

"Yes, I will have to go," Nigel said sadly. "I don't want to ruin it for the youths, but I can't allow them to go to their big dance without some sort of official protection, and a uniformed officer would truly ruin their experience."

I felt irrepressible. "Will you wear a tux?"

"A tux?" he asked.

"Don't you have formal suits in England?" I teased. "A tuxedo is a suit with a wing-tipped collar, a bow tie."

"Yes, of course we have formal wear in England. What a question! But I thought I'd wear my best suit. I'm not a youth, I have no date, and I'll be there on business. I don't plan to have fun."

His tone of voice finally soaked in. "Nigel, what's bothering you?"

He sighed. "I guess I'm feeling a tad homesick."

I glanced at the clock, 7:53 p.m., and quickly made a decision.

"Come join us for popcorn and a movie. No one deserves to be alone when they're homesick." I used my no-nonsense mommy voice. He chuckled and said he'd be right over.

I shouted up the stairs, "Shelly, Hannah, Mikey, come on down right now." They came tumbling down the stairs.

"What's wrong?" Shelly asked, worry lines wrinkling her forehead.

"What did I do this time?" Mikey demanded.

"I'm sorry, Mom," Hannah always apologizes first, then asks what she did wrong.

"Oh, kids, I'm sorry. No, no, nothing's wrong, you're not in trouble, and stop apologizing. I forgot to turn off my Mommy-voice, that's all. We have some things that need to be done, though, okay?" They nodded. "Mikey, make sure the guest bathroom is clean, please. Hannah, check the living room and pick up any messes in there. Then look for a good movie to watch. Shelly, please start four batches of popcorn. I'll be making coffee and juice. Any questions?" They looked a little shell-shocked.

Shelly asked, "Why are we doing all of this at eight o'clock on a school night?"

I answered, "Oh, I'm sorry. My brain jumped ahead of the explanation. Because Detective Hawksworth is homesick, and we're going to cheer him up. He'll be here any minute now."

Their faces lit up, and they scattered to get their jobs done. I smiled as I started the coffee. I was glad we all liked the detective. He was an interesting person to spend time with. *Right,* my inner voice said sarcastically, *he's interesting. Sure. And cute, and charming, and funny, and he has dimples...* I told my inner voice to shut up and go away as the lion's head knocker sounded a jolly rat-a-tat-tat.

I rushed to reach the door ahead of Hannah. "Honey, we can't just open it. Look through the window first and make sure you know who it is."

She nodded and complied. Her smile was enough. I opened the door for Nigel. He was wearing jeans and a polo-style shirt, a blue one that made his eyes pop. It made Hannah's eyes pop, too, and I had to remind her to finish her job in the living room. She blushed, nodded, and scurried away.

"Good evening, sir," I said gaily, wondering how bad I looked after my walk with Natalie. Inwardly, I shrugged and gave it to God.

Nigel picked up a curl from the right side of my head and moved it to the left where it belonged.

"There," he said with a smile, "now it's perfect."

I grimaced. "My brother used to do that for me."

Nigel laughed. "He was probably the only one willing to cross paths with such a tough young woman." It almost sounded like flirting, and I was a little confused by it. Maybe it was because he was lonely. I would have to be careful not to be encouraged by this mood of his.

Stop it, I told myself. *You don't want to get involved with the police again anyway, remember?*

"Hey, before we go in," I grabbed Nigel's arm. I looked at his face as he turned to me, and I almost stayed quiet. "I don't want to ruin the evening, but I saw Forrest Pearson earlier, and he looked like he wanted to talk. I don't know if it had something to do with Jamie or not, but I got the impression he might know something."

"Where did you see him?"

Shelly rushed past with two big bowls of popcorn. "Hurry up, you two, or you'll miss the movie."

Nigel said, "Half a mo'," and turned back to me.

"Natalie and I were walking." I told him about the conversation with Forrest and Elizabeth. "It was after he said he didn't kill Jamie. I told him to talk to you if he knows anything. He looked like he was going to say something, but he just thanked me."

Nigel ran his fingers through his hair. "Right. I'll talk to him again tomorrow."

Shelly grabbed one arm, and Mikey grabbed the other. "In the meantime, we're gonna have a great evening," Shelly announced.

"That's right," Mikey agreed, "and don't you forget it."

Nigel laughed and allowed himself to be dragged into the living room. We all piled onto the furniture and watched the movie

Hannah had chosen. It was a family favorite, and Nigel had seen it, too, so we talked more than we watched. It was a wonderful evening.

At ten, it was time for Nigel to leave. He was relaxed enough to hug Mikey and Hannah, and he gave Shelly an awkward one-armed hug that made her smile. "You'll get used to it," she assured him, "if you go to our church long enough. One-armed hugs are the norm there."

Nigel laughed. "Perhaps I'll learn a lot living here," he said genially.

I sent the kids to bed and walked him to his car. He took a deep breath and turned to me. "Thank you," he said with obvious sincerity. "I needed this very much."

Chapter 30
Tippling

Nigel glanced at the house and leaned against the car. "You have a wonderful family," he said softly.

"Do you have a family?" I asked quietly, hoping I wasn't crossing a line.

He smiled sadly. "I used to." He studied Mary's Peak north of town.

I thought that was all the answer I was going to get when he said, "I had a wife and two boys ages two and four. Someone broke into the house one night when I was on duty. Neighbors heard the screams and called 999, but we . . . didn't arrive soon enough. They either stole or destroyed everything I owned. And they killed my family."

I gasped. "Oh, Nigel. I'm so sorry."

He glanced at me and away again. "Thank you, but I don't want your pity."

"You don't have my pity!" I said sharply. Then I softened my tone. "You do have my sympathy and my friendship."

He didn't answer.

"How long ago did this happen?"

He sighed. "It's been twelve years. But the pain is so intense sometimes, it could have been last week."

"Yeah, grief seems to run in cycles, doesn't it?"

"That's what the counselor gurus tell one, but I don't know if they're right, or if they're singing platitudes in order to get one to face another day."

I smiled, and we stood lost in thought for a few moments. "I lost my best friend in a house fire when I was ten," I told him. "That was a long time ago, but the grief still catches me at times, even now. It's true, what they say, that the pain of the grief lessens with time, but it still seems to come back periodically, even though I have my wonderful friend Natalie. She doesn't *replace* Shelly, nobody could, but she is my best friend now."

Nigel glanced at the house again. "Your daughter is named for her?"

I nodded, remembering the fire, as I was sure Nigel was remembering the night he lost his entire family. My heart hurt for him.

He sighed. "You're right, though, that the pain lessens with time. The pangs are farther apart, and I recover from them more quickly, thank God."

I said, "I wonder how Jamie's mom is doing. This has to be ripping her apart."

Nigel shifted and I hoped asking about her wouldn't ruin the gentle moment we were sharing.

"She's tippling badly," he answered.

"Tippling?"

"Drinking alcohol to excess," he smiled. "We really are a people divided by a common language."

I smiled impudently up at him. "I'm willing to learn your language, if you're willing to learn mine."

Nigel laughed and looked at me so that my stomach did flip-flops. "Oh, I'm willing," he said softly. Then he sighed. "But on that note, I should go home. I am not a youth – a teen-ager, and I need not act like one. Look at you, shivering in the cool air. I should be ashamed."

I would have happily shivered for another hour. I liked the mood of the moment; but like Nigel, I shook myself and decided to act my age.

"I'm glad you came," I stepped back.

Nigel pushed away from the car.. The urge to be close to him was very strong, but I resisted. It wouldn't be appropriate, in the middle of an investigation. Besides, he may just be missing his family, and I didn't want to be a substitute. And I'd be mortified if he was sorry the next day.

Are you sure you want to be close to him? Or are you simply lonely, too? My voice of reason asked me. I wondered.

I took another step back. "Have a good night, Nigel. I'll see you again soon."

"Would you like me to do a perimeter check before I go?" He asked.

"I think we're good, thanks." I smiled. "I checked the windows earlier, and the doors will be locked as soon as I go back in."

"Are you sure? I would really like to know you're safe."

I nodded. "If it makes you feel better, then please do." I smiled as he shoo-ed me into the house. I watched through the window, and when he rounded the corner, we waved.

He waited until the downstairs lights were off before he started his car and drove away.

I dragged myself up the stairs and went to bed, confused, emotional, and very tired. My sleep was filled with images of Nigel, Jamie, and Forrest. And for some reason, my mother was there, too.

"WHAT DO YOU THINK OF this hair style?"

"Yeah, it's nice...how about this one?"

"Ooh, yeah, I like that one. Look at this one."

"Nah, she looks like a badger."

"Look at *that* one." Laughter.

Shelly and Amy were sitting at my kitchen table the next evening, hairstyle magazines all over. They were making final decisions on how to wear their hair to Prom. I left them to it, and when they finally came searching for me, I was upstairs, looking over my closet.

"I really should go shopping," I told them as they walked into my room. "Do you know I haven't bought anything new in at least four years? Except for this blue skirt here and the sweat suit I wore last night," I amended. "And Natalie bought those."

"We'll take you shopping," Amy offered immediately.

Shelly perked up. "Absolutely!" She agreed. "We'll dress you up, and you'll look beautiful!"

"Not that you don't look beautiful already," Amy amended.

"Right," Shelly answered. "You'll just look *more* beautiful!"

I smiled. "Thank you, girls. That is very sweet of you! I might just take you up on your offer - as long as you don't make me look like an old woman trying to look like a teenager."

They giggled, and I decided to talk to Natalie. She would help me dress my age.

Shelly and Amy dragged me downstairs to look at hairstyles.

"Mrs. B," Amy held up an open magazine. "Do you think you could do this for me for Prom?"

I looked at the French knot and nodded. "Oh, sure, hon, that's a pretty easy one."

Shelly held up another magazine. "Could you do this one for me?"

I looked at the simple hairstyle of curls, some in a barrette, some left hanging on the shoulder. "That's another simple one, Shelly, and it'll look gorgeous on you."

"But . . . " I studied the two pictures. "Girls, show me your dresses, please? In fact, why don't you put them on."

As I waited for the girls to come back, I thought sadly that Jamie should be having this kind of evening with a friend, too, preparing for Prom, discussing hair styles, and comparing dresses. I said another prayer for her mom.

The two girls came downstairs giggling. They weren't wearing their shoes, so the dresses dragged on the floor, and I smiled, reminded of the days when they played dress-up not so many years ago.

"Okay, it's just as I thought," I said. "Shelly, your dress was made for an older woman..."

She looked stricken. "No, no, what I mean is your dress was made for a runway model. Amy, your dress was made for a *teen* runway model."

Shelly said, "Oh, so my dress is a little more sophisticated, like it was made for a twenty-year-old, and Amy's is made for...what?"

"About an eighteen-year-old," I answered, sure that the two years between sixteen and eighteen would matter greatly. She looked satisfied.

"However," I continued, "these hairstyles are reversed from the dresses you're wearing. Look at yours, Amy." I pointed at the picture of the French knot. "This is supposed to be worn with a sophisticated dress on an older woman, a woman in her twenties. Like the dress Shelly is wearing.

"And this," I pointed to Shelly's picture, "is meant to be worn with a less sophisticated dress, a dress for a slightly younger woman, like Amy's dress."

I switched the pictures and laid them on the table, so that the hairstyle Amy wanted was in front of Shelly, and vice versa. "I recommend you switch hairstyles to go with your dresses." I sat in a chair and waited for the girls to think and discuss.

Shelly picked up the picture. "I think I see what you mean," she said. "If I did the French knot, I could have this sweeping back part. Could I have the tendrils on the side, too?"

I nodded. "Absolutely."

Amy watched Shelly study her picture. Finally, she picked up the other magazine. "And you think this would be good for me?"

I nodded again. "You even have the same color hair." Amy smiled.

The phone rang. Shelly reached for it and listened for a few moments. Then she turned to me. "It's Colleen. She wants to know if you can do her hair for Prom, too. Can she bring a picture over to show you?"

"Tell her to come on over."

I stood up. "Okay, girls, if we've made our decisions, you can hang your dresses up. Don't lose the magazines, please."

As the girls picked up their pictures, the lion's head knocker rapped out a rat-a-tat-tat. Shelly grinned and ran toward the door. "That's got to be Detective Hawksworth."

She opened the door to him, curtseyed to the floor, and rising said, "Welcome, my good man, to our humble abode."

Nigel crossed the threshold and said, "That's a beautiful dress."

Shelly grinned. "And with my hair and make-up the way I want them, *I'll* be beautiful, too."

Nigel bowed and said gallantly. "You are always an attractive young lady."

Shelly laughed. "I'm messing with you, Detective. Don't mind me."

"This family truly enjoys playing with words," he laughed.

"Of course," Shelly answered, "we're word people."

Amy wandered out of the kitchen to meet the English accent. Shelly introduced them, and the girls went upstairs, giggling.

I led Nigel into the kitchen, and he stopped at the sight of the table, strewn with hairstyle magazines. "What's all this in aid of?"

"This is preparation for Prom." I laughed as I gathered up the magazines and stacked them at the other end of the table. "Would you like a cup of coffee?"

"Have you any tea?" he asked.

I looked in the cupboard. "I have English Toffee Tea, Green Tea, Peppermint Tea, and Black Tea...all decaf, I'm afraid."

He sighed and teased, "I'll have to bring my own caffeine next time I come."

I apologized. "I'm sorry. I don't do caffeine. It doesn't do good things to me."

Nigel looked perplexed. "I haven't the slightest idea what you mean."

I felt my face grow red. "Caffeine does weird things to my heart and my breathing. I hate it. But I will buy caffeinated coffee and another coffee maker if you plan on coming around even after the case is closed."

"You'll purchase a percolator specifically for me? Why don't you just make a separate pot of coffee and fill a thermos?"

Exasperated at myself, my voice was more acerbic than usual. "Because I don't want more caffeine than is absolutely necessary. Look, a candy bar has enough caffeine to give me the jitters, about as much as three cups of coffee would do to you. That's just a candy bar. Imagine what a cup of coffee would do. It's irritating, and I'd rather not talk about it, okay?"

My attack left an uncomfortable silence in the kitchen. After a moment, I said, "I'm sorry. I have no idea why I lashed out at you like that."

Nigel walked over, put his arm around my shoulder, and smiled warmly. "No harm done."

I sighed and crossed my arms. "My body should work properly. And when it doesn't, I feel powerless."

Nigel nodded. "With your experiences, powerlessness would be anathema to you."

I smiled and felt my shoulders relax. "Thank you for understanding. And I am sorry I lashed out at you."

"I think perhaps we're tired...all of us. This town is being worn down by this murder."

"Is that why you're here? To talk about the murder?"

Nigel was amused. "I do think I will solve the murder without asking your advice."

I rolled my eyes. "I meant, do you have questions for the kids or me?"

Nigel grinned as the lion's head knocker sounded again. I moved to answer the door, calling up the stairs, "Colleen's here."

Nigel followed me from the kitchen. "Colleen?" he asked as I let her in.

"Colleen, this is Nigel Hawksworth." I gazed at him and smiled.

Colleen looked from Nigel to me. "I don't get it," she said. "What's the joke?"

I turned to her. "Colleen is an old-fashioned Irish term for a young woman."

Colleen made a funny face. "So when someone calls me by name, it's like they're calling me 'girl'. It's kind of generic, isn't it?"

Nigel quickly said, "Men usually use the term when the young lady is attractive. Ugly women have a completely different nickname."

"Oh," Colleen's eyes widened as she heard the accent. "You're the new detective, aren't you?"

Nigel nodded, and I asked, "Is that the picture?"

She handed me a picture of a French braid, loosely woven at the bottom and with pretty rhinestone pins stuck into it. "Very pretty," I told her. "Do you have the pins?"

She said she did, and I told her to take the picture upstairs to Shelly and have her put it with the other Prom hairstyle pictures so it wouldn't get lost. She ran lightly up the stairs.

Reentering the kitchen, I said, "Shall we start over? May I get you a cup of coffee or tea?"

Nigel shook his head. "How about we go to Cecily's?"

Chapter 31
Jamie's Home Life

I shouted at the kids that I was going out, and we left for downtown. I would have walked, but Nigel said he needed his car with him in case of an emergency.

"How do you stay in such good shape?" I asked as he buckled his seat belt. He had opened the door for me, and I was given the privilege of gazing at him as he walked around the car.

"Ah, you noticed, did you?" he grinned. I knew for certain he was flirting that time! "I use the equipment at the station in the mornings. Why do you ask?"

Uh-oh. I didn't want him knowing I'd been ogling him, but I had to answer. "Um, well, I mean, I was just curious."

Nigel laughed. "Right, we'll take the compliment as stated."

We arrived at Cecily's, and my face was so red, I thought it might explode. I needed a moment to compose myself, but along came Peggy Sue and Papa Jong, and I had to be sociable.

The four of us chatted as we walked through the parking lot but parted at the door. Nigel and I chose a seat as far from the front windows as possible. Peggy Sue and Papa Jong sat right up front where they could people watch. They were a funny-looking couple, she large and attractive, he at least four inches shorter and so much smaller all around. I wondered what their dinner together meant.

We ordered coffee, decaf for me and regular for Nigel. I'd fed the kids but forgotten to feed myself in the rush of evening chores, so I ordered a salad, too.

"Danielle, do you know much more about Jamie's home life than you've already told me?"

I chewed my salad for a moment, running everything I knew about Jamie through my memory. "I don't think so," I shook my head. "I know that she didn't get along with her mom. They argued a lot, usually about Linda's drinking or Jamie's rebellion. And Jamie avoided seeing her dad as much as possible. Is this what you're wanting to know?"

Nigel watched Peggy Sue and Papa Jong for a moment. "No, not quite. We just don't seem to be getting any further in the investigation. I thought going back through all our notes would open up a new avenue for us, but it didn't. So now I'm looking for some details of Jamie's life, hoping they'll help." He looked at me wistfully.

I laughed. "You look like Mikey does when he's hoping for an extra dessert." Nigel chuckled and relaxed back into his chair. I continued, "I take it your conversation with Forrest led nowhere?"

He grimaced. "He says he has nothing more to say, but I think you're right. He's holding back." He played with his knife. "I can't force him to talk, though."

"I'm sorry."

He raised his eyes to mine. "Why?"

I shrugged. "I don't like wasting your time."

He smiled. "Much of detecting is a waste of time. However," he sat forward. "Tell me a bit about Jamie's life, whatever you know. Surely something will spark an idea."

I wiped my fingers on my napkin. "That salad was good. You should have had one."

Nigel grimaced, and I took note that he wasn't a green food enthusiast.

After thinking a moment, I said, "You know that Jamie's grades dropped radically after a visit with her dad, right?"

Nigel sat forward again. "No, I don't. I knew her grades dropped periodically but not why."

"Well, Jamie was pretty much a solid B student, according to a friend of mine who teaches at the school."

"Which teacher?" He whipped out a small notebook.

"I should have said, 'she taught.'" I answered. "She moved to another state a couple of years ago."

"I need her name, anyway."

I gave him her name and the phone number she had while she lived here. "Anyway, Jamie was a B student. But a couple of times a year, like clockwork, she would be on academic probation and wouldn't be allowed to play sports. We finally figured out it always happened after a visit with her dad. At first, we thought she didn't like coming home."

Nigel raised his eyebrows.

I grabbed my coffee cup to warm my hands. "Then we began to look closer, and we noticed that she wore darker clothes when her grades dropped, too. We wondered if there was abuse going on, so my friend reported her suspicions to the school authorities. Someone investigated, we didn't know who, but the powers that be determined that Jamie's dad wasn't actually injuring her."

Nigel nodded. "If there is no witness and the child won't or can't say something, there is nothing authorities can do." He wrapped his hands around his mug. This conversation was giving us cold hands.

He continued, "On the other hand, if she was experiencing emotional or verbal abuse, they wouldn't consider her endangered." He stared at his mug. "Which is stupid."

"We wondered if he was watching R- or X-rated movies and making sexual and-or violent comments when she was with him," I continued. "We thought that might account for her behavior."

Nigel grimaced. "And then she told Hannah and Michael her dad was hitting her."

I considered that a moment. "Yeah, she did. But I never saw bruises on her. You took them through it pretty carefully, and if I remember correctly, she only said it once."

"He may have only hit her once," Nigel said.

I nodded slowly and said, "Maybe. I wonder –"

Nigel stood abruptly. I was startled, but I stood with him, willing to accept that he sensed danger or something. He took my elbow and guided me to the door. After paying and leaving a tip, we walked to the car. In silence.

Nigel opened my car door for me and I climbed in. Before he opened his door, someone approached. They talked for about a minute, and the other person walked away.

When Nigel climbed into his seat, I asked, "Was that the mayor? Is everything all right?"

He smiled at me and said, "Yes and yes." He started the car and drove down to the river on the edge of town. The moon glided across the little ripples of water, and a breeze ruffled the leaves overhead. It was melancholy. And peaceful.

Nigel turned toward me. "The people at the next table had stopped talking and were listening to our conversation. It deemed it time to leave."

I grinned. "Cecily's may not have been the best place for us to talk."

He grinned back but sobered immediately. "The mayor wanted me to know that George Graham is not only a major contributor of gossip in this town, but that he may just be the fountainhead of most of it."

I giggled. "He might be. He's such an institution, I never considered he might know something. He's so good at insinuating, never actually giving information. You know?"

Nigel nodded. "I will talk with him tomorrow, though. And with Larry Sneider."

I grimaced. "I understand he isn't all creepy-like. One of the teens said he helps out at the food pantry and he does some work on the local charity houses."

Even in the dark, Nigel's smile was attractive. "Are you looking for the good in him?"

I sighed. "Maybe."

Nigel started the car. As we rounded the corner toward my home, he asked, "Did you spend a lot of time with Jamie, like you do with some of the other teens?"

"I tried. She wasn't very interested, so I just made sure she knew I was here for her, if she ever needed someone." I looked at the lighted windows. "It seems she preferred my kids."

I was startled by the chuckle in the other seat. "It would seem your children are following in your footsteps. You should be chuffed with yourself, Mum."

"Chuffed? That's a new one."

He grinned. "Shall I educate you in British slang? It means, 'to be proud of yourself'. Or, in American, well done, Mum."

The praise startled me, and I blushed.

As soon as I got inside, I called Natalie. "Want to take a walk?" I asked.

"I have to iron my slacks for tomorrow, and there's a raisin nut cake in the oven," she answered. "You want to come over for some tea and cake?"

Before I left the house, I let Ramon out and checked on the kids. Amy, Colleen, and Shelly were practicing different dance moves, still preparing for Prom. I wondered what the boys did the week before

Prom. Did they even think about it, other than getting the tux? Hannah was reading a book, and Mikey was playing with his Legos. He had a great idea for a new invention and wanted to try it out. I let them know I'd be back 'some time' and that it was nearly bedtime.

Natalie had already finished the ironing and was eating when I arrived. My tea sat on the table with a piece of cake. "You walked?" she asked when I came in.

"You're only two blocks away," I retorted. "If I can't outrun a bad guy in that short time, I deserve to be murdered."

Natalie glared at me. "Not funny."

"You're right. I'm sorry."

She nodded and asked, "Anything new?"

"Nigel and I talked about the potential abuse Jamie suffered from her dad."

Natalie stared at her cake. "Oh, boy."

I nodded soberly. "We talked about the plummeting grades and dark clothes after she came home. Add in the sexual activity, and we have to wonder if there was more going on than R-rated movies."

"As if those aren't bad enough."

"Yeah, I know, but to be sexually abused . . ."

Abe walked in. "Don't tell me someone I know is being abused. I don't think I could go to school with someone and not do anything about it." He sat heavily next to his mom.

Natalie rubbed his shoulder comfortingly. "No one who goes to school with you anymore," she said gently.

Abe sighed. "Good. Wait. Do you mean the abuser has gone somewhere else?" He looked steadily at Natalie. "What are we going to do about it?"

Natalie's face lit up. "I'm so proud of you. But, honey, you can't fix this one. It's already been taken care of."

The sigh of relief was heartfelt. "I'm so glad." He jumped up and grabbed a huge slice of cake. As he walked out of the dining room, he asked, "Mind if I take this piece of cake?"

Chapter 32
We Have To Live Here

Natalie growled at him, and he laughed as he ran up the stairs. "That was easy," she commented as a door slammed.

I rolled my eyes. "If only all of life's problems could be solved so easily."

We moved into the living room, to softer chairs. "Your cake was good," I lied. Natalie's baking usually resembles sawdust and spices.

"Thanks. Where do you think this leaves the investigation?"

I sipped my tea. "I don't know. I honestly think Jamie's dad deserves to be hung, drawn, and quartered, but does it have anything to do with her murder? I mean directly, of course. You know what I mean." I flapped my hand at her.

"No, I don't know what you mean." Natalie was looking up the stairs. "They can't hear us, can they?"

"Should we talk outside?" I asked. Natalie looked up the stairs again and shook her head, so I continued, "But he's indirectly responsible because his abuse caused Jamie to be sexually active at a much younger age than she probably would have been otherwise."

"That's assuming she would've waited longer to be sexually active. Many girls start young nowadays," Natalie answered.

I shrugged. "I guess you never know, but I still think he's at least indirectly responsible."

"For her sexual activity, yes," Natalie tucked her feet under her. "And for the many emotional scars, too. But I don't think you can blame him for her murder."

"Okay, just for the sake of argument, let's say we can't blame him...for anything except what he's done to Jamie. What next?" I prompted.

"Well," Natalie jumped up. "Let me get paper and pen."

I groaned. "We've been through this exercise already," I called to her. "Oh, and did I tell you I saw Peggy Sue and Papa Jong at Cecily's Café this evening?"

Natalie plopped back onto the couch. "Why were you at Cecily's?"

"Because I don't have any caffeine at home." I smiled.

Natalie stared. "Nope, can't say I'm following you."

"Nigel stopped by. I didn't have any caffeine, so we went to Cecily's. I told him I'd buy a coffee maker and caffeinated coffee for him if he was going to continue coming over after the investigation was over..." I waited for it.

"Don't stop there!"

I grinned. "Well, he didn't get the hint, but he was amazed that I would buy another 'percolator', as he put it, just so he could have caffeine. I had to explain –"

"Right, but how did you end up at Cecily's?"

"Oh, we went for coffee. Peggy Sue was there with Papa Jong."

"They aren't dating or anything." Natalie waved her hand dismissively, unfazed by my implied criticism. "Peggy Sue isn't interested in a relationship. Besides, she's just gotten her daughter and grandson in her life."

I thought back to our conversation at baseball practice. "No, I don't think that's right. When we were talking, she sounded really sad about never having married. I think she would have liked to have had a family."

Natalie swirled her tea around. "I guess I never thought about it," she answered. "But this is off-subject. I have paper here. Let's decide who's guilty."

I shook my head. "The way I felt when I turned the Spruce Bruce in to Nigel, I don't feel like playing games. If we do this, we do it for real."

Natalie met my gaze and nodded. "Right. We do this for real. It's time to get to the bottom of this, and that means we don't let friendship stand in the way." She stopped a moment. "And I recall us saying the same thing before. Where did that list go, anyway?" She looked around her immaculate living room.

Ignoring her side comment, I soberly reminded her, "But we still have to live here when it's over, and if we hurt someone badly through questioning them, we'll have to live with it for the rest of our lives, and with them."

"Or until they move," Natalie countered with a smile.

"I'm serious."

"I know," she said with a sigh, "but you're so somber about it, it makes me want to tap dance or tell a joke. Okay already. I get that we have to be careful. Let's get down to it." She pulled out an old photo album, placed her paper on it, and headed it 'suspects'.

"After tonight's conversation with Nigel, I suppose I'd put Jamie's dad at the top of the list," I told her.

"I wouldn't put him at the *top* of the list," she mumbled as she wrote, "but I agree he belongs on the list. Reason?"

I set my empty cup on the floor next to my chair. "I suppose Jamie could have threatened to tell someone in authority about the abuse."

"Yeah, like the Spruce Bruce," Natalie scoffed.

"He's not the only police officer in town. Besides, I'm sure Children's Services would have investigated. Maybe."

Natalie nodded. "Yeah, maybe. I'll write it down, and on a scale of one to ten, I'd give him a three. Who's next?"

"Didn't someone say something about him not wanting to pay child support? And that he has a new girlfriend?"

Natalie sighed. "Yeah, but still a three. Again, who's next?"

"We already talked about Jamie's boyfriend, Forrest. He may have wanted to get rid of her so he could date Kelly Green. They could have argued and it escalated to the point of murder."

Natalie wrote it down. "Works for me, but do we know where he was that night?"

"Nigel says no one has an alibi."

"I'll give him a seven," she wrote. "Not lower because of Kelly Green, but not higher because we don't even know if he likes her, or if he has a temper."

"And the police must have nothing on him or they would be keeping him in a jail cell." I sat straighter. "Oh, I asked Shelly about him, about why girls might fight over him."

Natalie looked eager. "And?"

"I think you were right about him just being really nice. Kind, and compassionate, and maybe a good listener." I shrugged. "Shelly says he's all of those. And he's usually available to walk someone home in the dark."

"Wow. Nice kid. And that goes a long way toward winning a girl's heart."

I nodded. "Especially if she has a dysfunctional home life."

"Wait a minute, Abe's nice," Natalie objected. "Why aren't the girls fighting over him?"

I shifted in my seat. "Maybe it's because Forrest and the girls are from the same economic class." *How do I say, 'Because Abe's from a rich family'?* I prayed I wouldn't have to be more explicit.

Natalie nodded. "Makes sense." I sighed in relief. She crossed something out and wrote. "I'm dropping his number to a five, though."

"Sounds good to me."

"Right. So we have Jamie's dad and Jamie's boyfriend. What else of Jamie's do we have?" She grinned at me.

"We have Jamie's rival, Kelly Green," I answered her grin. "And it would be because she wanted Jamie's boyfriend."

"I'll give her a five," Natalie wrote it all down. "Teen-age hormones are notoriously out of control."

I laughed. "You must have been a fun teen-ager."

She sighed. "I was. I think I slammed three sets of hinges off my bedroom door before I moved out." She shook her head. "I'm surprised my parents still love me."

"I'm not," I retorted.

"Now," she turned back to the paper. "Who else do we consider?"

"The Spruce Bruce, of course."

Natalie thought about that. "I suppose so."

"I would think it's obvious. He and Jamie were involved in a sexually intimate relationship, which would have ruined his career and probably sent him to jail for statutory rape, if she had told anyone."

"But we don't know that he went beyond that."

"No, but we know even less about some of the others," I insisted.

Natalie shrugged. "I just don't want to write him on our list, simply because we don't like him."

I nodded. "I totally get that, but I think there is more evidence against him than anyone else, so far."

Natalie wrote. "All right, he's on the list. But I don't know what number to give him."

I sighed. "Same here. Let's skip a number on him, or you could just write, 'high' next to his name."

"I don't think he smokes pot," she murmured.

I laughed. "Something that means 'high number' or 'high on the list'. You know what I'm talking about."

Natalie grinned, then hopped in her chair. "The paper. The one the kids wrote at the party. Do you remember who was on it?"

An image of the paper drifted through my mind. "Officer Nichols."

Natalie wrote his name. "Right. Didn't someone write that he was seeing Jamie?"

"Hang on, let me think . . . no, someone drew a heart and crossed it out."

"That's pretty vague." Natalie chewed on the end of her pen. "Oh, wait. Did we also read something about Mr. Jacobs, the French teacher?"

"Yeah, we did, but didn't we decide that couldn't be true?"

Natalie scoffed. "We aren't passing judgment right now, just writing down suspects."

"Fine, write him down." I rubbed my eyes.

"He was on the paper, after all," Natalie murmured as she wrote.

"Oh," I bounced in my seat. "I remember. There was something on there about cheerleading."

"There was?"

"Yeah, don't you remember? It looked like cheerleading, and there was a TR dash O, and there was an X through it all."

"What in the world is that supposed to mean?"

I furrowed my brow in remembrance. "Shelly said something a few months ago about Jamie wanting to try out for cheer. I think they let her, but they had decided in advance not to accept her."

"Oh, yeah, I remember that. Jamie got really mad, because she had taken the try-outs seriously, hadn't she?"

"Yeah, and I think there was a lot of trouble about it."

Natalie tapped the paper with her pen. "So, what does this have to do with Jamie's murder?"

I threw up my hands. "I have no idea. It was on the paper."

Natalie threw herself back against the cushions of the chair. I did the same thing. "It always makes sense in books," I wailed.

Natalie chuckled and sighed. "Does anyone else go on the list?"

I pondered. "Her mom?"

"Nuh-uh. No way. Linda would *not* do something like that to Jamie. Not to her daughter," Natalie crossed her arms.

"Patricide, Matricide, Infanticide, they're out there. We see it on the evening news too often to ignore it, so I think Linda belongs on the paper."

"No!" Natalie's shoulders were hunched and she looked . . . frightened? Angry?

I stared. "No?"

"No. I refuse to put Linda's name on the list. There is no way she would have done that to her daughter. *You* might think a mother in this town is capable of killing her daughter, but I refuse to." She blinked at the tears that threatened to overflow.

"Whoa. Hey, Natalie, what's going on? Why are you so triggered?"

She stared at the wall behind me for nearly a minute, blinking back tears. Finally, her shoulders sagged, and she dropped her head. "Tabitha, oh, my baby girl, heard a rumor that Linda killed Jamie. She asked me how bad she would have to be for me to do that to her."

I took two steps, knelt down by her chair, and held her. "Of course, you told her you it would never happen."

She nodded. "But if one mom can, another can, too, right? That's Tabitha's reasoning."

"Not this mom. Not this family," I said firmly. "And Tabitha knows it. She probably just needed to hear it."

Natalie shrugged, sniffed, and sat up.

"Are you okay, now?" I asked.

She nodded and wrote Linda's name on the paper. "I hate this. I want my home town to be a safe place to live and raise my kids. And I hate, hate, hate even the *idea* that a mom would kill her child."

I returned to my chair and said slowly, "I think it would have to be a fit of temper. Not to mention, she may have been too drunk to do anything at all. And that would rate her about a one or two out of ten."

Natalie smiled through wet lashes. "You're trying to make me feel better." But she wrote it down.

"Tabitha will be fine," I assured her. "And so will you."

She nodded, and we sat silently for a moment. "Papa Jong."

"What about him?" Natalie sniffed.

"Put him on the list," I answered.

Natalie's mouth dropped. "Why?"

Chapter 33

I Hate The Idea

"Well, I just remembered. He said he was setting up a sunglasses display in his shop when we bumped into him, remember?" Natalie nodded. "But he already had one set up. I noticed it when we walked in. So..."

"So why would he say that? Wow. Good observation. But it doesn't necessarily mean he had anything to do with Jamie's murder." Natalie sat back again.

"No, but why would he then tell us what Jamie's mom told him? Was it genuine, or was it to distract us?"

"Maybe he was just looking for an excuse to tell us what he knew, hoping you would tell Nigel," Natalie suggested.

I thought about that. "Maybe. But why lie at all?"

Natalie jumped up and ran to the kitchen. She threw the cordless phone in my lap as she returned to the couch. "Call Detective Hawksworth," she commanded. "Find out what Linda told him. She is awake now, isn't she?"

I dialed and Nigel answered on the second ring. He sounded tired but alert. I suddenly realized I had no right to call him, and I didn't even know the time. I cleared my throat. "Hi, Nigel, this is Danielle."

He perked up. "Danielle, this is a pleasant surprise."

I felt awful and glared at Natalie. It was her fault I was calling him. "Well, umm, this isn't a social call, Nigel. I'm sorry to disturb you. It's just that Natalie and I were wondering if Linda Sneider was out of her coma, and if she's said anything."

There was a prolonged silence on the line. I decided I probably wouldn't need to go shopping for new clothes after all, since he would never speak to me again. I sighed in discouragement.

"She is awake, but she doesn't remember how she ended up in the hospital. The last thing she remembers is Papa Jong taking her home, so we think she's missing about three or four hours. That's not unusual in these types of cases. Are you and Natalie trying to help again? Because, as you know, I'm a trained professional, and I do know how to do my job."

Guilt washed over me. "I know. And I believe you are very good at your job, or our Sherriff's department wouldn't want you over here helping out. But Natalie and I were talking, and we were wondering about Linda. That's all."

Nigel chuckled. "You're a pathetic liar, Danielle. Stop trying."

The chuckle encouraged me, and I smiled. "Okay, I'll stop trying to lie if you'll stop reminding me how good you are. I can't stop helping now. Like I said before, this is my town, and these are my kids, and I love them an awful lot."

He sighed. "Deal." I thanked him for the information and said good-bye.

"Don't make me do that again," I glared at Natalie. "I like his friendship, and I don't want to jeopardize it by asking for inside information."

"Like you said, this is your town, these are your kids, and you love them an awful lot. You'll keep asking, because you can't help taking care of people. I think you were born a mother. How many dolls did you have?"

"Fourteen, and a play kitchen with table and chairs, and a doll cradle and high chair, and every accessory available at the time," I answered with a smile. "Okay, so back to work."

Natalie nodded. "So what do we know about Linda?"

I tucked my feet up under me. "We know that she got hit over the head with a clay flower pot and has been hospitalized. We know that she's awake, but she doesn't remember anything after Papa Jong took her home. I think that's all we know about her."

Natalie shook her head. "First, we know she's an alcoholic. We know that she and Jamie didn't get along very well. We know that she was looking for a fifth of vodka, already drunk. Sometimes people get drunk so they have the courage to do something difficult."

I nodded.

Natalie continued, "We know that Papa Jong said he offered her a ride home. He didn't tell us he took her home; just that he offered her a ride. And we know that she doesn't remember anything after she says he took her home. Did he take her home? Or does she remember him offering, and she assumes he did?"

I pondered this a moment. "I think we're going to have to assume he took her home. There must be corroborating evidence somewhere, like the neighbors seeing them arrive." I looked at my toes. They needed painting again. "Maybe Papa Jong hit her."

"Oh, come on, Danielle, Papa Jong's a nice guy. Give him a break."

I was shocked. "Do you realize you were the one who wanted to do this exercise, and you're defending practically everyone I suggest? Either we do this or we don't. We can't do it part way."

"Gah!" Natalie shot up out of her chair. "What I wouldn't give to take a look at Nigel's notes on this case. Why isn't he telling you more, anyway?"

I rolled my eyes. "You know why. We're doing our best, and that's going to have to be good enough. Without the police showing us their case file."

Natalie growled. "I'm done for tonight." She threw the photo album onto the floor and herself onto the couch.

"Don't you at least want to try to eliminate some of these people from our list?"

"Why don't you? I can't take any more right now." She turned and lifted her feet onto the couch, laying her head on a pillow.

I reached over and picked up the album and paper. For several minutes there was no noise as I went over in my mind everything we had learned. Abe walked through the room. He pointed at his mom and raised his eyebrows, asking if she was asleep. I shrugged that I didn't know and went back to my paper.

Finally, I sighed and set it down.

Natalie asked, "Any good?"

"Well, I think we can eliminate Officer Nichols and the French teacher."

"Mr. Jacobs?"

I nodded. "And I think I agree with you that Papa Jong lied about the sunglasses as an excuse to give me information to pass on."

Natalie nodded. "Anyone else?

I looked at the list of names again. "I think that leaves us with the four people we've always had – Jamie's dad, Jamie's mom, Jamie's boyfriend, and Jamie's rival."

Natalie flipped a hand. "We just don't have enough information."

I picked up the album. Turning pages, I saw that Abe and Tabitha were in early elementary school. There were sports and school program pictures, and vacation shots. I saw many of the kids who were Shelly's friends, all lined up, smiling, sometimes with teeth missing, sometimes with mud on their faces.

"Who's this?" I asked. Natalie lifted her head wearily and looked where I was pointing.

"Oh, that's Forrest Pearson. Don't you recognize the nose? Even as a kid, he had that hooked nose." She looked more closely. "Poor kid; must be hard living with that nose."

I nodded with a smile. "And that Adam's apple," I agreed. Closing the book, I stood to leave.

"Do you want a ride home?" she asked. "I'm not really comfortable with you walking."

"Thanks, but I have my pepper spray and flashlight. I'll be fine."

"All right," she said, unconvinced, "but text me when you get there, okay?"

I assured her I would.

As I approached my house, I noticed a car parked on the street, just past my driveway, and wondered if my flippant remark about out-running a murderer was about to come back and haunt me.

Peggy Sue jumped from the car. I sighed in relief.

"Aren't you ever home?" she demanded as I approached.

"Hi, Peggy Sue, what's up?"

"I need to talk to you," she said quietly. We walked into a silent house, except for two hungry cats, and I hoped it meant the kids were in bed.

As we entered the living room, I asked, "What's up?"

Peggy Sue fell rather than sat on the couch and announced, "Papa Jong wants to date me."

I grinned at her. "I'm so happy for you!"

"Are you kidding? Look at me. I'm large. You have to admit I'm large."

"Well, you're not fat," I said carefully. "Just tall and larger boned than he is."

She made a scoffing noise. "I didn't say I'm fat. I said I'm large. And he's small, really small. We'd look ridiculous."

"Peggy Sue, do you like him? I mean, are you two friends?"

She nodded. "Of course we are. He's funny and smart and interesting."

"Would you enjoy spending time with him?"

"Already do."

"So then, does the rest of it really matter?"

Peggy Sue jumped up and paced for a few moments. "What if he's a . . . I mean, what if he . . ." She stopped and whispered, "What if he's a killer?"

I asked as calmly as I could, "What do you mean? Do you know something?"

She paced again. "Well, you know that he took Linda Sneider home, and that's the last thing she remembers. What if that's because that's all that happened before she was hit?"

"You're saying that you think he may have hit her over the head?"

She shook her head and said softly, "I really can't believe he would do that. Not really. But it's what I'm afraid of." She sat down again, all of her vitality seemingly gone. "What am I going to do? If he did hit her, then he probably killed Jamie. If he didn't, I'm suspecting an innocent man, someone I really like."

Tears flooded her eyes. "I really want to go out with him, but if I suspect him and he is innocent, then I might ruin my chance to be happy with a really good man. But I just can't take the chance."

I gave her a quick hug. "Why don't you give it a few days? Maybe this will be over and done soon."

"He wants to take me to dinner again Sunday night. In Eugene this time. What do I tell him?"

"What did you say when he asked you?"

"I said I'd love to. But I'm not sure." She was up and pacing again. "I'm a grown woman, forty-four years old, a *grandmother* for crying out loud. And here I'm acting like a teen-age kid. I should be able to make up my mind."

I grinned. "I've just had a great idea. Why don't you let this rest for a couple of days. If this murder isn't solved or Papa Jong isn't proven innocent by the time he picks you up for your date, then either Natalie or I will double date with you." I wondered briefly who I'd ask. "How does that sound?"

"Oh, would you?" A beautiful smile lit her face. "That would solve everything. And I don't think Papa Jong would mind."

"And if he did, he wouldn't say anything about it," I said with a laugh.

Peggy Sue went home relieved in her mind, but I was left feeling intense pressure. This mystery had to be solved. I cared about these people whose lives were being affected. I was going to do something, if I could only think of what that something should be.

"In the meantime, Danielle, get to bed," I told myself. "Tomorrow's another day, and you have to be there for it." With a sigh, I turned off the lights, checked my doors with their beautiful new locks, and dragged myself up the stairs. All three kids were asleep, and soon I was, too.

I AWOKE AT 7:00 THE next morning, exhausted. My subconscious mind had been working on the problem all night long, and I felt like I'd been trundling a wheelbarrow around and around the house. I dragged myself downstairs and found the kids eating breakfast. Shelly had raisin bran cereal. Hannah was eating toast and peanut butter, and Mikey had a piece of cake.

Cake?

"Were did you get that?" I asked. A knot began to form in my stomach.

He shrugged, his mouth full. When he swallowed, he said, "It was on the kitchen counter. I thought you made it."

I looked at Shelly and Hannah in a panic. "Did either of you make that cake?" I asked.

Eyes large, they said, "No."

I shook the cake from Mikey's hand. It landed on the floor, and as I ran him into the bathroom, I told the girls, "Don't let the animals eat that."

I gave Mikey the ipecac and left him to throw it up. Back in the kitchen, sure enough, there it was. It looked like a coffee cake in one of those disposable pans.

"Did either of you have cake?" I asked. Both girls shook their heads.

Hannah began to cry. "I told him he could have it, Mom. I thought you'd made it for us for breakfast. It has raisins, and apples, and cinnamon in it."

I hugged her and tersely told her it was okay. Then I called Nigel.

He answered on the first ring, "Good morning, Detective Nigel Hawksworth."

"Nigel?" Fear had raised my voice more than an octave.

"Danielle, what is it?"

My vision blurred, and there was a roaring in my ears. I took a couple of calming breaths.

"Danielle! Are you all right?"

I tried to steady my voice, but it still shook. "Someone left a cake on my counter, and Mikey's been eating it. Nigel, they got in again."

"I'm on my way."

Shelly and Hannah were holding hands at the table. Mikey was still being noisy in the bathroom. I took another deep breath, sent the girls what I hoped was a reassuring look, and said, "He's on his way."

On wobbly legs, I went back into the bathroom, rubbed Mikey's back, and prayed. Just a few moments later, Nigel's car screeched to a halt outside our house. He banged the lion's head knocker. When I opened the door to him, he grabbed me in a hug, asking, "Is anyone hurt?"

I pushed away. "Mikey's throwing up the cake he ate. He only took a couple of bites before I found him. The rest is in the kitchen. None of us made it, but it was sitting on the counter this morning when the kids got up." Hands clenched, I demanded, "How long is this going to continue?"

His face grim, he answered, "It ends now."

As I quietly followed him, I felt a bit of the tension loosen. He glanced at the cake and the girls. Pulling out his phone, he barked orders for forensics to come to the house immediately. Putting his phone away, he asked the girls if they'd had any cake. They shook their heads again, fear still etched on their faces.

Chapter 34
This Ends Now

He knelt down between their chairs and took their hands. I blinked back tears. "We have to take this much more seriously than the last time someone entered the house," he said calmly. "We've changed the locks and *still* he or she got in. We'll go over the house bit by bit this time, and we'll test the cake for anything nasty that may be in it, although I doubt there is." He smiled reassuringly. "Whoever is doing this hasn't actually injured any of you, and we have to take that into account. However, you'll have to stay somewhere else for a time."

The girls looked at me. I tried to keep my face blank, because I couldn't give them a reassuring smile, and I didn't want them to see the fear churning inside. Who could be coming into my house? Why would they? What did they want? I just didn't understand.

Mikey came in from the bathroom, pale and shaken. "I took an extra dose, Mom, to make sure there was nothing left in my stomach. I'm happy to announce that it's completely empty." He eased himself onto a kitchen chair and stared at the table.

I bent down to hug him. "Mikey, I'm so sorry, baby. Will you please forgive me for getting involved in this? All of you?" I looked around at my children.

Shelly said, "Mom, you had to. And we asked you to, remember? This is our town, and the people who live here are our friends and family. We can't let this go on forever. Besides, God is protecting us, and we'll be just fine, especially if you keep that ipecac on hand."

Her feeble joke made the others smile, but not me.

"Mom," Hannah said, "this started *before* you got involved, remember? So there's no need to apologize."

I sighed and tried to smile. "I wish that made me feel better, Hannah."

"Right," Nigel said decisively. "Now it's time for you to pack your bags and head out the door. But," he held up his right hand like a traffic warden, "you'll pack one at a time, and with supervision."

We all nodded. This time, there was no argument. He asked, "Do you ladies prefer to have a woman police constable . . . officer to watch you pack?"

We looked around the table and shook our heads. "No," Hannah said, "we'd prefer you."

As she said it, the sickening thought went through my head, *Why do we trust him? We hardly know him.* I shook it off quickly. I wasn't willing to go there right now. Our friendship with him, like all of the rest of this mess, had to be left in God's hands.

Nigel and I went upstairs with Shelly to start the packing. We left Hannah and Mikey in the kitchen with orders to touch nothing. Each of the children packed with Nigel's and my supervision. Then it was my turn.

I had a moment of panic when I realized he would be seeing my underwear. I shrugged. *I don't care. There's too much at stake for me to think about anything but my precious children's safety.*

As we finished packing my bag, we heard the lion's head knocker on the front door.

Shelly called up the stairs, "Shall I answer it?"

"No, I will." Nigel called as he ran down the stairs and let the forensics team in. He issued orders, and as they got underway, he walked us out to the minivan. Opening the doors, he held us back so he could look inside. I wanted to cry; the van was a mess. There were fast food wrappers, school papers, and an old science experiment on the floor. Mentally, I sighed again.

"The cats!" I yelped. "And Ramon. And Asia."

"Asia?" Nigel asked.

"Our bird. Who will feed them if I can't come back to my house?"

The kids and I looked at Nigel. With a smile, he answered, "I'll come to your house once a day to feed the animals and change their waters."

Instantly, Hannah and Mikey hugged him. I didn't want to put him to more trouble, but as he'd said, there was no way I was coming here alone. Silently, we climbed into the van.

As he closed my door for me, Nigel said, "Someone will be over later this morning to interview you all, okay?" We nodded and he waved us off.

We stopped at the end of the street, and I announced, "Let's go to Auntie Natalie's house first, okay?" There were subdued cheers. "We need to let her know what's going on. And I think I need a cup of tea."

"Mom," Shelly asked, "are you going to drive me to school every day from Eugene?"

I sighed. "I guess so, Shelly. Unless the hotel in Junction City has a vacancy."

Mikey spoke up. "Hey, did you remember our school books?"

This time I groaned. "No, I'm sorry."

"That's all right," Hannah was quick to reassure me. "We can catch up when we move back home."

We had only gone a block when my cell phone rang. I handed the phone to Shelly, and she said, "It's Gramma G."

"Oh, my goodness," I whispered. Taking the phone, I answered with false cheer, "Hi,

Mom, how are you?"

"My question is, 'How are you?' Have those police solved the case, yet?"

"I'm fine, and the kids are fine. The police are still working on the case, but they are really close to having all the evidence they need."

"Sure they are," she shot back. "And when do they plan on serving the warrant? Tell me that. You and my grandchildren are living in a town with a murderer. Raymond, my daughter and grandchildren are living with a murderer."

"Hi, Dad," I called out as I rolled my eyes. The kids giggled quietly.

"Raymond, she says hello. But don't think I'm going to be sidetracked, young lady."

"Mom, I'm not living with a murderer," I answered her. The kids gasped. "Every one of my kids is very nice."

Mom made an exasperated sound. "Don't you get snarky with me, Danielle Grace. I know exactly where you're living. And I think you and the children should come out here to New Jersey right now and stay with us until the murder is solved. I'm sure your father agrees with me, don't you, Raymond? Tell her you agree with me."

Dad said something that I didn't catch.

"Mom, we don't need to leave town. The police have it under control."

"Raymond, she doesn't want to come," Mom said. "Tell her she has to... No, I'm *not* giving you the phone."

Taking advantage of the distraction, I said, "Hey, Mom, I have to go. We're running errands, and I'm sitting on the side of the road. I love you, talk to you soon," and pressed the off button before Mom could finish her protest.

The kids and I looked at each other and sighed in relief.

They giggled when I repeated the conversation, but the momentary uplifting of our spirits from my mom's call didn't last even the few seconds needed to reach Natalie's house. As we pulled into the driveway, Shea was taking the garbage can to the curb. "Morning," he called cheerfully. Our faces brought him over to the van quickly. "What's wrong?"

I explained, and he insisted we all stay with them. "I won't take, 'no' for an answer, and Natalie would be furious with me if I tried." He smiled gently as he opened the van door for me. "Besides, you're family. And family takes care of each other."

I was past arguing and agreed we would stay with them for a couple of days. Prom would be over by then, and if this wasn't cleared up, we would move to a hotel. God would have to provide the funds. Maybe Pastor Ted could help, too.

Natalie handed around mugs of hot cocoa and buttered toast. We munched quietly for a while. When there was enough food in our stomachs, I asked Shelly if she felt up to going to school. She would be late, but she would only miss her first class.

"Yeah," she said. "Now that I feel less afraid, I'm ready to tell everyone how close we were to losing Mikey, and how he threw up in the bathroom for, like, ten minutes."

"I did not. I didn't," he insisted. "Did I? You're not really going to tell people that, are you?"

Shelly tilted her head. "Maybe I'll tell them that you had to go to the hospital and get your stomach pumped."

"Shelly, don't exaggerate too much," I told her with a smile. She grinned at me as Mikey expostulated against being the butt of the joke.

I left the squabbling and called Nigel. "Please put my trash out to the curb. I probably shouldn't be worrying about something so mundane, but it does tend to overflow if I don't get it emptied."

"What time does the dustbin lorry come round?" he asked.

I pondered that a moment. "Would that be the garbage truck?" He grunted. "Does one grunt mean, 'yes'?"

He chuckled and said, more clearly this time, "Yes."

"About ten o'clock this morning."

"I'll get a team to sift the garbage right away."

"What do you mean, you'll get a team to sift the garbage right away?" I asked. *I don't want anyone going through my garbage,* I silently protested.

He explained patiently. "A team will have to go through your garbage to see if the intruder left something, like a packet for the cake, assuming it isn't made from scratch."

I thought about that. "It isn't store bought," I considered. "Because it's in a pan, so it must have a box. Wow, I didn't think of that."

Nigel chuckled. "Right. I am pretty good at my job."

"Of course you are," I cheered him on. "So get back to it, Mister, and stop gabbing with me."

He laughed as he hung up.

We got through the day. I let Hannah and Mikey read books and play video games. I thought it would comfort them. Shelly did an excellent job of dramatizing the incident to her friends. In fact, she did so well, a delegation of teens showed up after school. They wanted to help in any way they could. I was touched by their concern.

Since they insisted on helping, I considered how I could honor their need to *do* something. *It's so hard to feel powerless, Lord. What can they do for me that won't get them injured or in Nigel's way?*

They patiently waited until an idea popped into my head. "You can't help find the person who keeps getting into my house," I said. "Detective Hawksworth and our police department are doing that. But my younger kids are still fearful. Would some of you spend time with them this afternoon or evening?" They were all over that, batting around ideas.

"We could go to the movies," suggested a teen with his license.

"How about skating?" said another. "They're younger, and they might like that."

"Or we could take them swimming at that big wave pool in Springfield," another one suggested.

I intervened. "Why don't you decide what you want and can afford to do, and let me know by five o'clock, okay? Then you can pick them up after dinner. Please have them home by ten, so they can get a decent night's sleep."

Everyone agreed to that, and for another twenty minutes, they happily stood in the driveway discussing their plans to help out the "younger ones". Lenny came to the door and informed me that they were going to a G-rated movie and then to 'that totally awesome bakery place' in downtown Eugene. I wasn't sure Hannah would be impressed with their choice of movie, but I knew she would love to go with the older kids, especially to Sweet Life bakery, a family favorite. I thanked them and went in search of Hannah and Mikey to let them know. They were thrilled.

When the teens came after dinner, the numbers had swelled to nearly twenty. "Good gracious," I exclaimed. "Are you *all* going?" There were five minivans parked in the driveway and along the street, and all of the kids were standing around the front door.

Chapter 35
When They Leave, You Leave

Several of the teens tried to answer at once, and Edgar, with his megaphone voice, declared himself spokesperson. "As you can see, Mrs. B, you and your family are important to us. Besides," he grinned, "the more, the merrier." And all twenty or so teens cheered.

Hannah and Mikey walked outside and stopped short. Huge grins lit up their faces. Shelly walked out with Abe, Tabitha, and Danny, who had asked to go, too. They all climbed into the various minivans (*I didn't know there were that many minivans in town,* I thought) and drove away, whooping and honking to each other. I shook my head and smiled. There are times I really love my town.

When they had left, I couldn't take the waiting any longer and called Nigel.

"What's going on?" I asked. "I haven't heard from you all day."

"Officer Nichols stopped by for statements," he protested.

"Well, yes, but he isn't you. You have the answers."

"Right," I could hear his grin. "That's all I'm good for, is it?"

"Pfft, you know what I mean," I grinned back.

"We've been through your home and found nothing that indicates how the intruder entered."

I sighed in frustration as he continued, "I know how you feel, Danielle, and I'm sorry. But we must accept that he has a key or some kind of device for entering your home."

"Oh, man. You think he has a lock-pick?"

"Perhaps. Although the lock faces aren't scratched, so he may have a master key or even a duplicate key." He became brisk. "I should know more tomorrow when I've interviewed a few more people. You stay where you are and don't even think about moving home."

"Nigel," I said quickly, before he could hang up. "Prom is day after tomorrow. I need to be there to help the girls get ready. Besides, Shelly's date will want to pick her up there, and Abe will need this bathroom here to get himself ready."

"If you need to be home to prepare for the dance, then I'll be there while you are. When they all leave, so do you," he emphasized, "*even if you must leave the house messy*. Do you understand?"

I smiled. "Yes, Nigel." After hanging up the phone, I snuggled down on the couch and thought deeply about the case. There *must* be a reason for all that was happening. I *must* figure out what it is.

I fell asleep, and Natalie and Shea left me there until the kids came home at ten o'clock. They were full of their adventure, and I listened for nearly an hour to a detailed account of the movie and their trip to Sweet Life. Hannah had gotten the Chocolate Silk with raspberries, a chocolate pie-like dessert that was so thick, you could stand your fork in it. Mikey had chosen the Tiramisu, and Shelly had chosen the Nipple of Venus, a chocolate treat, simply because it had a naughty name. It also tasted delicious. They were happy and relaxed, and I had a kink in my neck.

Abe saw me rubbing my neck and moved behind me. Natalie had taught him, years ago, how to rub the kinks out of her neck and shoulders, and he spent some time rubbing mine while they all described their evening. It was heavenly. I offered to pay him, but he smacked the back of my head and continued rubbing. We all laughed and continued to visit.

Finally, they went to bed, and I made a mental note to send a thank you letter, cookies, something, to the teens who were so wonderful to my kids.

SATURDAY FINALLY DAWNED bright and clear, a beautiful day for the Prom. We were no nearer to finding out what was happening at my house, but we decided, without a word of discussion, not to mention Jamie's death and everything surrounding it for this one day. Shelly and Abe were excited as they breakfasted on eggs and toast. They chatted about where they were going to dinner and discovered they'd made reservations at the same restaurant. They considered sharing rides, the limo idea having fallen through, but decided they would be with different friends. It would be fun to see each other, though.

We went home at four o'clock, secure in the knowledge that Nigel had stopped by earlier to make sure nothing new had been left there to scare us. I had been a little afraid, anyway, of what kind of mess I'd find, but the police had left it clean. Really clean. Briefly, I considered having them clean my house every week. I decided they were probably too busy. And Tom and Jerry, Ramon, and Asia, our bird, were all happy, so Nigel had been doing a great job of feeding them. I wondered if he was giving them too much food, to make them so happy.

Shelly quickly washed her hair and plugged in the hot curlers, curling iron, and straightener. Then she blew her hair dry. A knock on the door announced Amy and Colleen. I did Colleen's hair first. The braid was a quick five minute job with curls taking another five minutes. She looked beautiful as she waltzed out the front door to finish doing her make-up at home.

There was a lot of noise as the girls chattered over the sound of the blow dryers, but we heard the lion's head knocker at five when Nigel arrived.

I gasped. He was dressed in a dark suit with white shirt and burgundy tie. His hair had been trimmed, and he was freshly shaved. And he wore cologne. With his dimples, dark hair, and blue eyes, dressed in that suit, I almost swooned. My reaction made him laugh.

"Say not a single word, my lady," he said with a sweeping bow. "Your eyes speak volumes." I blushed and invited him in.

As we entered the kitchen where Amy and Shelly were doing their hair, there were shrieks of pleasure as they proclaimed over the noise how handsome he was. The sheer volume of hair accessories and appliances brought Nigel to a halt.

"You're using all of these?" he asked naively.

The girls laughed. "Of course," Shelly answered for them. "You don't think we just naturally look good, do you? Not like Mom," she continued enviously. "She always looks good."

Amy rolled her eyes. "Yeah, I wish I had naturally curly hair."

I shushed the girls and tested the dryness of their hair. Amy was ready for her simple part-up, part-down hairstyle. As Nigel settled himself in a chair to watch, Amy and Shelly exchanged glances.

"Let him watch," I told them. "Obviously, he doesn't have a sister," I raised my eyebrows at him, and he shook his head. "So, it's probably time for him to realize just how much effort and time go into a woman looking her best." The girls rolled their eyes, then giggled and nodded.

An hour and a half later, the girls' dates were at the door. Amy and Shelly were double dating. Both boys were handsome in their tuxes and had parents in tow. Amy's mom had arrived just a few minutes earlier. We took pictures in the living room and in the front yard in front of a fir tree which made a beautiful backdrop. Nigel stood in the background watching it all.

Finally, the picture taking was over, and everyone left. I stood on the porch and sighed with regret. "Are you alright?" Nigel asked.

I smiled up at him. "I'm fine, just a little sorry my baby is growing up so fast. It seems like just last week I was holding her on my hip." I hugged myself.

Nigel placed his arm around my shoulder comfortingly. "And yet, I recall hearing mothers of infants wondering if it will ever end, the cycle of feeding, cleaning up nappies, stepping on toys."

"Nappies?" I asked, momentarily distracted. "Oh, right, diapers. Well, at the time it does seem endless. I suppose, now that I don't have to get up in the middle of the night, every night, I remember it as being a small phase of my life. And I miss it. Even the diapers." I smiled again and we moved back into the house.

"Would you like a cup of coffee?" I asked. He would, so I made some. "Any news?"

Nigel sat again at the kitchen table. As he spoke, he quickly shuffled the mess into a semblance of order. "I interviewed George Graham. He made a couple of suggestions, but, like you said, most of it was insinuation."

I handed him his coffee mug. "Did he say anything you can share with me?"

He shook his head. "Not really. I'm not sure it has anything to do with the murder, and I shouldn't spread gossip."

I grinned. "Please don't."

Nigel laughed and continued, "I also spoke again with Forrest Pearson. You were right, he has something on his mind, but I think he is weighing his loyalties."

I grimaced. "Poor kid."

"Poor kid, yes," Nigel nodded, "but he's old enough to know right from wrong. I only hope his loyalty doesn't get him into trouble."

I nodded, and we sipped our coffee in silence.

He grunted and set down his mug. "Absolutely nothing new has been learned over the last two days. I am not showing myself to be a brilliant detective in this case. I don't know if it's because this is a difficult case or if it's because I'm not accustomed to your culture, or even if it's because I don't know the people of this village well. I suppose it could be any one or a combination of all those reasons."

I eyed him levelly. "I know it isn't because you aren't a good detective."

He raised his eyebrows. "How can you know that?"

I smiled. "As I said before, my country wouldn't want you here if you didn't have a good record. Besides, I've had a chance to watch you work. Boy, have I ever!" I rolled my eyes and he laughed. "And you're doing a good job."

Again he asked, "How can you know that?"

"I may not be a trained detective, but I am a writer, and writers observe people. And I've been observing you." My ornery voice said, *And how.* I swallowed a laugh. "You're doing a good job."

Nigel smiled his thanks, and we moved on to other subjects. We chatted until 7:30 when Nigel needed to head over to the dance and keep an eye on the kids.

As he stood at the door, patiently waiting for me, I wandered around the house for a few minutes, straightening up the mess left from the whirlwind of hair, make-up, and dresses. Finally, we said good night, and grabbing the camera, I headed back to Natalie's, carefully locking the house against my invisible intruder who could enter at will.

I pondered why that rang a bell as I drove back to Natalie's house.

"Want to take a walk?" Natalie asked as I opened her front door. I held up the camera, and she grabbed it. We ran to the computer, slid in our SD cards, and looked at each other's prom pictures, reminiscing about our children's childhoods before heading out for our walk. By the time we left, it was dark.

Chapter 36

A Siren Tore Through the Night

We both carried flashlights and pepper spray as we set out. There was no wind, not even a breeze, and the stars shone brightly through the scattered clouds.

"I'm a little nervous being outside after dark," I commented. "Is it because I know Nigel is out of town?"

"There's an unsolved murder in our little town." Natalie rolled her eyes, then looked at me sideways. "But sure, that could be it."

"How did I get used to him so quickly?"

She was silent a moment. "Maybe it's because he's a good man."

I smiled as I thought about that. "Yeah."

As we walked, we compared notes on our children's preparations for Prom. Abe had worn a tux with a pink bow tie and cummerbund. His date's dress was strapless and barely reached her knees. It was a pretty dress, but it wasn't as pretty as Shelly's, Natalie and I agreed.

We were quiet for a few minutes, and my mind drifted from Prom to murder.

"Jamie should have gone to Prom tonight," I said quietly.

Natalie sighed. "I was just thinking that Linda should have enjoyed this evening with her daughter."

As the shadow of the elementary school reached into the street, I suddenly saw in my mind's eye an image of Linda Sneider lying on the ground amidst the shards of a clay pot, and I knew. I knew! I knew who had killed Jamie, who had hit her mom on the head, and why. I could see the images and hear the snippets of conversation of the past weeks as they slid into place.

I picked up the pace and headed toward Peggy Sue's house in the old new development to use her phone. I needed to call Nigel. I needed to tell him what I'd figured out. Natalie jogged to keep up with me.

"What's going on?" she demanded. "Why are we running?"

"I know," I whispered. "I know who did it, and I know why. Come on."

She jogged beside me, panting. Dropping her voice to a whisper to match mine, she demanded, "Who? Who is it? Tell me." She grabbed my arm. "Danielle, talk to me."

I slowed to a fast walk and enumerated on my fingers. "Natalie, think about it: The Adam's apple. And the nose. The fight Kelly and Jamie had. Linda's strange message to Papa Jong. That weird confrontation at Dairy Mart. The person who can enter my house at will. Oh, my goodness, and Peggy Sue's daughter. All of it."

Natalie panted quietly for a moment. "What do they have to do with anything?"

"Secrets. It has to do with secrets," I answered. Images were still flashing through my mind. The party paper. The Spruce Bruce. The two people at the town silo.

That's when I noticed we were at the grain silo again, and I heard his voice. I grabbed Natalie's wrist and stopped dead. Turning off our flashlights, we listened carefully, but we couldn't hear the words. As silently as possible, controlling our breathing, we crept closer. I desperately wished Nigel were in town.

Finally, we were close enough to hear what they were saying. The two people were on the other side of the silo. They couldn't see us.

"...Forrest," We heard. Then, "Can't you see I'm..." murmurs, "for your own good."

A different voice answered, murmuring just as quietly, "...and you need to let me do it myself." It was a woman's voice, or rather, a young woman's voice, perhaps a teen-age girl. It was female, anyway. *Drat! I need to hear better, Lord.*

A man's voice said, "Don't mess it up this time. It's our last chance."

They talked some more, but we couldn't hear anything specific for a while. I thought the wind shifted; we couldn't hear their words as well. Until they turned the corner of the silo, and we were face to face.

"Mrs. Baker," Forrest Pearson's silhouette said. "I didn't know you were here." Little Kelly Green moved to the right of us, as if she wanted to leave unnoticed. Natalie moved a step with her. Kelly stopped.

"Good evening," I said with frantic cheerfulness. "I got a rock in my shoe and was trying to get it out. We heard voices, but we didn't know who was back there." I looked desperately at the sky. "Beautiful night, isn't it?"

The silhouette of Forrest said, "Yes, it is a beautiful night." Something gleamed in his right hand. I pretended not to notice. "I suppose it's a good thing we caught you here," he said conversationally.

Desperately, I said, "Yes, I suppose so. Detective Hawksworth will be here any moment now, and I'm sure he'll want to talk to you. Don't you think so, Natalie?" I glanced at her, and from the corner of my eye saw the flash move toward me.

Natalie's reflexes were lightening quick. She had the cap off and was spraying pepper in his eyes just as the knife swiped through my jacket sleeve. It fell harmlessly to the ground as he screamed in pain. Kelly started to run, but I grabbed her flying hair and held tightly to the enraged tigress.

A siren tore through the night. As I fended off the scratching and punching, I searched for who was screaming and saw Natalie with her mouth wide open. I punched her shoulder and yelled, "Use your cell phone!" She stopped screaming and grabbed at her pocket. Profanity and moans drifted up from the ground as I wrapped my arms tightly around Kelly, pinioning her arms.

"I forgot I had it," Natalie said breathlessly. I'd forgotten, too, until she screamed. She dialed 9-1-1. She must have gotten the same operator I'd had, because she yelled, "I am calm!" before giving the information a second time. I kept a tight hold on a struggling, cursing Kelly Green and watched Jamie's murderer writhe in pain on the ground.

In less than a minute, a police car screeched to a halt in front of us. The lights of the car were full on us as the officer jumped out and rushed to give first aid.

Natalie's mouth opened as she saw who was on the ground, clawing at his eyes. "But . . . but that's not Forrest," she said. I dragged Kelly over to the side of the car, and Natalie followed.

"Of course not," I answered. "It's Forrest's dad. He looks so much like Forrest that we mistook him a couple of times, remember?"

"But that's *Jamie's* dad," Natalie protested.

"Isn't he just?" I answered softly. Natalie gasped. Kelly finally stood silently, glaring at us.

"Are you saying that Jamie was dating her . . . her half-brother?" Natalie stammered.

I shook my head. "I think it's a little more complicated than that. Isn't it, Kelly?"

Natalie and I looked at her. She had calmed down, but she still glared. Suddenly, she burst out, "Jamie had no right to date Forrest. It was wrong, but she just didn't care. So our dad had to tell Forrest, 'cause he didn't know. And *still* Jamie didn't care. The idiot. It's disgusting. I'm glad she's dead."

Natalie's mouth dropped open. "*Our* dad?"

We stared at her in disbelief until a noise distracted us.

The officer was pouring water into the man's eyes as he cursed, the knife unnoticed. I figured he'd see it soon enough. A moment later, Nigel's car pulled to a halt behind us, and he ran over and grabbed my shoulders. "Are you alright?" he asked. "Did he harm you? Did I get here in time?"

I nodded, still holding the arm of a now-quiet Kelly. "We're not hurt at all."

"Thank you, God." A sound like a sob escaped Nigel as he gave me a quick hug and walked away.

"But Nigel . . . Grr."

"What is he doing here?" Natalie wondered as Nigel walked away. "Why isn't he watching over the kids at Prom?"

He walked quickly over to the officer and asked for information. I wasn't sure how he would have any, since he hadn't asked us any questions, yet. But the officer stood to confer with Nigel.

Quick as a flash, Jamie's dad reached out to the knife and stabbed Nigel's leg, burying it into his thigh up to the hilt. I screamed as Nigel fell to the ground. The police officer flipped Forrest's dad over and quickly handcuffed him before rushing to Nigel's aid. I shoved Kelly into Natalie's arms.

"Hold her!" I ran to the police car and grabbed the radio transmitter. Glancing at the dash, I read into the mic, "Car one-one-two A, officer down! Repeat, Car one-one-two A, officer down with a knife wound to the leg. Send an ambulance at once."

Someone answered, "Roger that, Car one-one-two A. Ambulance is on its way." There was a short pause before I heard, "Who is this?"

But I didn't have time to explain. As the town's emergency siren called our volunteer paramedics to the scene, I ran over to Nigel. He was on the ground, groaning softly, the knife still in his thigh. The officer had returned to Forrest's dad. Jamie's dad. What a mess. "You have the right to remain silent. Anything you say can and will be used against you in a court of law..."

I sat next to Nigel and gently lifted his head onto my lap. Stroking his hair, I crooned to him as I would to my children. He was deathly pale but stoic.

"You'll be okay, Nigel," I said to him softly. "That siren means they're sending help right now, and you'll be just fine."

He smiled through his pain and lifted his hand to my cheek. "If it makes you feel better, I won't pass out." I could have cried with relief. I'm not sure I didn't.

For a few minutes, I just rubbed his hair and sang softly. Then I remembered to ask, "What are you doing here? Why aren't you at the dance?"

He answered, "I was watching the kids dance and noticed Forrest Pearson. As I stood there, I realized where I had seen him before, or someone very like him. And just like that, the pieces fell into place, and I knew who had murdered Jamie. I even thought we had the evidence needed to procure a warrant."

He shifted a bit and groaned. "I'm so sorry, Danielle, but there is a sharp rock under my left buttock. Can you remove it, please?" I giggled as I fished for the piece of gravel. He sighed in relief. "Thank you."

After a moment, he continued. "I thought a bit longer about the clues we had gathered, and I realized the youths didn't need me there; they were safe. So I drove back for another interview with Larry Sneider. When I heard the 9-9-9 call, I knew you were in trouble."

I pretended to punch his arm. "It's 9-1-1, and I'm not always in trouble," I said, and he smiled.

"Not always, but I had a feeling you were this time." He shifted and groaned again. "And I want you to stay out of my next case, please."

"Absolutely," I assured him.

Very soon more police arrived, then an ambulance and then another one. Lights flashed, rescuers talked, police asked questions, so many questions, and the whole evening became dream-like. Larry Sneider was led, handcuffed, to a police cruiser, his eyes red and streaming. Kelly was placed in the back of another cruiser, but she didn't wear cuffs.

Finally, Shea arrived with the car and drove us to Albany Hospital where they had taken Nigel. The precious man had called his mother to stay with the younger kids who were already asleep.

Two hours later, we were still sitting in the hospital waiting room. I thought of all the questions I'd been asked by four different police officers, and I knew there would be at least one more officer, a detective from England, who would want to hear my story, especially my reasons for talking with a murderer. At night. Behind the grain silo. Even I knew it was stupid.

I was sure Nigel was mad at me. I told Natalie so several times. When Shea finally returned from the vending machines, I told him, too.

Shea said, "Please stop saying that. If he's mad at you, he's an idiot. You had no idea those two were there, and if you stopped to listen, well, you had no idea some goofy teenager would go for you with a knife."

Natalie looked at him in protest. "He isn't a teenager, he's a grown man."

Shea looked confused. "Forrest Pearson is a grown man?"

I bit my lip to hide a smile as a nurse entered. "Detective Hawksworth is all stitched up and recovering just fine," she said cheerfully. "He's demanding a word with someone named Danielle. I presume that's you." She looked at me with a smile. I glanced at Shea and Natalie. They gave me a little shove, and I followed the nurse to Nigel's room leaving Natalie to untangle the mess in Shea's head.

As I entered, my heart was in my mouth. I knew he would be okay physically, once the muscle healed, but I felt like I had caused the attack to happen. If I hadn't been there, Nigel wouldn't be in this hospital bed recovering from a knife wound.

"Hi," I smiled as I approached the bed carefully. "How are you feeling?"

Nigel smiled at me. His face was pale, his wounded leg elevated on pillows under the covers, but his eyes were bright, and his beautiful dimples were in evidence. "Relax, Danielle. It's just a knife wound in the leg. I'm not going to come a cropper."

Tears welled up. "I'm so sorry. Can you forgive me for being there and placing you in danger?"

"Do I need to? Were you there intentionally?"

"No," I shook my head. "Natalie and I were taking a walk. We heard voices around the other side of the silo, and they sounded like Forrest and someone, maybe Kelly. So we stopped to listen." I blushed.

Nigel grinned. "You were eavesdropping."

He shifted slightly, grimaced in pain, and reached up to touch my cheek. I remembered he'd done that when he was lying on the ground next to the silo. I placed my hand over his, enjoying the warmth on my cheek. "Since you need to hear it, then of course I forgive you," he said softly. He gently pulled my face down and pressed his warm lips to mine, taking my breath away.

As I stood up again, a nurse said, "Obviously you're feeling better, Mr. Hawksworth." She smiled cheerfully as she fluffed his pillows. Looking me over, she said, "Don't stay too long; we don't want to wear him out, now, do we?"

I blushed again, and she laughed softly as she left.

"I really should go," I said, watching his droopy eyes. "Pleasant dreams." He smiled drowsily at me. I took his hand and held it until he was asleep and went in search of Natalie and Shea.

We headed home; Abe and Shelly would be there soon. We could tell them all about the excitement tomorrow. Tonight belonged to them.

At midnight exactly, not five minutes after we shuffled wearily through the door, Shelly and Abe tangoed in. They were laughing uproariously, and it took us several minutes to get a coherent story from them.

"It was so much fun," Shelly said breathlessly.

"We gathered that," Natalie said, smiling.

Abe bowed to his mom. "May I have this dance?" he asked. Natalie stood and danced with her son. As they twirled around the room, Shea asked Shelly to dance with him. She batted her lashes and laughed, and they danced around the room, too. I sat on the couch and smiled with all my might.

After the impromptu dance, Abe and Shelly took turns telling us the details of the night. "I tried to dance with Detective Hawksworth, but he wasn't around when I looked for him," Shelly said. "I wonder where he went." She looked at Abe.

He said thoughtfully, "I saw him leave about 8:30, and he didn't come back. Besides," he finished, "he's too old for you. He probably doesn't even know how to dance anymore."

"That's all you know," Shelly retorted. "He's British. The Brits practically invented dancing"

I laughed out loud at that, and the party broke up. Shelly and Abe went upstairs to put away their party clothes, and Natalie followed them up to maintain propriety. I was just too physically and mentally fatigued to do it myself. I dragged my tired body into the downstairs guest room and fell into bed. As sleep enveloped me, I hoped his kiss wasn't a side effect of pain meds.

Chapter 37
You Know All the Answers

A few days later, Nigel was out of the hospital enjoying a few well-earned days off, and we had a welcome home party for him with Shea, Natalie, and the kids. We gathered in my living room for pizza. We'd told the kids who was guilty; the entire town knew by now, but very few people knew the how and why. That would all come out at the trial, the police said.

When Nigel told me, I giggled at the police department's naiveté.

"Mom," Shelly started the conversation. "We know who killed Jamie. But how did you figure it out?"

I grinned in triumph at Nigel. "You needed me," I said to him. He just grunted, his mouth full of pizza. I pulled Ramon the Wonder Dog away from Nigel's plate. The animals seemed to be happy we were home again.

Nigel swallowed and said, "If you remember, we seem to have figured it out at the same time." I just looked at him, and he grinned. "But you're right; I did need you. So, go ahead and take the honors of explaining. I'm going to develop a mutually beneficial relationship with this pizza." And he devoured another huge bite as we all laughed.

"Well," I began, "one night, Natalie and I were walking our loop. You know, around town." Everyone nodded impatiently. "We saw Forrest and Kelly in the parking lot next to the grain silo in the middle of town, but we couldn't be sure it was Forrest because he looked a little different. It took me until last night to figure out that he looked different because the man was older, more filled out. Forrest is still a teen-ager. He won't grow into his 'man muscles' until he's in his mid-twenties. It was his dad."

There were several, "What?" noises. Abe's voice came out on top. "But Forrest doesn't look a thing like his dad."

I nodded and shook my head. "I know. We all thought Forrest's dad was the man married to Forrest's mom."

"Whoa. He isn't?" Abe continued as spokesperson.

"No, he isn't. Mr. Pearson is Forrest's step-dad. Even Forrest didn't know that his biological father was someone else, until a couple of weeks ago."

"Why didn't he know?" Shea asked. "I'd think they'd let him know. For . . . for about a dozen different reasons."

I nodded. "You would think so. But Peggy Sue hid a teen pregnancy from us. And several others have, too."

"Obviously," Shelly snorted.

I continued, "It's something that goes with you into your adult life, the mistake of getting pregnant before marriage. Or getting someone else pregnant. I remember the story of the woman who, at sixty-something years old, was still being criticized for getting pregnant in high school. I'm sure I'm not the only one who knows that story."

I looked around at my family, both biological and honorary. "We're secure, all of us here, in our relationships with each other. Not everyone has the blessings we have."

Shea nodded and asked, "So what happened? Why did Jamie's dad kill her?"

I looked at Nigel. He flipped his hand at me and said, "Go ahead, you know all the answers," and took another huge bite of pizza. *The size of his grocery bill must be enormous*, I thought.

I turned back to the group and smiled sadly. "I was talking with Linda Sneider yesterday," I said. "I thought she could fill in a couple of gaps for me."

"We never asked her questions," Natalie said.

"Of course not," I shot back. "Who interviews a grieving mom about past secrets?" She nodded. "Anyway, she told me that Jamie's biological dad lives in Okinawa, a soldier she had a short affair with just before she married Larry Sneider."

"Larry?" Natalie asked. "Was that his name? Did I know that?"

I answered, "You knew that."

"What you don't know isn't worth knowing, honey," Shea answered with a hug.

The kids laughed and started asking Natalie what she knew. Playfully, she smacked at them, and they laughed louder.

"Stop it!" I finally yelled. "Or we'll be here all night." They settled down good-naturedly, and I continued. "Larry never knew Jamie wasn't his biological daughter, and he thought Forrest and Jamie were half-brother and -sister."

"Holy moly," Shea rumbled. "What a mess."

I nodded. "There's a proverb I hate but is usually true: Old sins have long shadows. It was certainly true in this case. Anyway, Mr. Sneider tried to tell Jamie she couldn't see Forrest anymore, but he wouldn't explain why. Jamie, always ready to rebel, refused to stop seeing him. Forrest was told, and Kelly Green who is another of Larry's children –"

"A prolific man," Shea observed. I agreed.

"Forrest and Kelly were told, but for some reason, Larry never told Jamie."

"According to the report of the interview," Nigel cut in, "he said he wanted at least one of his kids to live a life of innocence, so he didn't tell her. He thought he had enough authority over her that he could dictate her behavior and attitude." We rolled our eyes in unison.

Shelly spoke up, "Well, *that* worked out well for him, didn't it?"

I continued, "The thing is, Linda told Jamie who her biological father was, so Jamie wouldn't accidentally date a brother some day. But she didn't tell Larry, because she didn't want to lose his respect."

"After all this time?" Natalie asked.

I shrugged. "I think she still carries a torch for him."

Natalie shook her head. "What, he's somehow attractive to women, too? Like Forrest is?"

I smiled. "I suppose it's hereditary."

"And Jamie didn't say anything, because she thought her 'dad' was being overbearing and misogynistic," Nigel said. "According to Larry Sneider. Maybe she thought he knew."

"Secrets," Natalie murmured. "That night, before we saw them at the grain silo, you said it was all about secrets."

I nodded.

Shelly shivered, "Shoot, if I ever needed an object lesson in why secrets are bad . . ."

"So the night he killed her?" Abe wrapped a comforting arm around Shelly's shoulders.

"The night he killed her." I sighed. "Jamie's attitude enraged Mr. Sneider and he grabbed the closest piece of clothing, that dress, wrapped it and his hands around her throat, and...stopped her mouth. Forever."

Hannah's soft heart was touched, and she cried softly for her one-time friend. I rubbed her hair and glanced over the group. Mikey and Danny leaned up against each other, each supporting the other in more ways than one. And Abe had his arm around Shelly, the gesture of a friend and brother. Tabitha was snuggled up against Shea.

Nigel finished the story. "When Danielle started asking questions, and even when she wasn't the village was spreading rumors that she was, Larry Sneider cast about for some way to scare her off."

"So," Natalie interrupted, "the black rose and the coffee cake were just a sort of war on nerves?"

Nigel nodded. "Those, and the break-in, the confrontation at Dairy Mart, *and* the times he phoned. He just wanted to scare her away from the investigation." He looked at me with a mixture of pride and irritation. "It didn't seem to work, though, did it?"

"Was there anything wrong with the cake?" Natalie insisted.

Nigel shook his head. "They aren't done running tests, yet, but so far as they can determine, the cake was fine."

Shea asked, "Hang on. Where does someone buy a black rose? They're kind of rare, aren't they?"

I nodded, "They are. They're so rare, they don't exist in nature." I looked at Nigel. "So, where did he get the black rose?"

Nigel wiped his mouth on a well-used napkin. "There are several ways he could have gotten a black rose."

"You said they don't exist," Shea said.

Nigel nodded. "In nature, they don't. But you can make them, either by buying a rose bush and diluting black food coloring in the water you use for it—"

"Like we did with the carnation for science!" Mikey spoke up. "Remember, Mom?"

I nodded.

Nigel continued. "Or he could buy a special flower paint, but it's difficult to procure, unless you're a florist. Or he could have purchased a black-tinted or painted rose from a florist."

"So, which one did he do?" I asked.

Nigel grinned. "None of them."

"What?" several people asked.

Nigel's grin grew. "You have a very . . . interesting person living on Cobalt Street who is growing black roses in her back yard. He stole one from her."

We all groaned, and Shelly said, "Of course he did."

We waited a moment, hoping for more, but Nigel merely looked smug and a bit sleepy.

"You know Mr. Graham's opinion of George Jr," I took up the story again. "Mr. Graham doesn't like to leave him in the hardware store alone because he gives things away."

"'That son of mine,'" Shelly imitated Mr. Graham, "'will give away the deed to the store if I don't get back there soon.'"

Everyone grinned and nodded, and I continued. "Well, Larry Sneider talked him out of an extra key to our house so he could leave the rose." I turned to Natalie. "I thought of that when I headed back to your place after doing the girls' hair for Prom. Someone could enter at will...like they had a duplicate key to my house."

I picked up the last slice of pizza. "Actually, Gramma G gave me the hint."

"Your *mother*?" Natalie laughed. "I can't imagine in the tumble of words that you heard something useful."

I smiled. "She told me about her manicurist whose house was broken into by someone who had made a duplicate key. I wondered who might have a key to my house, besides Mr. Graham and his son who are honorable people. And then I thought of George Jr who is easily talked out of things, like merchandise. When we changed the locks, Larry Sneider simply talked George Jr. out of another key."

"You changed the locks to your house?" Natalie asked. She absently shoved Jerry (or was it Tom?) off the coffee table with her foot.

"I told you," I said.

"No, you didn't. If you had, I'd have thrown away the one that doesn't work anymore."

"I was sure I told you," I answered, picking up the cat. I stroked him behind his ears and was rewarded with a heavy purr.

"You can decide *later* whether or not you talked about it," Shelly informed us. "Tell us how you figured it all out."

I put the cat down. "Well, we were taking a walk after you all left for Prom, and the elementary school cast a shadow. It kind of looked like a hooked nose, and I suddenly realized that Forrest and Mr. Sneider have the same nose. And the same Adam's apple, the same color hair, the same body build, everything. In fact, there's no way a youngster like Forrest could look so much like a man who isn't his father, so he must be. His father."

I put the pizza slice, now flecked with cat hair, back in the box. "It was like a kaleidoscope shifted and all the pieces fell into place. I saw that Forrest was Larry Sneider's son, so the relationship between Forrest and Jamie as boyfriend and girlfriend shouldn't be happening. Kelly must have been arguing with Jamie because she knew, and she'd only know if she, too, was a child of Larry Sneider."

I shook my head. "But I thought that if Kelly and Forrest knew, then Linda must know, too. Only she didn't stop the relationship, or even try to. I wondered about that, which led me to asking myself if Larry Sneider *wasn't* Jamie's dad. But maybe he thought he was. And then I thought about the aborted or miscarried baby. Was it Forrest's? And if it was, would Jamie's dad try to stop the conception of another baby, even if it meant killing Jamie?

"One thing was sure," I finished. "I understood how the murder could take place. When we heard Forrest's voice behind the silo, I knew we had to listen. But it turns out Forrest has his biological father's voice, too, and it was Larry who was talking."

"Man, if they were so much alike, you'd think they would have noticed," Abe declared.

Shelly answered, "Everyone seems to be related to everyone else in this town, somehow. If Forrest looks like someone, we're all going to assume they're, like, cousins or second cousins or nephew and uncle three times removed or something. Besides, they didn't spend much time together, so it's not like their similarities were all that obvious."

We nodded sagely. Those who have lived here for more than a couple of generations are careful who they date.

Abe spoke up next. "So, did Mr. Sneider hit Mrs. Sneider over the head with the clay flower pot?"

I nodded.

"Why? I mean, it kind of seems like a dumb thing to do."

I smiled. "It kind of was. But I think Mrs. Sneider hinted that he could help the police, and he was afraid she knew more than she did. But he couldn't ask, because if she didn't know as much as he feared she did, he would tell her more than she should know. But he couldn't talk to the police, like she hinted he should, because he knew more than he wanted the police to know, but he couldn't tell her that . . . I think he panicked and did something stupid."

"Something else," Abe said, rubbing his forehead.

Shelly smirked. "That's an awful lot of pronouns, Mom."

I pretended to swipe at her. "That whole incident was a bit confusing, even to Mr. Sneider, I think."

Nigel snorted and nodded.

"Wait," Natalie held up a hand. "Didn't we hear Kelly say something like, 'Let me do it'? And didn't Mr. Pearson say it was their last chance?" She looked from Nigel to me. "What was that about?"

I'd wondered about that, too, so we all turned to Nigel. He had just stuffed a last bite of pizza into his mouth, so we had to wait while he chewed. Like, fifty times. "Right. What they *told* us is, Larry Sneider wanted Kelly Green to try to scare you again, Danielle. She was to do something – they refused to say what it was – to convince you to stop investigating."

"I wasn't really doing anything!" I rolled my eyes. "Seriously, the people in this town."

Natalie grinned. "I'm pretty sure we've had this conversation before."

Nigel continued, "But it seems possible she was supposed to actually hurt one of you."

We sobered instantly. Shelly asked quietly, "Do you really think she would have hurt us?" Abe leaned over and kissed her forehead. I rubbed Hannah's hair. Danny put Mikey in a headlock, and they both tumbled over. The tension broke, and we laughed.

Nigel's beautiful blue eyes looked into mine. "Probably not." He looked around the circle and smiled. "Officer Nichols was allowed into the interview room with her for a few minutes, and he did a surprisingly good job."

"Good for him," I said softly.

"Kelly said she 'talked big' to her new dad, whatever that means, but she hadn't really done any of the things he wanted her to do."

"Oh, good," I exclaimed softly. "She's spent a lot of time here, and I'd hate to think she could hurt us." Shelly and Hannah nodded.

"Kelly and Forrest are in a lot of trouble," Nigel had Ramon on the couch beside him and a cat stretched out across his stomach and chest. "But I'll try to persuade the judge to grant them leniency because the whole mess was started with their parents' lies."

Ramon licked his hand, and Nigel petted him absently. "We don't know whether or not they are accessories after the fact. Forrest says he didn't know who murdered Jamie until the interview Saturday night. He was afraid he could guess, and that was the look you intercepted the other evening, Danielle." I nodded. "We think Kelly knew at least a week ago. But they were being manipulated and – in many ways – controlled by their biological father. They were caught in the middle, and they aren't very good at deception. Which tells me they are being raised by good parents."

"Poor kids," Shea murmured.

Nigel nodded. "If the judge allows, I will ask for a suspended sentence." He looked at our confused faces. "What do you call it when a person is convicted but not imprisoned for a crime?"

I thought a moment. "I think you mean probation." The faces in the room cleared.

"Ah, yes, of course," Nigel continued, "probation. I will ask for probation. And State-mandated counseling. They and their families have suffered a lot."

Shelly sighed. "We have, too."

Nigel smiled. "Yes, you have. It's time for your lives to get back to normal."

Shea stood. "I think it's time for us to go home," he said good-naturedly. "If life is going to get back to normal, we should start with getting to bed on time."

He turned and looked at me. "Unless you have any other surprises to share with us tonight?"

I shook my head. "I think we've covered everything pertaining to the murder, and I have no other surprises."

"Good," he said with a grin. "I need to rest my brain."

Chapter 38

Let It Go to Voicemail

We all laughed and picked up pizza boxes and other party paraphernalia. Nigel urged the animals to the floor and tried to help, but I pushed him back onto the couch. "Put your leg up. You only get to act like a hero for a little while, so enjoy it."

He chuckled. "I wrote to my mum about you," he said under the noise. I stared at him. He sat back and smirked.

The Shalligan family finally left, and I sent Shelly, Hannah, and Mikey to get ready for bed. I checked the kitchen for any residual mess, shooed Ramon out the back door, and returned to the living room and Nigel. Shelly was hugging Nigel good night, and Hannah and Mikey were waiting their turns.

When they all left, Nigel's eyes were moist. "I never knew what I'd missed out on," he said quietly. "I imagined it, but I never knew."

I smiled. "They like you. They admire you. And best of all, they respect you."

"Oh, Lord," he prayed, "don't let me fall off the pedestal."

I laughed. "I don't think you're on a pedestal. I think they're right to respect you. And to like you, too." I shrugged. "I like you."

He hobbled over to me. "I like you, too, Mrs. Baker," he said quietly. His arms wrapped me tight, and I looked into his beautiful blue eyes.

I thought he was going to kiss me, and my heart jumped. But just as his face started toward mine, my cell phone rang. Groaning, I pulled it out of my pocket.

"Oh, *Mother*," I groaned.

Nigel laughed and said, "Let it go to voicemail. You can call her back." But his cell phone rang at that moment. With a groan that matched mine, he pulled it out. "It's the station."

"Let it go to voicemail," I answered teasingly. "You can call them back."

He made a face and answered. Sighing, he pressed the off button and said, "Several flats . . . apartments have been burglarized at a retirement facility in Albany. They're short-handed tonight, and they want me to come in and help out. Even though I'm convalescent."

"Are you going to?" I asked quietly. "The doctor said you should have another three days of rest, at minimum."

He smiled. "They're setting up a couple of chairs, so I can sit and interview people with my leg up. I'm very sorry, Danielle, but I'm going to have to go."

I smiled. "That's okay, I know the drill. I'll see you when I see you. Right?"

He moved closer to me and asked, "Will this make the wait a little easier?" And he kissed me until I was breathless.

And like the wind, he was gone.

Acknowledgements

They say it takes a village to raise a child. "They" are correct. It also takes a village to publish a book. With that in mind, I would like to acknowledge and thank my village:

Carina, Thomas, Jennifer, Boaz, Caleb, and Micah - my wonderful children - thank you for your patience while I was writing, your support of my endeavor, your positive and constructive feedback, and your genuine excitement as your mom finished this project.

Michelle Leach - thank you for prodding me to finish this book, for designing the book cover, and for the positive and constructive feedback through the whole process.

Bobbie Christiansen and Judy Peters - thank you for being my Alpha readers, helping to form this story into a novel, filling clue gaps and encouraging me to continue writing. Without you, this book would be languishing in my computer, half-written and very sad, indeed!

Wade Anderson - my wonderful, supportive husband - thank you for giving me the freedom to write. I may not always stop writing so I can make meals, load the washer, or run those errands, but you are patient through it all and oh, so proud of me. Thank you!

About the Author

Debbra Anderson lives in a small town in Western Oregon where she spent more than 25 years in the homeschooling community. Now that her children are grown, she is enjoying her morning cup of tea - uninterrupted. *The Hawk Circles* is the first in her new Danielle Baker and Nigel Hawksworth series.

Read more at https://www.facebook.com/DebbraAndersonAuthor.

Ingram Content Group UK Ltd.
Milton Keynes UK
UKHW041355060323
418112UK00001B/170